TWELVE O'CLOCK HIGH

W. RICHARD SHEPHERD

Order this book online at www.trafford.com
or email orders@trafford.com

Most Trafford titles are also available at major online book retailers.

© Copyright 2023 W. Richard Shepherd.
All rights reserved. No part of this publication may be reproduced, stored in a
retrieval system, or transmitted, in any form or by any means, electronic, mechanical,
photocopying, recording, or otherwise, without the written prior permission of the author.

Print information available on the last page.

ISBN: 978-1-4907-9812-7 (sc)
ISBN: 978-1-4907-9813-4 (hc)
ISBN: 978-1-4907-9814-1 (e)

Library of Congress Control Number: 2019917820

Because of the dynamic nature of the Internet, any web addresses or links contained in
this book may have changed since publication and may no longer be valid. The views
expressed in this work are solely those of the author and do not necessarily reflect the
views of the publisher, and the publisher hereby disclaims any responsibility for them.

Any people depicted in stock imagery provided by Getty Images are models, and such
images are being used for illustrative purposes only.
Certain stock imagery © Getty Images.

Trafford rev. 10/31/2019

 www.trafford.com

North America & international
toll-free: 844-688-6899 (USA & Canada)
fax: 812 355 4082

CONTENTS

Prologue vii

Chapter 1	The Old Man	1
Chapter 2	The Rate Of Attrition	23
Chapter 3	Eggs For Breakfast	51
Chapter 4	Shambles	63
Chapter 5	Rally Point	83
Chapter 6	Pamela	113
Chapter 7	Achtung!	133
Chapter 8	To All Men	155
Chapter 9	Missing In Action	171
Chapter 10	Widewing	185
Chapter 11	Twelve O'clock High	207
Chapter 12	Threshold	235

PROLOGUE

THE GREEN TOBY

In the summer of 1949, Mr. Harvey Stovall left his suite at the Hyde Park Hotel and strolled toward Piccadilly enjoying himself. First, he had just cabled good news to his partner in the firm of Stovall & Stokes, the go-gettingest legal team, he reflected, in Columbus, Ohio. Second, he was faced with a free day in which to poke about London.

Stovall paused at the intersection of Piccadilly and Bonds Streets, more out of curiosity than from an intent to make a purchase, and observed the latest in men's hats in the window of Scott's, hatterer to his Majesty the King. That black Homburg, he thought, would certainly create a stir in Columbus, but he'd better stick to his own conservative brown Stetson.

Involuntarily he appraised his reflection in the window, which mirrored a prosperous citizen, a trifle heavy about the middle, with gray hair and the shrewd, tired eyes of the overworked American businessman, a dark blue double-breasted suit, a dark red carnation in the lapel and neatly shined black shoes. He re- called, with a pang, that he had been leaner when last he walked these ancient streets.

Sauntering through the Burlington Arcade, he recognized the shop in which he had once bought an old silver cigarette box as a wedding-anniversary present for his wife, Martha. He was about to enter and explore the establishment when he stood suddenly transfixed, his eyes drawn by a green enameled Toby on display in the window.

Vigorously modeled, with a well formed satyr handle, the mug depicted a robber, with a Robin Hood hat and a black mask over the eyes. Stovall hurried into the shop with such precipi- tance that he jostled a gnarled gnome of a man just inside the door.

"Wot's the bloody 'urry, mate", said the gnome, who resembled one of the Tobies on the wall shelf behind him? "I'm the proprietor 'ere."

"Excuse me", said Stovall, making no effort to conceal his excitement, "I'd like to see that green beer mug in the front window."

"It's Tobies you're after, sir? Allow me to show you a rare salt-glazed Toby I 'ave 'ere . . ."

"No, no", said Stovall impatiently, "the one in the window, please." "Right you are, sir."

Grumbling to himself, the gnome crawled into the window and fetched the Toby, watching with evident disapproval while his customer examined it eagerly.

"That one's been knocked about a bit, sir", he persisted. "Not in it with this fine collection of Staffordshire Tobys over 'ere."

"Where did you get this", asked Stovall? The proprietor searched a huge ledger.

"An auction at Archbury", he said. "After those bloody Americans left." Stovall's eyes lighted up.

"How much will you take for it?"

"I 'ates to take advantage of you, sir. Now if you'll allow me to show you a Staffordshire in perfect condition . . ."

"I want this one. How much?"

"Well, sir. Wot do you say to fourteen bob? Frankly, there's not much value to it."

Instantly Stovall's expression hardened into a glare and color mounted his cheeks. Mistaking this sign for sales resistance, the proprietor added hastily:

"Call it twelve bob."

"Fourteen bob is very reasonable", said Stoval, quietly.

He counted out the money and watched while the proprietor wrapped the jug carefully in excelsior, placed it in a box and tied it with a stout cord. Then he thanked him, hurried outside and hailed a taxi, instructing the cabby to take him to the Hyde Park Hotel. It was his intention to leave the Toby in a safe place be- fore he resumed his stroll. But halfway to the hotel he changed his mind.

"Paddington Station", he said.

Almost before his decision had fully crystallized, he found himself aboard a train bound for the village of Archbury in the Midlands. Two hours later he walked through the winding old streets of Archbury, direct to a pub called the Black Swan, borrowed a bicycle from the bartender, slung his package to the handlebars, and pedaled out of the village along a country road lined with hedges and shaggy houses with thatched roofs. Breaking in and out of the scudding clouds, the sun gradually thawed the chill from the air, and a light breeze cooled Stovall's forehead, moist from the exertion of pumping the bicycle up the occasional hills. More than once he felt a little foolish, and won- dered, whether or not, if he should turn back.

Certainly he, Harvey Stovall, was a methodical rather than an impulsive or emotional man. Furthermore, it annoyed him that he had brought the package along; if he should took a spill, he might break it. But he pedaled steadily on, glancing down now and then to insure that the metal clips were protecting his trouser cuffs.

After a while, he turned off on a side road, propped the bike against a hedge and strode slowly a hundred yards out onto an enormous flat, unobstructed, field. When he halted he was stand- ing at the head of a wide, dilapidated avenue of concrete, which stretched in front of him with gentle undulations for a mile and a half. A herd of cows, nibbling at the tall grass which had grown up through the cracks, helped to camouflage his recollection of the huge runway. He noted the black streaks left by many tires, where they had struck the surface, smoking, and nearby, through the weeds, which nearly covered it, he could still see the stains left by puddles of grease and black oil, on one of the hard-stands, evenly spaced around the five-mile circumference of the perimeter track, like teeth on a ring gear.

And in the background he could make out a forlorn dirty gray control tower, topped by a tattered gray windsock, and behind it two empty hangers, a shoe box of a water tank on high stilts and an ugly cluster of squat Nissen huts. Not a soul was visible, no- thing moved, save the cows, nor was there any sound to break the great quiet. And yet Harvey Stovall, standing there against the green landscape, was no longer alone.

Nor, to him, was the suit he wore still blue. Rather it was an olive drab, with major's leaves on the shoulders, as befitted the Adjutant of a heavy bombardment group.

A gust of wind blew back the tall weeds behind the hard-stand nearest him. But suddenly Stovall could no longer see the bent-back weeds through the quick tears that blurred his eyes, and slid down the deep lines in his face.

He made no move to brush them away. For, behind the blur he could see, from within, more clearly. On each empty hard-stand there sat the ghost of a B-17, its four whirling propellers blasting the tall grass with the gale of its slipstream, its tires bulging under the weight of tons of bombs and tons of gasoline needed for a deep penetration raid.

In the large Nissen hut used for briefing, now deserted and covered with dust, he saw the gathering of a ghostly company of 250 pilots, navigators, bombardiers and gunners, encumbered in their bulky flying clothes, life vests and oxygen masks, straining to hear the words of a ghostly Intelligence officer as he indicated a target on the map.

In the Group Commander's quarters, with its luxury of a bathroom, and a fire grate, now rusty and cold, he saw two ghosts wandering about, one of whom had broken under the pressure of great events.

In the station hospital, there were no rows of beds in the ward, and the operation room was vacant. But he knew that many ghosts assembled there in the small hours of the night, to speak of frostbitten faces and hands, of wounds inflicted by jagged flak and exploding 20 millimeter cannon shells, and of survival.

In the Adjutant's office, Stovall recognized a middle-aged ghost, himself, examining the papers that flowed across his desk. Telling the tale, in brief reports and in cold figures, of the ordeal of the rest of the ghosts who populated a small, self-contained universe, bounded by the limits of this deserted station, in which they had endured a terrible hour, and in which demoralization had threatened American arms, with a shameful and disastrous defection.

Regaining his composure, Stovall walked back to the bicycle, perplexed at the nature of the emotion that had inspired the first real tears he could remember shedding since his youth, and then he understood. They were born, not of a sentimental wallowing in Auld Lang Syne, but of the clear realization, emerging through the perspective of time, that here, on this one station, America might have lost the war. That this one rotten apple, decaying at a critically early juncture, almost spoiled the whole barrel.

Americans only remember victories. Little did they know how perilously close the sequence of events at Archbury Field had come to destroying, in its cradle, the future giant of air power which, even according to its victim, was the decisive factor in Nazi Germany's plunge to defeat?

He mounted the bike, pedaled down the runway, scattering a formation of plover, turned off at the far end, and followed a narrow concrete road to an outsize Nissen hut which had been the Officer's Club. Seeing that the door stood ajar, he leaned the bike against the entrance and place his hand on the rusted door-knob.

He had to shove with his shoulder before the door, having warped on its creaking hinges, finally scraped inward, sending a hollow reverberation through the empty room. Cobwebs shrouded the windows and a layer of dust powered the floor.

Stripped of its furniture and pictures, the room was lifeless, save for a pair of rats which streaked away from him, and disappeared through the hole under the mantelpiece at the far end, near which was a faded square where a radio had once stood against the wall. But here, too, Stovall could see many ghosts - ghosts of the aircrews who had found, in this room, a haven where they could relax, order a drink, shoot craps and listen to the radio.

His roving eyes came to a halt on the mantelpiece, and imperceptibly his shoulders straightened and his whole body stiffened.

Abruptly he returned to the bicycle, removed the package from the handlebars, untied the cord and lifted out the shiny green Toby.

He reentered the club and walked purposefully to the mantle, where, with his handkerchief, he cleaned a spot in the thick dust.

And then, with the reverence of a man laying a wreath on the tomb of the Unknown Soldier, he placed the Toby with precision on the clean patch in the center of the mantelpiece, so that the masked robber faced out towards the empty room.

He walked swiftly to the door, where he turned around for a last look at the Toby, which stared back at him with a malignant leer. Then, having seconds thoughts about leaving it behind, he retrieved the mug and carefully returned it to its box.

Once more, as he was about to leave, he looked back and noticed the faded square on the wall where the radio had been. He then closed the door and mounted the bike for the ride back to the village. And as he pedaled slowly away, he imagined that he could again hear a cryptic broadcast that had once blared from that radio, one evening, in those first few months of 1943.

CHAPTER ONE

THE OLD MAN

"This is Lord Haw Haw, speaking to you from Berlin."

There was a rustle of magazines and newspapers being tossed aside by the combat crews lounging near the radio, in the chilly Nissen hut. And drinks were held unsipped, as the glib voice of England's suave traitor continued with his broadcast from Herr Goebbels' propaganda ministry.

"Tonight I bring a special greeting from the fighter pilots of the Luftwaffe to the 918th Bomb Group in England. Congratulations on your safe arrival at Archbury. We've been expecting you since you left Kansas, and our U-boats have been counting your B-17s on the flight from Iceland to Prestwick, Scotland. We're sorry that you lost one in the drink off Bluey West Two, but the U-Boat that picked up the crew reports that all of them are in good spirits . . . and most talkative.

So, here's luck on your first mission, and a friendly tip to your Group Commander, Colonel Keith Davenport. I say, Colonel, have your Adjutant, Major Stovall, correct the clock above the radio in your Officers' lounge, it's four minutes slow. Pleasant dreams, chumps, and take it easy. We'll be seeing you."

Forty pairs of eyes swung, first to the clock, then to their wrist watches and finally to the tall bony figure of Colonel Davenport, who had been leaning on the radio cabinet, and who now switched off the dial with a snap. The fatigued, mostly unshaven young faces looming above the flight jackets and flying clothes focused on him expectantly.

Davenport, who likewise needed a shave, appeared more tired than anyone. Dark smudges showed under his eyes, and his left eyelid twitched nervously, as he met the questioning glance of a yellow- haired pilot who wore his crushed hat tilted back.

"How about that, Colonel", asked the young man, uncertainly? "It sounds like a gag."

"That was no gag, Bishop", said Davenport, with a shrug and an awkward imitation of a smile. "The 918th has apparently already made Goering's hit parade. Especially, Major Stovall."

Everyone looked at the Adjutant, who stood nearby wearing a rather unhappy expression that matched a sudden craving, unprecedented in his tea-totaling life, for a strong shot of whisky.

"What do you say, Harvey?", Davenport continued, "Do you keep our clock on time from now on, or do we get a new adjutant in the Group?"

Disconcerted, Stovall groped for an answer amid the flurry of nervous laughs that followed the colonel's effort at humor. Then Davenport led Stovall to one side.

"Let's go over to my office, Harvey", he said, inconspicuous- ly.

On their way to the door, the pair passed a heavyset navigator with LT. HEINZ ZIMMERMANN stenciled on the breast of his flying jacket. Zimmermann had not looked up once from the red -hot stove, at which he had been staring, during the broadcast. After the colonel and major had passed, he deliberately spat on the stove.

Outside, the night was cold and damp against a man's face. Even if there had not been a trace of the fog which muffled the occasional blinks of Major Stovall's flashlight, shielded with blue tissue paper, no low-flying JU-88s would have detected a crack of light, to betray the existence of an American bomber station, in the solid blackness. The two officers picked their way cautiously through the mud, past the still unfamiliar layout of the Administration Block of Nissen huts. Past a slithering bicycle, and finally past the guard, who rose awkwardly to attention from behind his unpainted wooded desk, in the hall of the Ops Block, shielded just inside by a blackout curtain.

As they walked down a narrow hall, hung with signs reading S-2, and S-3, and ADJUTANT, Davenport spoke over his right shoulder.

"What a lousy dirty dump", he said. "They can take England and ram it, and jam it."

Stovall sympathized acutely with Davenport's irritation, because he knew that it was not prompted by personal discomfort. Throughout the endless and maddening difficulties that had plagued the Group during its months of training, he had never once known this conscientious West Pointer to think of himself. But he sensed that Lord Haw Haw, spokesman of an implac- able enemy, sweeping everything before it toward Stalingrad, and waiting across the North Sea for Davenport's green boys, had unduly disturbed the Old Man. If the colonel had a flaw, reflected Stovall, it was that he felt too much like a father toward his forty-eight air crews, and that he had over identified himself with his men. Incessantly worrying about them.

Under the stress of combat, would Davenport try to spare the crews the ultimate hardships and sacrifices? Would losses overly upset him, and would he thereby lose his efficiency as a leader? Stovall comforted himself with the reminder that HE was a civilian soldier . . . and that such misgivings might well be stemming from his own inexperience of command.

He followed the colonel through a green door lettered C.O., groped with the blackout curtains to insure that they were tightly drawn and switched on the office light. Far away, in the village of Archbury, the two men could hear an air-raid siren's wail, rising and falling.

"That's just what we need", grumbled Davenport. "A few bombs dumped on the 918th to prove that that Lord Haw Haw guy wasn't fooling."

"Night intruder, maybe", said Stovall, while the colonel fished in his desk until he came up with a sealed pint bottle of bourbon. "Snooping around that R.A.F. airdrome near here."

Davenport unscrewed the bottle cap, sniffed the bourbon and held it out toward Stovall. "Join me?"

"Afraid I still don't drink, Colonel", said Stovall, and to himself: "You're not going to find the answers to your problems at the bottom of a brown bottle."

Some hint of disappointment in his eyes caught Davenport's attention.

"I know what you're thinking, Harvey", he said. "Not until after our first mission, I used to say. Well, tonight, I kind of feel that for us, the war has begun."

The siren's wail died out, uncovering the distant drone of engines in the sky, as night fighters of the R.A.F. shooed the visiting German away. The colonel swallowed two swigs, and wiped his mouth with the sleeve of his flight jacket.

"Better have one."

Davenport held out the bottle again, but the Adjutant shook his head. "If you don't mind, sir", he said.

"Okay", said Davenport. "Now, how in hell did those monkeys find out so much about us?"

Stovall scratched his head.

"Well", he said, "there's the crew they said they picked up."

"Any Nazi sympathizers on that crew?"

For a moment Stovall looked as though he hadn't understood.

"Colonel", he said, in a persecuted tone, "are you still riding me about that navigator . . . Zimmermann?"

"Maybe", said Davenport. "Of course", he added, "he wasn't on that crew."

"If he isn't on the level", said Stovall, "then the F.B.I. and Counter-Intelligence are all wet. They couldn't have given Zimmermann a cleaner bill of health."

"And yet, his old man was a big wheel in the German American Bund."

"I'm satisfied that he always hated his father", replied Stovall. "He left home when he found out about it, you know. He real- izes he's still suspect and he's plenty eager for combat . . . . to live down his family's stigma."

"He'll still have to convince me . . . what with that Nazi background. Maybe we'd better keep him restricted to the station and detail somebody to keep a close check on him."

"I'd strongly recommend against that, Colonel. Eventually it would attract attention, probably ruin him with the rest of the men in the Group . . . none of them know he was ever under any suspicion."

"Of course", said Davenport, reluctantly, "I wouldn't want to hurt one of my guys by any hasty action."

He took another shot of whisky and replaced the pint in his desk.

"I've got the finest bunch of young men that ever came out of the U.S.A. But you'd better issue another memorandum on base security. Everybody, from cooks, M.Ps., to ground crews and officers, to you and me, have got to clam up more. I don't know where you'll dig him up, but put an M.P. at the Officers' Club, too."

"Yes, sir."

Davenport lifted one of his green painted phones.

"Might as well see if I can operate one of these scrambler phones", he said to Stovall, then, into the receiver: "Operator, get me PINETREE."

There was a two-minute wait, during which Stovall studied the gloomy expression on the homely, fatherly, face of his thirty-eight-year-old commander, whose cheekbones were creased from the oxygen mask he had worn on that afternoon's practice mission. It was the face of a man unable to conceal the heavy load he was carrying.

"Hello", said Davenport. "PINETREE? I want to speak to Colonel Savage." There was a pause.

"Hello, Frank? This is Keith Davenport . . . . thanks . . same to you. Say, can you scramble? Okay, I'll scramble now."

He waited several moments, then pressed a switch on the phone's base. "Hello, Frank. Yes, I can understand you."

Davenport's voice was traveling through the wires in garbled form, to thwart any line tapping, and was being unscrambled automatically at the other end.

"Can you make me out? Okay? Look, Frank, I've got a problem . . . if you're going to be there for the next half hour . . . . Roger that."

He hung up the phone, took his trench coat off a wall hook, slipped it on, and slung his gas mask over his shoulder.

Stovall beamed, "I see that you've read that poop-sheet from headquarters I put in your basket, about wearing gas masks."

"Yes. And from the looks of that IN basket, those cookies at PINETREE are out to win this war with mimeograph machines. It's not like Frank Savage, either; he's always hated paper work."

Stovall helped Davenport adjust the straps of the mask so that it hung properly.

"Memorandum thirty dash six", he said. And then, "Isn't Colonel Savage kind of low ranking for a commanding general's job?"

"He's only the acting C.O. Until some hot-shot general from the Pentagon shows up.

Frank is strictly a stick and rudder man. But he got the dream assignment, leading the first ten missions here, and built himself a reputation back home. That was before the German fighters started playing rough."

Davenport leaned against the doorway, taking out a cigarette, and Stovall saw that the conversation had stumbled over one of the colonel's pet subjects.

"Personally", continued Davenport, "I was surprised to see General Pritchard give him that first Bomb Group. Savage handles men like Simon Legree."

"You've served with him before, sir", asked Stovall, casually trying to hide his eagerness for a glimpse behind the scenes of military politics?

"Off and on", said the colonel, "since we were lieutenants in the 3rd Attack Group at Barksdale Field."

His expression showed that the recollection was exciting. "What sort of joker is he", prompted Stovall?

"Well, to begin with, he's a good-looking bastard. He's part Indian. And nobody's neutral about him. You either like him, or you hate him. Personally, I couldn't help liking him. He's lousy at a desk job, but he's a damn hot pilot. He won a D.F.C. in peacetime, which takes some doing. Dames love him and I wish I had a dollar for every quart of whisky he's drank."

"Sounds like an interesting guy to meet."

"You don't meet Frank Savage. You collide with him." Davemport lit his cigarette and ejected a puff like a snort.

"Life is funny, Harvey. Tonight he's my boss and yet, just a few short years ago I was ordered down to Barksdale to relieve him of command of his squadron. He had been flying his boys ragged and sweating the ground personnel like a road gang.

You'd thought there was a goddamn war on the way he ran that outfit. Keerist, were they glad to see me!"

"Is he a West Pointer", asked Stovall?

As soon as he had uttered the words he felt embarrassed, but the colonel missed the implication.

"No, he came in as a reserve officer. And then he finally got a regular commission."

Davenport turned to leave then added. over his shoulder.

"See if you can take the mens' minds off that blast from Berlin. How about cooking up a christening party for the Officers' Club next Sunday? Something to keep my family happy."

After the colonel had left, Stovall sat heavily on a corner of the desk and lit his pipe. He had a sense of unreality, and he couldn't rid his mind of the illusion that the Group was still in training. That it would always be in training. He tried to visualize the twenty-five hundred men, whose records he kept, as a finished weapon, which had been brought face to face with the enemy at the logical moment. But the picture wouldn't focus. There simply hadn't been enough time to yank these young- sters off the sidewalk, throw their schoolbooks away and trans- form them into airplane commanders, with a quarter of a million dollars' worth of four engine bomber, and ten lives, thrust into their hands. Or enough time to tap a bellhop on the shoulder and, presto, come up with a ball-turret gunner, skilled in the art of shooting to kill.

Until now, he thought, I've wondered how I'd ever catch up with my work. But soon there will be decorations, missing-in-action reports, shipping home the personal effects, gathering the material for those telegrams which will read: . . .

"The Secretary of War deeply regrets to inform you . . ."

I've been working harder than I ever worked in my life, and yet we haven't even started.

He glanced through the connecting door to the filing cabinets in his office. There, he thought, is the first part of the story, the vital statistics. Now comes the last part.

What a seat for a spectator, for the Keeper of the Records. From the womb to the tomb.

The all-clear was sounding in the village as he went to his desk.

"Sergeant", he said to his chief clerk, "it may be all clear in Archbury, but I'm afraid it's going to be a long time before they sound the all-clear in this office."

"The major", replied the clerk, "can say that again."

From his back seat of his staff car, as he and his driver drove through Archbury, Colonel Davenport glanced toward the Black Swan. Four soldiers, with their arms around the waists of four W.A.A.F. girls, looking particularly broad-beamed in their slate-blue R.A.F. uniforms, passed under the muffled light above the entrance and disappeared inside the pub, singing . . .

"Bless them all. Bless them all. The long and the short and the tall." The colonel smiled to himself, and to the driver he said.

"Looks as though the 918th is getting Anglo-American relations off to a fast start."

"Yes, sir", said the corporal, as the car continued on, it's shielded lights barely reflecting the doorways along the left-hand side of the cobbled street. "They tell me that you've got to cultivate the local talent to get eggs with shells on. The two go together. Dames and eggs, and eggs and dames."

But the colonel's mind, freed for the first time in days from harassing details, had already begun to rove in broader sweeps. For the first time he was conscious of a question in his mind about the wisdom of having pulled every string at his disposal to grab that prize plum . . . command of a Bomb Group.

If it hadn't been for his West Point classmate, newly promoted Brigadier General Ed Henderson, on duty in the Pentagon, he'd never have gotten the Group. Everybody wanted the chance to make a combat record that counted. It was nice to be the boss, and take the bows, while you were back in the States. But it cut both ways.

Over here it was possible to fail, to get killed, playing guinea pig in an American bombing experiment that a lot of military minds didn't believe in. The British, for instance. They were sold on night bombing, where you had the protection of the darkness. They thought the Americans were crazy to go in naked by daylight, for the sake of greater bombing accuracy.

Did Frank Savage, up at headquarters, who had already had a taste of it, or General Spaatz, or Hap Arnold, or even General Marshall, really believe that the handful of B-17s, sitting on their wet hardstands in England tonight, could challenge the skeptics with results good enough to justify building up a much larger Air Force here? Nobody knows, he told himself.

Twenty minutes later the colonel stepped from his car, in the driveway, before a huge stone structure that resembled a castle. A crescent moon had risen, shedding enough light to illuminate sweeping lawns, avenues of linden trees, and a pond clustered with wild ducks and three swans. Formerly a girls' school called Wycombe Abbey, the towering, blacked-out edifice, was now the headquarters of the American Bomber Command, known by the code name PINETREE.

Colonel Davenport opened the great oak door, pushed aside the blackout curtain and found himself in a brilliantly lighted hall, high-ceilinged and austere with its Gothic arches. So this, he told himself, is where they fight a plush war. With hot showers, and tea time at four o'clock. Where lieutenants have breakfast, are promoted to captains at lunch and majors by dinnertime.

He showed the sentry his A.O.G. card, then walked through an anteroom marked

COMMANDING GENERAL

And, seeing that the door to the office was open, he thrust his head inside, however, the room appeared to be empty.

"Have a seat", said a casual voice that seemed to come from the ceiling.

Davenport stepped inside and saw Colonel Savage standing, precariously, on top of a tall bookcase from which he was reaching out to tack in place the corner of a ceiling-high map of Western Europe, mounted against the wall on beaver board.

"Short of help around here", asked Davenport?

"Help is short everywhere", replied Savage, without interruping his hammering, "when there's a war on. You can usually do it yourself by the time you get hold of a corporal."

He tapped the last brad in place and then, in one simultaneous movement, he tossed the hammer down at Davenport, without warning, and executed a spring to the floor, landing with the cushioned spring of an athlete. Unprepared, Davenport made a grab for the hammer, but dropped it.

Same old Frank, he thought; tosses the ball to you and takes it for granted that you'll catch it. Savage gave Davenport a hard handshake, pushed him toward a chair, settled himself behind his desk and confronted his visitor with a quizzical expression, predominated by friendliness and sympathy.

"Keith", he said, "I know that look - that harried look of the new Group Commander. As if you'd just had a barbed-wire high calonic."

"Well, anyway, I've got a problem", said Davenport.

Savage laughed and motioned toward his IN and OUT baskets.

"That's full of problems", he said. "I'll listen to yours if you can give me a new one. And I don't mean a shortage of spare parts. Nor, generators burning out when the turrets are tracking at once. Nor, turbos and props running away on take-off. Nor, shortage of privates for K.P. and guard duty. Nor, machine gun stoppages and defective tracers. Nor, chuck holes in the runway and wheels breaking through the hard-stands. Nor, lack of hang- er space for night maintenance. Nor, powdered eggs, pregnant W.A.A.F.'s, cold shaving water, honey buckets instead of plumbing."

He stopped to take a breath.

"That IN basket is full of freezing oxygen masks, freezing guns, freezing Plexiglas, electric flying suits that short out and burn a grid on your butt. It has eighteen different kinds of eng- ine malfunctions at high altitude, gunners that can't hit anything but their own wing man, and losses that have gone up from zero to five percent on shallow penetrations into France. And, that's just a sample."

He grabbed the basket with both hands and flipped it upward so that the top papers fluttered back into place like a deck of cards.

"Now, give me a new problem."

"I've got a new one, all right", said Davenport. "A bad one. Did you hear Lord Haw Haw tonight?"

"I never listen to the son-of-a-bitch", said Savage.

"For Christ's sake, Frank", responded Davenport, impatiently, "Berlin knows we're here, knows my name, even knows our clock is four minutes slow."

Savage looked with frank incredulity at the alarm written on the other man's face. "Do you mean to tell me", he said, "that you drove through this blackout just to tell me that?"

"But, . . but", - Davenport was nonplused - "what do you make of it?" "So they've got spies", laughed Savage. "So, you can't hide a bomber station. So, we've got farmhouses right alongside the perimeter track. So, Americans like to talk."

"Yeah, they talk", he said, with a flush of guilty recollection. "And I let a few of them go on pass - hanging around that pub in Archbury."

Davenport stood up, took a few nervous paces and lit a cigar- ette. Suddenly, there was a knock on the door and an aide step- ped inside.

"There's a Flight Leftenant Mallory to see you, sir", said the aide. "Please ask him to wait."

Before the aide could reply, Davenport spoke up.

"It's not a him, Frank", he said, pointedly. "It's a her." "Then ask her to wait", said Savage.

When the aide had withdrawn, Savage made a wry face at Davenport.

"Why can't we fight a war over here", he said, "without having the joint loused up with babes during working hours?"

"It all depends", said Davenport, again speaking pointedly. "This babe, you haven't seen." They exchanged glances for a moment. A twinkle came into Savage's eyes.

"An operational piece of equipment, eh", he asked?

"If you mean is she a beautiful girl, the answer is yes."

"You've only been here a short while. Where did you find her?"

"Her old man is Lord Desborough - our airfield is on their family estate. They dropped in on me for a neighborly call."

"She's a real dish?"

"On the plus side of a real knockout. Not the kind you ever keep waiting in an anteroom for more than three seconds."

Savage stared at Davenport, remembering for a moment.

"Right now", he said, "I'm not interested in dames - not even one like that. I want to know how you guys are getting along down there in the mud - what we can do to help you?"

"Well - I guess we're doing okay, so far. All except this security business. That's what's worrying me right now."

Savage stood up and walked over to the fireplace, tall, broad of shoulder, back and arm muscles showing through his uniform jacket. If his easy movements suggested a former pro-ball player or a man with American Indian blood, it was because he was both. His wavy hair was black, except for a fringe of gray at the edges, and his face was bronzed and much younger looking than might be expected at the age of thirty-six.

As Savage turned to face him, Davenport felt a faint annoyance at this man's exceptional asset of rugged good looks, and at the power of those eyes. One minute, when he smiled, they pulled at you; a minute later they knocked you back, as though he had reached out and pushed you. They were doing that now.

"You want to know about security?"

The words came with emotional conviction.

"Bear down on loose talk, of course. But as soon as you are operational, there will be only one kind of security that counts, and that is. Have you got a bunch of pilots that can hold a tight formation? Can your gunners shoot straight? Can you put air-craft commanders in the air that won't turn back from a target as long as their wings stay on?"

Openly irritated, Davenport ground out his cigarette in an ashtray that had an aluminum model of a B-17 mounted on it.

"Sounds like a fight talk, Frank", he said. "Do you think that's what I need?"

In spite of old rivalries, Savage had always liked Davenport personally. His expression softened. "You're right, Keith", he said, finally. "Where do I get off lecturing you? It's just that I've been over here longer, I guess. I'm sorry."

"Aw, balls, Frank", responded Davenport, mollified. "I realize you've had a lot of combat experience."

Savage reached down and pulled out a bottom desk drawer.

He lifted out a Green Toby Mug, modeled in the likeness of a masked robber, and set it on the desk.

"Take this old fellow along with you, Keith", he said, deliberately changing the subject. "Maybe he'll bring you as much luck as he brought me." "A beer mug?"

"I had a better use for it. Mister Security. He worked for me when I had the 901st Group. We stuck this mug on the mantelpiece in the Officers' Club as a signal that we were alerted for a mission. The boys finished their drinks and went to bed. Any visitors hanging around were none the wiser."

"We can use that idea", said Davenport, picking up the Toby. "Thanks, Frank."

"You're welcome to it". said Savage, as he stood up, "but don't bust it. Someday I'll want it back for a souvenir."

The two walked together out to the anteroom, where a W.A.A.F. officer sat with her head bent over, looking at a magazine.

"Hi there, Flight Leftenant", said Davenport. "How's everything at Desborough Hall?" She rose and stood at attention.

"Rather quiet, Colonel", she replied. "But I imagine your chaps will liven things up for us a bit. Several are coming by this weekend for some tennis."

As the young woman smiled at Davenport, Savage felt something like a shock go through him. A beautiful girl always gave him a thrill. But this girl was literally stunning.

"May I present Colonel Savage", said Davenport? "This is Flight Leftenant Pamela Mallory." She turned her wide, violet eyes toward Savage, who reached out and gave her a masculine handshake.

"Sorry I was busy", he said, cordially, "but I have to make sounds in there like a commanding general, until my new boss gets in. I'm just pinch-hitting."

"Pinch-hitting", she asked, quizzically? "Substituting."

"Oh - of course, Stupid of me." She hesitated.

"To tell the truth, my business was with the commanding general, but -."

"But maybe this guy will do", interposed Davenport, who was observing with interest the difficulty with which Pamela was concealing a flustered reaction to Savage's disconcerting gaze.

She gave a little laugh, and said. "I'm sure he does very well - as a pinch-hitter."

"If you'll excuse me", said Savage, as he was moving toward the door, "I'll be right back." "That's perfectly all right, sir", responded Pamela, formally.

As the two men disappeared, her eyes followed Savage's retreating figure intently, for a moment, then with a quick shift of her eyes to the aide, who looked away, she returned her attention to the magazine.

"See what I told you", asked Davenport, as he and Savage approached the front door?

"Not bad", said Savage. "What a break for you. You're parked on the most strategic spot in England. But don't go messing around with targets of opportunity, Keith. Stick to the primary".

"She's way out of my league, Frank."

Davenport extended his hand out to say good-bye, then paused.

"I almost forgot to ask you. Who's the new Bomber Com- mander?"

"Ed Henderson. He left London an hour, or so, ago. He's probably blundering around High Wycombe now, in the black- out, with a green driver." "Henderson?"

Davenport's face broke into a smile of pleased surprise. "Well, I'll be damned."

"Yeah", said Savage, dryly, "your pal Ed Henderson."

Davenport felt a warm glow at this unexpected news, of a friend in court. In addition to being the classmate who had used his influence to get Davenport the 918th Group, it had been Henderson who had switched Savage and him, to be in command of the 13th Attack Squadron.

It was the kind of development that would have been an odd coincidence anywhere, except in the Air Corps, where a small cadre of men, as intimate in peacetime as a family, were now running an enormous operation. If you tossed any three of them together, you were sure to have similar complications, rooted in the past.

But to Savage, it seemed that Henderson's arrival was carrying any coincidences a little too far. He had always believed that Henderson's love of the Old School Tie had cost him the command of his squadron.

"I'd like to wait and say hello to him", said Davenport, "but I ought to get back. Give him my best. Tell him I think it's great news."

"Yeah, great", remarked Savage, noncommittally, as Davenport climbed into his staff car.

Savage watched Davenport drive off and then started to re-enter the Abbey, then changed his mind and strolled across the driveway, where he stood on the grass, breathing deeply of the wet night air. Through the trees he could gradually make out the church steeple in the ancient town of High Wycombe.

How long will it be, he wondered, before the steeple bell, and all of the bells in England, silent since they had been reserved by the government as the official warning of the invasion, would ring out again in victory? If ever.

This British Isle was still terribly vulnerable, a ripe apple which could be had - which the German High Command ought to invade at any price. If they understood the potential dagger that was being aimed at their heart by a few men in this old - girls' school. Or, Savage asked himself, would it be a rubber dagger, bending because its human metal was not hard enough.

He walked back to his anteroom and rejoined Flight Leftenant Mallory.

"Come right in, Miss Mallory", he said, showing the way to his office, but without noticing the hint of disapproval in her expression, when he failed to use her military title.

As she sat down by his desk, he became aware of an unmilitary scent of gardenia. And he noticed that she did not cross her legs, but sat rather stiffly with her feet together.

Despite the camouflage of a W.A.A.F. uniform, no one could have mistaken Pamela Mallory, even at a distance, for a man. There was too much bosom, too small a waist, and the racehorse ankles were too slender. Her face, straight of nose, unusually pale, and framed by her chestnut-colored hair, that curled in a roll above her slate-blue collar, was rather a small setting for her eyes.

Her eyes were enormous, and Savage couldn't help but noticed that their whites had the bluish tinge normally seen only in small, and healthy, children.

"Care for American cigarettes?" "Like anything", she said, pleasantly.

It was the first time he had heard this odd expression. "Here."

He reached into a drawer, taking out two packs. "I'm a cigar smoker. These are for you."

"Oh, no, . . . thank you", she said, quickly. "But, may I try just one of yours, for a change?"

Savage sensed that he had touched her pride. It was that English pride, so vulnerable to the invading horde of Americans, with their abundance of cigarettes, chocolate and salted peanuts, their superior rations, their high pay, their lavish tips to London cabbies, and their wealth of all material things that were now scarce in an austere Britain. He offered a light for her cigarette.

"I know how busy you are, Colonel Savage", she began, in a crisp, official tone, "but I came to your headquarters on a rather important matter."

"I haven't got a thing to do but listen to you", said Savage, smiling. "You see, sir, - I'm in DDI-4-B."

She saw that he was in the dark about what she just said.

"Signals", she amended, "radio. What we're doing is in a SECRET classification that won't permit me to go into details, but perhaps that won't be necessary. The point is, is that I get information every day that may be very valuable to you and your staff."

"Sounds great", Savage looked skeptical.

"Yes, sir", she agreed. "How would you like to receive accurate information on German fighter reaction to your daylight bombing strikes?"

"We'd grab at it", he said, still regarding her with uncertainty. "And just how do you mean, fighter reaction? Our crews give us pretty good reports on how the Germans react."

"I mean a lot more than the enemy fighter tactics your crews see. I know most of the German fighter pilots by name, where they live, where they rearm and refuel, what they talk about - what they say about you. By that I mean, you Americans."

She had Savage's rapt attention, now. "Mind telling me more", he asked?

"Unfortunately, sir, I can't", she responded. "I think you can readily understand why security is so tight. If the enemy found out we are getting this information, the source would dry up."

"Sure, I can see that. But you've got me on the edge of my chair. I've never heard a word about - what it is you're doing."

"And that's the way we need to keep it. For now, I can pass on the information to you, without telling you how we get it. Of course, you'll have to get an okay from the Air Ministry."

"Hell, that'll take a couple of months."

"Possibly, sir. Channels, and all that. But meanwhile, I don't see why we can't arrange something between us informally."

"I'm all for that. Nuts to the red tape."

"All right, but I'm going to need one thing from you. Otherwise, I can't be of a maximum assistance to you."

"Sure, what is it you want."

"Your routes and control times, as far as possible in advance, before each of your missions." Savage's mouth opened.

"Are you kidding me", he said?

"No, sir, not at all. It's absolutely necessary that we know your routes and times." Savage abruptly stood up. All of the early skepticism had returned to his face. "Just a minute", he said. "That's information we don't give to anybody - except the combat units. I'd get court-martialed if I let any of it out."

"Perhaps I'd better wait and discuss this with your new general", she quipped. "He'd tell you the same thing."

Savage stared at the girl for a long moment, nonplused.

"I don't get it", he continued. "If the R.A.F. wants that kind of secret dope from us, why didn't they send an officer over here to see me, Miss Mallory, instead of a - ."

He stopped, groping for the right word, his eyes involuntarily dropping to the un-masculine contours of her uniform jacket.

"Flight Leftenant Mallory, if you don't mind, sir. And do I really have to remind you that I am an officer? And I dare say that women in the W.A.A.F. have been entrusted with much more confidential information during the past three years than anyone in your headquarters, Colonel Savage."

"It all sounds cockeyed", persisted Savage, in a tolerant tone, ignoring the girl's pique. "We're worried enough, as it is, about possible leaks of our Field Orders. Sending you a copy would be one more chance for a leak. No, - I'd have to see this request in writing from the Air Ministry, Miss Mallory."

"You've called me Miss Mallory twice, now, Colonel." "I'm sorry."

"And I thought you Americans, most particularly, detested red tape. Go ahead, then, and get it in writing - a couple of months from now. Meanwhile, I'm sure I could have helped you. I'm sorry to have troubled you, sir."

She stood up.

"Hey, not so fast", said Savage, hurrying around his desk. "Don't get me wrong. I'm extremely interested in what you've told me, and I appreciate your coming here. I'll look into it thoroughly - and get a request in for coordination, right away."

"Why hurry", she asked, coolly? "perhaps it will be a nice, long war."

Savage flushed as she gave him a brief handshake, rendered a side-wheeling R.A.F. salute, and then left. He slowly returned to his desk, sat down and stared at nothing in particular, scratching his head. Then he rang for his aide.

"Ask the communications officer to come in and see me", he said. "Maybe he'll know what that glamour girl was driving at. She just might have something."

"How do you like this layout", asked Savage?

Shifting his small body in his easy chair, Brigadier General Edward Henderson glanced appreciatively around his quarters on the second floor, which had formerly been occupied by the head mistress of Wycombe Abby. He saw a handsomely furnished living room, large enough for entertaining his British opposite numbers with official cocktail parties, a double bedroom and guest room, a door leading into a spacious bathroom, and plenty of coal in the brass scuttle, handy to the blue and red flames curling in the fireplace.

"First rate", said Henderson.

The two had just settled down with their cigars and Scotches. How easily, thought Savage, he adjusts himself to new surroundings. Already he looks as though he belongs here, and in a uniform with a star.

It had not escaped Savage's notice that although Henderson's promotion was less than a week old, his new star and shoulder patch were embroidered in silver and gold on all the uniforms and overcoats, which the R.A.F. batman was carrying to the closet in the bedroom. His slacks had a straightedge crease and the polish on his jodhpur boots glistened like glass. Even his cross-country bags, neatly stenciled with his new rank, were of special gabardine material instead of the canvas of the standard A-2 bag.

"What's the lowdown on this show", asked Henderson, brisk- ly?

"The newspapers", said Frank, "have been putting up almost a thousand bombers for me. But all I've been able to put over the target, on our biggest mission to date, is less than a hundred ."

"You know how it is, Frank", said Henderson, with an airy wave of his hand. "It'll be months before production really hits its stride. Meanwhile, we can't let the people back home get discouraged. They need good news. And this is the only spot from which Americans are fighting Germans."

There was no agreement in Savage's expression.

"Flak", he continued, "is getting worse. And those yellow-nose Focke Wulfs are pressing home their attacks. Losses are running three to five percent higher. And bombing accuracy is falling off." "What's your solution?"

"Fighter cover to the target and back. More nose guns. More bombers. And more replacement crews.

That North African show is still robbing us of the buildup we need. Down at the Groups, the combat crews are getting cynical about the lack of replacements, and discouraged about their chances of completing a tour. They've begun to figure out the percentages."

"What about the weather?"

"Awful! Sometimes we have to scrub a mission as many as seven or eight times, trying to outguess the stinking weather over the Continent.

It's maddening to the crews. They might fly eight missions on the ground for every one in the air. I believe that's their big- gest beef, but there isn't anything we can do about it up here." "Do you think our daylight bombing may turn out to be a fiasco?"

Savage pondered the question before answering.

"A lot of people think so", he finally said. "But here's the way I see it. With a big force we could get better results. But, if they won't give us that big force until we've proved the case for daylight bombing with what we have, then we're sunk.

Personally, I believe we can do the job in spite of all the ob- stacles, if we can develop the right leadership. Good Group

Commanders are going to be your number-one problem. So far, it's been a case of a good Group Commander - a good Group. A weak Group Commander - a weak Group. Right there is where we'll win or lose."

"I agree with you on that", said Henderson. Incidentally, has Keith Davenport gotten here with the 918th?"

"Yes, sir. A few days ago. He sent you his regards."

"I'll watch that outfit with a lot of personal interest. Davenport's tops at handling men."

Savage offered no comment.

"And speaking of jobs, Frank, you are the one who ought to have this job. You've earned it in combat, while I've been shuffling papers in the Big House."

The atmosphere between the two men became charged. Henderson's statement was literally true and they both knew it.

"I'm not kicking", said Savage, quickly. "I guess I'll always be a Squadron Commander at heart." "If you don't mind my saying so", said Henderson, smiling faintly, "you turned out to be a better Group Commander in combat than a Squadron Commander in peacetime."

Savage's eyes, always the color of granite, assumed the same texture. He held Henderson's glance until the latter looked away toward the fire.

"Let's call that a matter of opinion", said Savage.

"In any case", Henderson went on smoothly, after a pause, "I envy you. You've won everybody's admiration with the way you led the first Group here. That critically important first Group. Eight missions before you lost an airplane - when the British Bomber Command figured you'd lose seventy- five percent at a crack."

"Thanks", said Savage.

"Your star is already in the mill, you know", continued Henderson. "I hope it comes through soon. You deserve it."

To himself, Savage said: "You're not kidding, brother."

Henderson went over to the sideboard and mixed two fresh highballs, remaining standing after he had handed one to Savage.

"Look, Frank", he said. "Quite honestly, how do you feel about serving under me - again?" Savage dangled his glass from his fingertips. Then looked straight into Henderson's eyes. "I'd be a damn liar", he said, "if I told you I was happy about it."

"I anticipated that you'd feel that way", remarked Henderson, pokerfaced. "So, I discussed it with General Pritchard. His feeling is that even if it's a shotgun wedding, we've both got to sweat it out for a while. With your experience, I'm going to need the hell out of you in Operations, and he wants you right where you are - as A-3."

He looked over the rim of his glass at Savage as he sipped his Scotch, then said. "I told him I was in complete agreement with him."

"Well, if that's the way the Old Man wants it", Savage said casually, "that's always been good enough for me."

CHAPTER TWO

THE RATE OF ATTRITION

A woolly blanket of late winter fog, which had been lingering over the British Isles for two weeks, grounding the bombers, had finally moved east.

At Army Air Force headquarters in the suburbs of London, behind a broad glass-topped desk on which was a polished name plaque with the words, lettered in gold, . . .

MAJ. GEN. PATRICK E. PRITCHARD, sat a grizzled, sharp-eyed man who did not need the Command Pilot's wings on his chest to identify him as a veteran airman. He was nearly bald, from wearing a flight helmet, and he had the look that accrues to some men after thousands of hours spent in a cockpit - hours that have instilled the habit of meeting emergen- cies, resourcefully. He was dictating an official report to his boss in Washington, D.C.

"By all rights", he was concluding, "there should have been a constant morale problem this winter, because of losses, low replacement rate, unflyable weather, and rugged living conditions. On the contrary, morale is strong, even in our Hard Luck Group, the 918th, where the rate of attrition has been higher than in the other Groups."

Some eighty miles away, while the general was dictating, the first of the B-17s returning to Archbury from the day's mission, to the submarine pens at Lorient, was banking into its final approach. Two ambulances sped toward the end of the runway in response to a red flare fired from the bomber, signifying that there were wounded aboard.

At one of the hard-stands, a crew chief and his assistant shaded their eyes toward the gliding Fortress with special con- cern, for they had identified the number on the tail. This was their ship.

With his free hand, the crew chief was holding the leash of a mournful-eyed Dachshund named Corporal Kesselring. His master, Lieutenant McKesson, the pilot of the incoming B-17, had started the Dachshund out as a private, but had recently promoted it to corporal, whereupon the animal had run away. The crew chief had found it that morning living with the mess sergeant.

"Boy! Will Lieutenant McKesson be glad to see Corporal Kesselring", he said to the assistant crew chief. "But", he continued, squatting down and petting the Dachshund. "I'm afraid he's going to bust you back to private, old fellow."

The dog rolled its sad eyes up to the sergeant, then returned its eager attention to the runway. The sergeant lifted the animal up to the crew chief's stand, where he hoped the pilot would spot his mascot sooner.

The Flying Fort settle down into a bumpy landing, rolling clean to the end of the strip, and taxied off a few yards along the perimeter track, to clear the way for the other returning B-17s in the landing pattern. Before the propellers had stopped turning over, both ambulances were alongside the nose, on which had been painted eleven bombs, one for each mission the aircraft had flown since the 918th's first operation, two months earlier. While, over the waist hatch was the legend:

WHERE ANGELS AND GENERALS FEAR TO TREAD

Major Don Kaiser, Group Flight Surgeon, motioned the stretcher bearers under the nose hatch and reached up to assist as the body of the pilot, Lieutenant McKesson, was lowered through the opening. The job was complicated by the fact that the man was a beefy six-footer and that he was resisting violently, the back of his head having been blown away and exposing his brain.

Examining the wound quickly, while strong but tender hands restrained the pilot on the stretcher, Major Kaiser turned to the navigator, Lieutenant Zimmermann, who had just dropped out through the hatch.

"How long since he was hit?"

"Over two hours ago", replied Zimmermann. "Feels more like two hundred to me." The flight surgeon whistled and shook his head.

"I wouldn't believed it if I wasn't looking at it", he said.

"Easy with his right leg", snapped Zimmermann, to a medical corpsman as the stretcher was being lifted into one of the waiting ambulances! "It's broken below the knee. And, Major - somebody'd better sit on him. I've been holding him down for the past hour."

Unheeded by the cluster of men around the ambulances, the second B-17 to land came hurtling down the runway with its brakes and flaps shot out, and approached the far end with no apparent deceleration. At the last moment, the pilot cut his port side engines, gunned his starboard engines, and ground-looped the big airplane off the concrete and onto the muddy turf, oppos- ite the first B-17, where it spun completely around before coming to rest, with its right wing crumpled. In a jiffy, all ten members of the crew, including Colonel Davenport, emerged.

"Everybody's in one piece", Davenport shouted to Major Kaiser! "Don't bother about us!"

Kaiser waved back and was about to climb aboard the ambulance when Lieutenant Zimmermann put a detaining hand on his arm. To the flight surgeon's practiced eye, which had noted and been impressed by the navigator's stolid calm up to this point, it was obvious that something was now happening to the young man's composure.

The Doc observed the color draining from Zimmermann's swarthy cheeks and a suffering expression in his eyes, deep-set under jutting black brows and a low forehead.

"What do we do with an arm, Major", he asked, as though the words couldn't possibly be making sense? "We've got an arm in there - the top turret gunner's."

"Where's the rest of him?"

"In a French hospital, I hope, sir. I bailed him out."

The flight surgeon turned to a medical corpsman in the ambulance. "Give me a blanket", he said, then to Zimmermann, "I'll take care of it."

He climbed up into the nose of the airplane and, in a few moments, he reappeared. Zimmermann turned his back and looked the other way as the flight surgeon carried a long, slender object, wrapped in the blanket, over to the ambulance.

Then the ambulance pulled away and headed for the hospital, followed by the second ambulance, which had picked up three frostbitten gunners from the waist hatch.

In the B-17's cockpit, Lieutenant Jesse Bishop, co-pilot at the take-off, but the airplane commander at the finish, was starting up the inboard engines in order to taxi the airplane to it's hard-stand, when the assistant engineer tapped him on the shoulder.

"The truck's waiting, sir", he said. "Why don't you let me taxi her in for you." Bishop shook his head and said. "I've got it sergeant."

At the hard-stand, Bishop remained in the cockpit for several minutes, laboriously filling out the Form One, ignoring the shrill barking of Corporal Kesselring below, where the crew chief still held him by the leash. Then Bishop made his way aft from the blood soaked flight deck, through the bomb bay, past the clutter of spent shell casings in the waist, tossed his parachute out the waist hatch, to the ground, and clambered out after it.

Zimmermann, his coveralls spattered with the drying, dark stains of another man's blood, stood waiting for Bishop. Neither flyer said a word as they walked with deathlike lethargy to a jeep, which Zimmermann had flagged down.

"Let me off at the hospital", said Bishop, then, noticing the chaplain's cross on the driver's collar, he added. "Excuse me, Captain. Could you please drop me there?"

"That's right where I'm headed for myself", responded Chaplain Twombly, a strong featured officer who looked more like a squadron commander than a man of the cloth. He had made a point of being accepted as one of the guys and had succeeded rather well.

"You're always the first person I spot", said Zimmermann, as they drove off, "out there on the perimeter track when we're on final approach."

"I believe that's where I ought to be", said the chaplain.

He pointedly avoided any questions about the mission, waiting for his passengers to talk of their own accord.

"How did you make out in the poker game last night", inquired Zimmermann, after a pause? "The church", responded the Chaplain, "won three pounds ten."

He smiled as he replied, but his thoughts were grim.

Before leaving the perimeter track, the jeep passed a B-17 that was just disgorging its crew. The first man out kneeled down and kissed the ground.

Glancing back at Bishop, Chaplain Twombley said:

"The ground feels pretty good after a mission, doesn't it?"

Bishop ignored the question. He had removed his flight helmet and the wind was ruffling thought his thick yellow hair, matted above his forehead with sweat. His vividly blue eyes had a glazed stare and his young face was a gaunt mask, as if from a sudden encroachment of old age.

He passed his fingers through his hair, rubbed his eyes with his balled fists, and stroked the skin of his cheeks where the re- cent grip of the oxygen mask still itched. When he pulled a cigarette from a pocket of his flying coveralls he tried to light it from a book of matches.

The Chaplain noticed that the young man's hands began shaking with a course tremor, as he failed to get a light after three tries, merely burning the side of the cigarette paper.

"High octane", said the Chaplain, as he slowed the jeep down and produced a storm light that flamed like a blow torch.

Bishop got his cigarette lighted and continued to stare blankly ahead, without thanking him, but Twombley felt rewarded that he had been able to do something, anything, for this pilot, who's terrifying day's work had so visibly congealed him. To the Chaplain, this disheveled, unutterably weary twenty-one-year-old boy was a sacred thing - a tragic human sacrifice, condemned by the proved superiority of his body and character, to bear the maximum load that could be placed upon each.

When the jeep reached the site of a group of large, interconnecting Nissens that comprised the station hospital, Bishop jumped out and walked quickly to the door with the Chaplain, disappearing inside. And then, in less than a minute, he reappeared and nodded to Zimmermann.

"He's had it, Heinz", he said, with simple irrelevance. "Son-of-a-bitch", said Zimmermann.

The words were reverent the way he spoke them.

Bishop started off down the road, his hands in his pockets, his feet shuffling.

"Hey, Jesse", called out Zimmermann! "Where you going?" Bishop didn't turn around and just shot back, "the club."

"What about Interrogation", called out Zimmermann, again, in a tone which declared that a man didn't skip Interrogation any more than he would skip a Briefing for a mission.

"To hell with it", shouted Bishop, over his shoulder.

He entered the lounge of the Officers' Club, which was empty except for a corporal, who was setting out glasses at one end of the bar. As Bishop approached, the corporal smiled apologetical-ly.

"I'm sorry, sir", he said. "Bar's not open for half an hour."

"Give me a Scotch. A double one."

"I'd like to, Lieutenant. But those are my orders."

"On second thought", said Bishop, as if he hadn't heard the corporal, or didn't care, "make it a double-double."

"You'll have to wait, sir", persisted the soldier, who was anxious not to antagonize the officer. "It won't be long", he added.

But Bishop showed no irritation, nor any awareness of his surroundings. He leaned one elbow on the bar.

"I heard it snap - like a dry stick", he said, dreamily. "How's that, sir", asked the corporal, puzzled.

"His leg", said Bishop.

The corporal scrutinized Bishop with uncertainty. He couldn't help noticing the resemblance between the features of this dog-tired combat man in front of him, and the pilot in a colored poster on the wall by the bar. The poster showed a rosy cheeked, almost girlishly handsome, smiling youth, posing in flying clothes for an aircraft manufacture's ad, which bore the slogan:

"Who's afraid of the New Focke Wulf?"

Underneath was the penciled notation: "I AM", followed by the signatures of all the pilots in the 918th, with Colonel Davenport's at the top. The corporal, glancing again at the sweet-faced boy in the ad, thought: That's the way this guy must have looked back home. But look at him now.

"Pour the drink", said Bishop, suddenly, in a flat voice." The corporal squinted at the clock.

"That clock's been slow - once before, that I know of", he said. "I guess I can take a chance." He went over and set the clock ahead a half hour.

"Soda?"

Bishop nodded and watched closely while the bartender poured a double-shot into a glass, filled it with soda, and handed it to him. He took a swallow.

"I sure wish you could get ice over here", remarked Bishop, absently. "You could hear it snap, like a stick", he continued. "I had to yank hard."

"I just came from the sack, sir", the corporal said. "Did we lose any this afternoon?"

"Any? Don't you mean how many did we lose! Are you new around here? He took a second swallow of his whiskey and soda.

"We lost four", he said, "four that I know of. The usual number. And everybody else caught a working over."

"Four", said the corporal, shaking his head. "It don't hardly seem right."

Bishop carried his drink across the room and set it on top of a scarred, upright piano. He ran his fingers over the yellowed keyboard, then struck the opening crashing chords of the Warsaw Concerto, a new favorite in England. While the room began to fill with the music spurting from Bishop's fingers, a captain came in, stood and listened for a moment, then went over to the bar.

"I'm looking for Lieutenant Jesse Bishop", he said. "Couldn't find him at Interrogation." "I guess that's him", said the corporal.

The captain ordered a mug of beer.

"From what his crew told me", the captain continued, "he's due for a Medal of Honor. Boy, what a story!"

He paused to listen to Bishop's playing. "And he's some musician, too."

"Yeah. You ought to see it when the place is full. They even turn off the radio and everybody shuts up", said the corporal.

The captain walked over to Bishop and placed a hand on the young lieutenant's shoulder. "Mind if I interrupt you for a minute", he asked?

Bishop struck a sharp chord in an off key, stopped playing, and looked up. The captain stuck out his hand.

"Reynolds, Public Relations, Bomber Command", he said. Bishop made no move to shake the man's hand.

"I know this is no time to bother you, but they gave me a hell of a story on you at Interrogation, and if you can spare me just five minutes, I can button it up. Incidentally, congratulations -"

"We've got a Group P.R.O.", said Bishop. "Go talk to him."

"That's not the same. Believe me, these personal-interest stories do more good back home than -"

"We've still got a Group P.R.O." The two locked eyes.

Twelve O'clock High

"Listen, Lieutenant, I hate this job. But, just the same, it is my job to get your story." Bishop reached for his glass, took a drink, and swung around on his stool.

"Okay", he said, "I'll give you a story. This Group has been shot to hell. We've got a swell Group Commander, but can he turn fog, rain and clouds into weather good enough to fly format- ions through, and bomb through? Can he order up new aircraft and fresh crews when nobody gives him any? According to my home town newspaper we're making fifty-thousand aircraft a year. Where are they?"

He interrupted himself to glance, with some irritation, at the beer mug which the captain had rested on the mantelpiece.

"Would you mind taking that beer mug off the mantel?"

"Sure."

The captain shrugged, swallow some beer, and put the mug on top of the piano.

"Give us another month", continued Bishop, resuming his out- burst, "and we'll put up a maximum effort of one B-17."

The captain sipped his beer "You know that's not the story I want", he said. "I understand how you feel, but -"

"You do, do you? That's fine. Then go down and have a look at the battle damage from today's strike. Talk to the line chief, Sergeant Nero, and ask him how long it's going to take to patch up holes you can drive a cleat track through - without enough parts, or tools, or maintenance men. Just plenty of mud, Then go to the other bases and ask them if they're any better off. And then go back to your boss and ask him who dreamed up the cockeyed idea that we can bomb Europe from this cranberry bog. If you don't believe me, you ought to hear Colonel Daven- port, off the record. He feels the same way."

"I'll tell you what", said the captain, in a soothing tone. "I've got a photographer right outside. We'll forget the story for now, but let me get just one shot of you."

"Why don't you drive over to the hospital and get just one shot of the back of Lieutenant McKesson's head?"

The captain absentmindedly placed his beer mug back up on the mantelpiece.

"I asked you before", said Bishop, "to set that beer mug down somewhere else."

"For God's sake", responded the captain, anger beginning to get the better of him, "what is this mantel? An alter, or some-thing?"

"Just put it down somewhere else."

"You like to give orders, don't you, Lieutenant?"

"Haven't you desk-jockeys got anything better to do than come down here and heckle people? Why don't you go back to PINETREE and start a softball tournament, or something."

"Any other suggestions, Lieutenant?"

"Yes. Take a powder, before you miss the high-tea hour at Bomber Command."

"All right, Lieutenant. I can get piss'd off, too. I didn't come down here to ask you guys for anything. I'm trying to do something for you - to get you the recognition you deserve. But, if you don't have enough pride in your own outfit to co-operate with -"

Bishop sprang to his feet at the word "outfit".

"You've said enough", he cried, "you silly-looking son-of-a-bitch."

He drove his fist hard into the captain's jaw, knocking him back several feet. The captain absorbed the punch without going down, flushed deep red, he raised his own fists, and then slowly dropped them to his sides.

"Thanks", he said, slowly, "Mister Combat Fatigue."

He held Bishop's burning stare for a moment before turning on his heel and walking out the door, all the while rubbing his chin. Bishop reached for his glass with a shaking hand, noted that it was empty and walked to the bar where he ordered another drink from the wide-eyed corporal.

As Bishop was swallowing the first sip, the 918th's Air Exec., Lieutenant Colonel Ben Gately, entered the lounge. He went over and picked up Colonel Davenport's green Toby from the radio cabinet and carried it to the mantelpiece, where he carefully placed it in the center.

Bishop stared across the top of his glass at the Toby and then, in one lunging motion, he swept his hand down the whole length of the short bar, sending glasses and bottles crashing to the floor. Gately, too startled to move, watched as Bishop lurch past him and out of the club.

Lieutenant Heinz Zimmermann, still in his flying coveralls and leather jacket, but with his black hair slicked down with water in testimony of a hasty effort to tidy up after his summons over the Tannoy loudspeaker system to the Group Adjutant's office, braked himself to a halt before Major Stovall's desk, and uncorked a vehement salute. Stovall returned the salute, but did not motion the apprehensive lieutenant to an empty chair, an omission which, even more than the Adjutant's icy expression, told Zimmermann that his superior was boiling mad.

"Well, Zimmermann", he demanded, removing his glasses, "what's behind that brawl at the Officers' Club?'

The lieutenant's face, with its heavy Germanic bone structure, was capable, at times, of looking stupid. But now he looked positively oafish, as he glowered back at Stovall.

"You mean last night, sir", he groped. "Between Major Cobb and Dean?" "No, I don't. I mean your roommate, Lieutenant Bishop. A half hour ago."

Zimmermann stared back, disbelievingly, at Stovall, as the latter continued. "He called a visiting superior officer a dirty name and socked him." Zimmermann looked bewildered and amazed.

"Why, I can hardly believe that, sir", he said. "I've never heard Jesse use a cuss word. He doesn't know any. He's a clean kid in every way."

His voice assumed a confidential note as he sought to regain his ordinarily friendly footing with the Adjutant.

"Fact is, Major", he continued, "I don't think he's ever even had a piece in his life." Stovall harrumphed, then frowned.

"I'm not interested in his sex life", he said. "But I am interested in why he blew his top." "I can't understand Jesse doing a thing like that. It's not like him, sir."

"I'm getting sick and tired of these fights in the club", said Stovall. "Half a dozen in the past week. If necessary, I'm going to close that goddamn bar permanently." He picked up a paper clip and bent it back and forth several times, angrily, between his fingers. "This one", he resumed, "I'd like to settle without bothering the colonel. He's got enough grief." He stared at Zimmermann's honest, troubled features, as he felt his hot temper beginning to cool.

"I don't know why I'm taking things out on you, Heinz", he said. "You didn't have anything to do with it - I just thought you could help me. Bishop flatly refused to say a word. I finally had to send him back to his quarters."

"Then that's where I'd better go", responded Zimmermann. "I never should have left him alone." He moved as if to leave.

"Not so fast, Lieutenant", said Stovall. "Here, have a seat. Tell me what's behind that kind of outburst, from the gentlest person in this Group."

Zimmermann sat down, reluctantly.

"Jesse's had three rugged ones in a row, sir", said the navigator, hesitantly. "And today's was the worst."

"The topper?"

"That's what I mean, sir."

"I heard that McKesson got it today", said Stovall. "But I don't know any of the details."

"Well, sir", started Zimmermann, in a dull, tired voice, "we were crossing the enemy coast when a bunch of 190s hit us out of the sun, from TWELVE O'CLOCK HIGH. I thought they'd got- ten us on the first pass, because there was an explosion in the cockpit, just above my head, that shook the whole ship. I turned around just in time to see the top-turret gunner slip down through the flight deck hatch and fall to the floor at the rear of the nose compartment, screaming at the pilot to land - right now."

He gulped, then continued.

"His right arm was blown off at the shoulder and he was spouting blood all over himself, and on the inside of the ship. I tried to give him a shot of morphine, but it was forty below zero at twenty-five thousand feet when I took my gloves off. I bent the needle and couldn't get it in. I couldn't tie a tourniquet on him, either, because the arm was off too close to the shoulder. I bandaged him the best that I could, but he had to have medical attention right away.

With no oxygen and three hours of flying ahead, I knew he wouldn't make it. So I put his parachute on with the ripcord in his good hand and I dumped him out the nose hatch, hoping that the French would rush him to a doctor. His chute opened okay.

"Did he know what it was all about?"

"Yes, he knew, but he was game. Do you mind if I smoke, sir?"

The Adjutant handed him a cigarette, which Zimmermann lit with steady fingers. Then Stovall waited patiently for him to continue.

"What about Bishop", he inquired finally?

"I'm getting to that, sir", said Zimmermann. "All this time the ship was gyrating around in the formation, but I figured it was violent evasive action. The bombardier had been busy with the nose guns and then he was getting set to toggle his bombs. The target area was pouring up smoke and we clobbered it with a few more eggs, right down the middle.

Then we went back to our nose guns, but most of the attacks were coming from the rear. The innercomm was shot out, but I learned latter that all the gunners, except the ball turret, had passed out from lack of oxygen when the system was shot out in the first attack. Finally, when we were starting back across the Channel, I went up to check with the pilot and look things over."

Zimmermann took a deep drag out of his cigarette.

"I found Lieutenant McKesson slumped down in his seat with one foot jammed in the damaged pedals. He was sitting in a mess of blood and the back of his head was shot off. It had happened almost two hours previously, when the FWs made their first pass.

A 20 millimeter had entered the right side of the windshield in front of Lieutenant Bishop, shattering it. It missed Jesse but split open the back of Lieutenant McKesson's skull. We were flying number two in the formation, so he would have been looking to his left.

35

What Jesse told me was that McKesson fell forward over the controls, wrapping his arms around the wheel, and causing the ship to nose down sharply, smack into the middle of the low squadron. Bishop grabbed the controls from his side, avoided a collision, and pulled back into formation. He did it by brute force against the struggling of McKesson, who was half conscious - and Mac had plenty of muscle.

With no innercomm Jesse couldn't call for help. And he thought that the waist gunners, the radio, and the tail gunner had bailed out because their guns had ceased firing, but he kept on to the target.

McKesson couldn't see, and he didn't know what was going on, but he never stopped fighting the controls by instinct. Bishop couldn't see out, either, thought the shattered windshield, except straight up and out to the sides. He had been keeping one arm crooked through his own control wheel to fly the ship and stay in formation. Meanwhile, he'd been continually pulling McKesson off the controls with his other hand."

Zimmermann paused, took another drag from his cigarette, then continued. "Jesse told me he couldn't see well enough to land from his side and we'd have to move Mac out of his seat. It took at least fifteen minutes, with McKesson fighting us all the way. Bishop finally had to reach down and jerk Mac's leg sideways to pull it free. He couldn't help breaking the leg.

Finally, one of the gunners revived enough to help me get McKesson down into the nose compartment. Where I had to hold him down until we got back to the field. Another gunner helped Bishop by lowering the gear and flaps, and we landed okay. Now I guess I'd better get back to the quarters and see how Jesse's making out."

Zimmermann stood up and saluted the major. Stovall cleared his throat twice before he could speak.

"I've been spending too much time behind this desk, Heinz", he said, returning the young man's salute. "Tell Bishop not to worry. I'll cook up some kind of official reply that should sat- isfy those bastards up at PINETREE."

After Zimmermann had left, Stovall leaned back in his chair, feeling numb and a little nauseated. His mind tried to cope with the enormity of what he had just heard.

He projected himself back to the familiar surroundings of his home in Columbus, Ohio. To a world where a man who could knock a baseball out of the park was a hero, and where the collision of an auto and a streetcar was of front page interest. And then he tried to reconcile the coexistence of that normal world he had left, with this strange world of Archbury. Where the same breed of human beings lived through such utterly fantastic exper- iences as Bishop's, this morning.

He recalled the occasion during World War One, when he had driven his bayonet through a German soldier. And how he felt at the time, that he had survived a supreme test of his moral fiber under stress. But how could he compare that act with the feats of Bishop, during his hours long ordeal?

He found himself thinking about Colonel Davenport in a kinder light. For some time now he had been increasingly critical in his own mind, of the colonel's leadership. From his standpoint as the adjutant, ever conscious of the regulations and immersed in reports, the 918th had been steadily sliding downhill. Salutes were a rarity, quarters were dirty, uniforms slovenly, discipline lax, and griping universal. And Davenport seemed to overlook it, failing to call the Squadron Commanders in and rack them back. But how could Colonel Davenport be expected to be bothered about things like that when he was concentrating on operations, on the desperate struggle for survival in the air?

A flood of shame came over Stovall, as he recalled how successfully he had insulated his thinking from the realities of operations, content to plug along in his own rut. Little wonder that the crews switched the conversations to nonflying topics when- ever he, the ground-pounder, the retread ground officer from another war, joined a group at the club. He told himself that he must do better.

He picked up his pen and began signing a new batch of Personal Effects inventories, nearly all of which had omitted certain small items: a love letter from a girl in London, overlooked in a back pants pocket, which could stab a young widow's already broken heart. A contraceptive, in the side pocket of a nineteen-year-old gunner's blouse, which could further sadden a mother's tragedy. These things Stovall always scrupulously removed.

Then, at the sound of crunching tires near his window, he glanced out in time to watch Colonel Davenport climb out from his car, his face darker than usual with dejected exhaustion.

Davenport had just finished a quick tour of the station, after Interrogation, during which he had inspected the bomb dumps, the worst of the battle damaged aircraft, and the repair hangers. He scraped the mud off his shoes with a stick, then went directly to his office, where he found the Air Exec and the Flight Surgeon waiting for him.

"The warning order just came down", said Gately. "Snafu'd as usual. It says that we're the low Group at nine thousand feet."

Davenport looked at the sheet of teletype and frowned.

"They must mean nineteen thousand", he said. "That's bad enough, but nine thousand is what those flak gunners dream about. I'll call PINETREE about it. Any other good news?"

"Yes", said Gately.

He was a slender, spruced up uniformed West Pointer, with a thin mustache, brown eyes, and a dissipated look.

"I broke your number three iron"

He indicated the golf club on the colonel's desk.

"Nice going", said Davenport. "When did you find time to do that?" "You know me", remarked Gately, casually, "I always get in my one hour of physical training, as per orders. I busted the club after Pamela beat me on the last hole this morning."

Davenport controlled his annoyance.

"I've just come from the line", he said. "Sergeant Nero thinks we can put up eighteen tomorrow, with some luck. But there won't be any spares. How about crews?"

"We've got twenty-three", said the Air Exec, "but half of 'em have been going for the last four days in a row. They'll be asleep at the Briefing tomorrow. Isn't that right, Don?"

He turned to Major Kaiser.

"Can't be helped", said Kaiser, a little curtly.

Davenport glanced from his Flight Surgeon back to Gately.

"Better get back to Ops, Ben", he said. "I'll be over as soon as I find out about that altitude." After the Air Exec had gone, Davenport asked Kaiser.

"You think Gately's all right to fly tomorrow?"

"Yes, sir", said Kaiser. "His cold is no worse than plenty of others that are going to fly, but he asked to be grounded again", his voice was eloquent with disapproval.

Davenport scratched his head and tapped a pencil on his desk, striving to reach a decision. "What did you tell him", he asked?

"Frankly, sir, I couldn't justify excusing him on any medical grounds."

Davenport sat down heavily behind his desk, his mind busy with a battle he had fought many times. He had ample reasons for firing Gately. The man was trying to coast through an easy war, crowding in all the tennis, golf, women, and social life that were consistent with a nominal discharge of his duties.

Since the Group's arrival in England, he had logged more hours at a card table in the Officers' Club, cleaning up off junior officers, than at the controls of a B-17. Whenever Gately led a mission, he usually aborted with mechanical trouble or turned back on account of weather.

But, on the other hand, Davenport always recoiled from the prospect of relieving him. As an experienced staff officer, he was useful in many ways.

Davenport admitted, to himself, that he didn't like to delegate much authority where operations were concerned, and Gately wasn't the aggressive type of Air Exec who might have gotten in his hair. Furthermore, there was the matter of Gately's three-star general father on the Joint Chiefs of Staff. This war wasn't go- ing to last forever, and there was the future to think about.

He looked up and saw the Flight Surgeon's eyes on him, questioning.

"Well, Don", he started, "I honestly don't know why I haven't relieved him. He's only led two missions that counted. He's weak in the air and, what's more, he knows it. But he's a good staff officer and he takes a big load of the details off me on the ground. Hell, if I asked for a replacembent, I'd probably get some cast-off that was even worse."

"If you keep him, Colonel", said Kaiser, "I don't believe it's advisable to condone his grounding himself against my repeated recommendations."

"I'll have to be the final judge of that", responded Davenport. The stocky Flight Surgeon braced himself.

"Colonel", he said, "you and I have got to wrestle this thing out. May I speak bluntly, sir?" "Go ahead."

"I'm a doctor and a psychiatrist. As such, I am responsible to you for the mental and physical health of your combat crews. All of them are suffering from a greater or lesser degree of anxiety and stress. Acting only as a doctor, it would be simple for me to remove the cause of the emotional disturbance immediately . . . by grounding the lot of them.

But, I am also an Army officer and I am obligated to the furtherance of the military mission. Therefore, I cannot ground a man until I am convinced that he has reached the limit of his capacity - or that a very little further stress will make him dangerous to the success of the next mission, or to the lives and safety of his crew and aircraft.

There is only one honorable way out for most of these men, except the completion of a full tour of duty. And that is injury or death.."

"I'm aware of all that", said the colonel. "What's your point?"

"Briefly, this. I believe that the policy in this Group has given too many individuals an out. They have learned that even after I have certified them fit to fly, they can trot around to the front office and be excused. As a result, we have too many men in the hospital or sick in quarters.

Too many men who think they can't fly above ten-thousand feet. Too many cases of frostbite and, incidentally, I am opposed to awarding any more Purple Hearts for frostbitten hands. It's too much of a temptation to a gunner, who's getting shaky, and sees an easy way to hospitalize himself for several months. I don't believe that my viewpoint is cold-blooded. I just believe that the colonel has been over lenient.

Gately is the main case in point because he sets an example for the others. And I feel that it is my duty to make a stand about him."

Davenport, spots of color on his cheekbones, stood and paced back and forth, hands thrust deep in his pockets. He turned to Kaiser.

"Gately is my business", he said, "but Lieutenant Campbell is yours." "What about Campbell, sir?"

"He did a swell job of leading the low squadron today", said Davenport. "But he won't ever lead it again. Somehow, nobody noticed that he wasn't with his crew at Interrogation today, until it was almost over. They looked for him at his quarters and at the club, but couldn't find him. Finally the bombardier went back to the aircraft, twenty minutes ago, and found him still sitting in the cockpit. He never left it."

"Was he injured?"

"No. He was just sitting there, whistling and singing 'Old Man River'. And he was just as happy and carefree as a bird."

Gradually the words sank in on Kaiser. "Gone nuts", he asked?

"Completely", said Davenport. "His mind was gone."

"I must take the blame for Campbell", said Kaiser, in a crushed voice. "I should have seen it coming."

"That's just it", shot back Davenport! "How can you tell?" He made another circuit of the floor.

"You think I'm too lenient. But somebody's got to stand up for these boys. Up at PINETREE they're just a bunch of numbers on a blackboard. To me they're flesh and blood. How can the military mission succeed if you demand the impossible of human beings?"

There was knock on the door and then an enlisted man entered carrying a tray with a coffee pot and several cups on it.

Daven- port eagerly poured two cups of black coffee and drank half of his own in one gulp.

"That's getting to be your regular diet, isn't it, Colonel", commented Kaiser, glad for the interruption? "Coffee and cigarettes. Your diet last night and again tonight, And you haven't had your clothes off for three nights."

"I can take it", said Davenport. "But how long do you think these boys can take it? Like Jesse Bishop. Operations tells me he flew unassisted for two hours today with a fatally wounded pilot fighting the controls - before that Heiny navigator, Zimmermann, went up to help him."

"Yes, I know. I admit it was a miracle."

"And that's what they want up at Bomber Command, isn't it", said Davenport? "Miracles." "They're getting them, too", said Kaiser. "We're finding out every day that a man's tolerance for severe stress is unbelievably high."

"And I suppose you'd okay Bishop to go again tomorrow?"

"If he's medically all right in the morning, yes. Because, once I start grounding a man after a rugged mission, you won't be able to get a single aircraft off the runway. They'd all rather go to London than to Lorient."

As Davenport listened to the Flight Surgeon his face grew bleaker and grayer. "You're back on that same phonograph record", he said.

"I can't help it, Colonel. When we have enough replacements to keep the Group up to strength, I'll favor more liberal use of rest homes. There's a lot about combat fatigue we're still learn- ing. But, if we go soft now, when we need every crew, the 918th will be out of the fight."

"I know, I know", said Davenport, beginning to lose his patience again. "I'm tired of arguing with you. And I've got to get on the phone. So, if you'll excuse me."

"Yes, sir", said Kaiser.

As he started to walk out, the doctor stopped halfway to the door for one more try. "You'll rest up tomorrow", he said, hopefully, "and send Gately?"

"Goddamit, NO", yelled Davenport! "It's a target I can't delegate to anyone else - certainly not Gately. Now beat it and let me run this Group."

Davenport picked up his scrambler phone and called Colonel Savage at PINETREE. "Do you mean GENERAL SAVAGE", asked the clerk at the other end?

"Since when?"

"Since yesterday, sir. One moment." Savage came on.

"How's it feel to be a general, Frank?"

"It worries me plenty. I must have bitched something up royally to get a star for it."

"Not necessarily. But anyway, nice going. Say, Frank, I want to check an error in the Field Order. It said nine thousand."

"That's right. It's no error."

"But crimeny, Frank, that's murder. Which side are you guys fighting for?"

"We haven't been getting enough hits from high altitude.. So, just once, we've got to go in low. Then we can say we've tried everything."

"You sure can."

"We agree with you that it sounds like non-habit-forming tactics. But there's only one way to find out."

"And another thing - why are we the low Group again?" "A toss of the coin."

"Well, maybe you need to get a new coin", said Davenport, with exasperation. Davenport paused to pour himself another cup of coffee.

"You know we took a beating again today", he continued. "I can't even put a full Group in the air tomorrow."

His voice rose out of control, so that Stovall, in the next room, couldn't help overhearing him. "When are you going to give us a break? Nobody can keep this up. I'm asking you right now to let us stand down for a few days."

Savage didn't answer immediately. Then he said:

"I admit I'd be unhappy in your shoes, Keith. But do you realize what your saying?"

"Yes. I'm telling you that there's a limit! This maximum effort business has already gone to far!" "Look, Keith", said Savage, in a conciliatory tone, "in this kind of a deal, if we ever get down to one B-17, and one crew left - we'll have to send it."

"That's brave talk from someone sitting behind a desk."

"Now just a minute, Keith. You're talking hysterically - you don't sound like yourself." "I'm not - ", responded Davenport.

"Look, Keith . . . I'll call you back."

Savage hung up before Davenport could finish. With his lips quivering, the colonel placed the phone slowly back into its cradle, then picked up the instrument and slammed it down into the wastebasket beside his desk.

Ben Gately stuck his head in through the doorway, perceived the colonel's agitation, and started to withdraw.

"Now what", snapped Davenport?

"I just wanted to ask who the colonel will fly with tomorrow", asked Gately, lapsing into the formal third person?

Davenport flung himself wearily back into his chair, trying to regain his composure. He considered his answer, for a moment, while the unaccustomed flush in his cheeks receded, leaving the former gray pallor to accentuate the dark bags under his eyes.

"I'll lead the mission with Jesse Bishop's crew." "Very well, sir."

Gately left and, after a few moments, Stovall appeared, standing respectfully just inside the office door.

"Colonel", he said. "If you should happen to have a pint in your desk, I'd like a - a snort." Davenport looked at Stovall in amazement, then he reached down, pulled open a drawer, and produced a bottle of whiskey. He smiled sadly at the Adjutant's timid expression.

"So, you finally caught a cold, Harvey", he said, opening the pint bottle and handing it to Stovall. Stovall took a swallow, coughed explosively, and wiped his smarting eyes.

"Just a slight sore throat coming on", he replied. He tilted the pint up again - a smaller sip this time.

"Heap good medicine", he said. "Better have one yourself, Colonel."

In General Henderson's office at Bomber Command, where Frank Savage had just concluded his telephone conversation with Keith Davenport, there was an uneasy silence. Major General Pat Pritchard, the third officer present, puffed on his cigar and peered intently through the smoke. First looking at Henderson and then at Savage, observing that the brand new brigadier general had not yet exchanged his eagles for stars.

"Keith's been under a hell of a strain", said Savage, finally. "Looked ninety years old the last time I saw him."

Pritchard removed his cigar and turned to Henderson.

"I've kept out of this, Ed", he said. "But after hearing one end of that conversation, I can't keep out of it any longer. The 918th has been a sick Group - you and Frank have called it a "Hard Luck Group"

- for a long time now. Perhaps you still feel that you can justify keeping Davenport, but I can't justify a weak Group to my bosses forever, when no remedial action has been taken.

Something is basically wrong down there, and in my book that's always meant the commander."

"With the general's permission", said Henderson, "I'd like to give Colonel Davenport just a little more time. Make absolutely sure it hasn't been a long streak of bad breaks.

We haven't got a Group Commander that works harder, or flies more missions - and frankly, I'd be stumped to try and find a replacement.

Also, Keith is popular in the Group. The air crews worship him. I'm afraid of what could happen to the morale if I had to relieve him."

"What morale", asked Pritchard, dryly? "We're not staging popularity contests over here. Maybe what we need is more Group Commanders who aren't so popular. What do you think, Frank?"

Savage looked uncomfortably over at Henderson, who stared back noncommittally. The easiest thing, he knew, would be to agree with Henderson and duck the issue. The latter's defense of his friend had not surprised Savage, but it had disgusted him.

Ostensibly, he reflected, Henderson was being loyal. But actually he was betraying a dangerously harmful flaw in his capabilities as a commander. He was demonstrating that he was incapable of admitting a mistake, or of rectifying it.

Pritchard, on the other hand, he told himself, was a more typical kind of West Pointer. One who could rise above his personal loyalties, and think as a man fighting for his country.

Savage watched as Pritchard stared through rings of cigar smoke at the ceiling. This was the cagey old boy whom you had to get up early in the morning to fool. This was the general who had startled his West Point colleagues by bringing over a staff largely composed of newly commissioned civilians,

because he believed that you could teach an intelligent man the Army, faster than you could teach some professional Army man an ability.

They had been dubbed "Pritchard's Amateurs". But in this new kind of war, where conditions changed every day and you had to throw away the book, the amateurs had been confounding the critics. This was the general who, behind that benevolent expression of his, excelled at guessing what the other fellow was thinking.

Savage braced himself to answer the general's question.

"If we leave Davenport down there much longer", he said, earnestly, "I'm afraid he's going to crack up. Whether it's his fault or not, the fact remains that his Group always suffers the worst losses. I like Keith, . . . but I don't think it's fair to him, or the Group, to postpone putting him out of his misery until it's too late."

He glanced, anxiously, back and forth between his two listeners. Pritchard noticed Henderson's face growing reddish.

"Ed, . . I realize", he said, "that Davenport is an old friend of yours, and that you have a lot of confidence in him. That makes it hard."

"I'm not going to let that sway me for a moment, sir", replied Henderson, smoothly shifting gears into the voice of the model commander. "But there are so many factors. For instance, I have to ask myself, am I partly at fault? Has my staff given the 918th all the support and co-operation its needed? Are there conflicting personalities involved? I don't believe so.

I think we've done our part. But just the same. I'd like to do a little soul searching before I kick a man out and break his neck."

Now it was Savage's face that was turning a bit red. The operations of the Groups were his direct responsibility, as head of A-3. And it struck him that Henderson's remarks were calculated to raise a subtle question in Pritchard's mind.

"I still have confidence", concluded Henderson, "that Davenport can pull the 918th out of its hole. If anybody can."

Pritchard sent a puff of cigar smoke toward Henderson and watched it dissolve.

"We'll see how things work out tomorrow over St. Nazaire", he said. "A couple of good missions. With no losses. Might put them back on their feet."

Pritchard stood up.

"Meanwhile, I'd better get some sleep for an early start, if we're going to visit all the stations tomorrow."

The general needed rest. It was a rare night that he had been able to sleep for five uninterrupted hours since the day he had landed in England. Arriving with no bases, no crews, and no aircraft. All he carried with him was an order in his pocket, which boiled down to: "Build an Air Force!"

At 0230 hours many lights were burning behind the black-out curtains at Archbury Field. At Operations. At Intelligence.

In the combat mess hall the cooks were already unpacking crates of oranges, and preparing eggs for breakfast (special pre-mission fare) before the 0330 briefing. But most of the station was still sleeping, heavily.

Heinz Zimmermann lay awake in the dark, listening to Jesse Bishop, who was tossing and mumbling in the next bed.

"Pull up", cried Bishop, sharply jerking to a sitting position!

Zimmermann thought that Bishop had awakened, but Jesse simply slumped back, turned over, and clawed at his pillow.

"Flak", he called out! "Flak! . . Bail out, Johnny, bail out! . . . Sure, Mac, I heard you. I see him. A yellow-nose 190 at two o' clock low . . . Watch your leg, Mac. Easy now, I've got it . . Oh, gawd, I didn't mean to snap it. It snapped, Mac . . . I'm your friend, Mac. You know I'm your best friend . . . There's the Channel. I swear, it's the Channel."

Zimmermann smoked a cigarette, tried to doze off in spite of his roommate's mumbling, then gave it up. He walked over and sat down on the edge of Bishop's bed, then shook the tortured boy's shoulder.

Bishop awoke with an instant startled reaction, almost leaping from the bed. "Okay", he groaned, "I'm coming."

"No, Jesse, it's not time yet. You were having nightmares. Turning twenty-five-hundred R.P.M. That's why I woke you."

"Pulling a mission, I guess."

"You've been flying a lot of night missions lately."

"Ah, let a guy sleep, will ya?"

"All right. But I've been thinking. I can fix it with the Flight Surgeon if you don't think you ought to -"

Bishop sat up, fully awake.

"Are you crazy", he asked? "Crazy in the head?" "Okay, okay", said Zimmermann, soothingly.

He returned to his own bed and pulled his blankets over his chunky body. Clad in his flight coveralls, and normally a heavy sleeper, Zimmermann always made it a point to retire completely dressed before a mission. With his flight gear piled neatly on a chair beside him, he wouldn't have to grope around in the dark after being awakened.

On top of the pile was his pearl handled revolver, which he always carried with him. "They won't capture me alive", was the way he put it.

Bishop laid quietly now, but still Zimmermann couldn't drown his mind to sleep. He got up and stepped outside onto the boardwalk, which was slippery with frost. His breath exhaled in plumes as he looked up at the few stars that were visible through rifts in the gauzelike cirrus clouds.

"What are you doing up, Heinz", asked a voice behind him?

He turned and recognized Lieutenant Butch Roby, his crew's bombardier, who lived in the next room. Roby flicked away a glowing cigarette.

"Can't sleep, I guess", said Heinz.

"You're slipping", remarked Roby, moving over towards Zimmermann. "And I thought you were one of those guys, with rocks in their head, that liked combat."

"I can't say that I like it", replied Heinz. "I just hate those damn Nazi bastards."

"Me", said Roby, "I don't hate anybody. The way I see it is - this is just a job - to get over with." "A lot of guys feel that way. Sweating out their twenty-five missions. But if it takes a hundred, that's okay with me. I never told you, but I've got German blood in me on both sides." "Everybody knows that."

"Yeah?"

Zimmermann was genuinely surprised. "Just what do you know?"

The pair walked in silence for awhile. When suddenly Roby remembered something.

"Say", he said, "you forget to pick up your personal bomb loading last night. I'll go get it."

When the bombardier returned from his quarters, he was carrying a cluster of tiny incendiary bombs, which Zimmermann was in the habit of tossing out over the targets, as a little extra dividend.

CHAPTER THREE

EGGS FOR BREAKFAST

Towards noon, later that morning, the traffic pattern above Archbury Field was empty, except for a solitary Percival Q-6, which was circling to land. Major General Pritchard was at the controls of the small plane, lent to him by the R.A.F., until the Americans could import their own staff aircraft. Brigadier General Ed Henderson was the only passenger, and not too happy of one.

Why, Henderson was thinking as they glided toward the runway, did the Old Man insist on flying himself? He had too much on his mind to be coping with an unfamiliar airplane. Henderson looked sideways at Pritchard's scowling face, a cigar butt clench-ed in his mouth, and wondered if the Old Man was satisfied with the briefing they had attended at one station, and the take-off they had watched at a second.

There had been raucous boos at the briefing, after the announ-cement that three Groups were going over St. Nazaire - "FLAK CITY" to the crews - at nine, ten, and eleven thousand feet, res- pectively, to get hits on the concrete submarine pens. Twenty-three thousand feet would have been more to their liking.

And, at the second Group, the taxi plan had gotten screwed up when one B-17 sank a wheel into the mud, just off the perimeter track, and had to be hauled out by a cleat track. But all the aircraft had managed to get off on time.

The combat crews had seemed unusually on edge, and there had been a thinly veiled atmosphere of hostility towards generals. But Henderson hoped the Old Man would attribute it to the fact that the men were still full of fight.

Pritchard sat the Percival down onto the runway rather awkwardly in the slight cross-wind, forestalling an incipient ground loop with a tardy, but effective, yank on the hand brake.

"When are the Brits going to get around to toe brakes", he muttered, as he straightened out the little plane's roll."

While the Q-6 trundled past the deserted hard-stands of the 918th, Henderson began to worry, anew, about Davenport. The latter had been fourteen minutes late at the take-off, due to a last minute change of the bomb loading, in the revised Field Order. Yet the other two Groups had managed to switch bombs in time.

Why was it that the 918th was always the one to get caught short? He still refused to admit, even to himself, that Davenport was incompetent - that he could have so grossly overestimated him. He hoped that Davenport had been able to make up most of the lost time by taking short cuts to the Wing rendezvous point,

and that he could keep his losses down today. If not, how could he avoid relieving him?

Things must have been in a worse mess than he realized on his last visit to Archbury, in Davenport's absence. Had that smooth-talking Air Exec - Lieutenant Colonel Gately - sold him a Persian rug? He recalled Gately's closing assurance that: "Morale is very high", and how he had relayed that estimate up to General Pritchard in London.

A "Follow Me" jeep guided the Q-6 to a parking area in front of the Control Tower, where the visitors were met by Major Stovall, who was concealing, behind his snappy salute, a sensation of acute discomfort. He had been notified barely in time, of the coming visit, his shoes needed a better shine, and there was a spot on his "Pink" slacks. Furthermore, he was struggling with the novel misery of his first hangover.

"Would the generals like to go up to the tower", he asked, hopefully? And praying inwardly that the visitors would not ask to inspect the station.

"Perhaps later, Major", said Pritchard, cordially. "I believe that we've got time to look around your airfield first."

"Very well, sir", responded Stovall, trying to look pleased.

Then, noticing that the untidy sergeant at the wheel of the waiting staff car made no move to open the door for the generals, the Adjutant hastened to perform the courtesy himself.

"Where's your Air Exec", asked Henderson, as they drove off?

Stovall thrust from his mind a quick mental picture of Colonel Gately's departure that morning, with a tennis racket under his arm, as soon as the bombers were airborne.

"Wing Headquarters, sir. A conference."

It was only half a lie, Stovall told himself, because Gately had promised to drop off some reports at Wing - being that it was on the way to Pamela's house.

"And the Ground Exec, Colonel Brown", asked Henderson?

"The colonel is still in the hospital, sir. I'm acting Ground Exec until he gets well."

Henderson frowned, but lapsed into silence. Stovall's relief was short-lived, for General Pritchard turned to him.

"How many got off this morning, Major", he asked? "Seventeen, sir. But I believed that two aborted." Pritchard looked at Henderson.

"Fifteen over the target", he said, "if, they all get there."

A half hour later, on top of the control tower, Pritchard and Henderson stood at the railing, scanning the cloudless sky. Both were in a foul mood, but Pritchard wore the grimmer expression.

Henderson glanced at his wrist watch. "Should be any minute now, sir", he said. "Yes", said Pritchard.

He removed the cigar from his mouth.

"Ed", he asked, "after what we've seen around here this morn- ing, would you say that we still have a fighting outfit here at Archbury?"

Henderson's face grew flushed.

"I'm afraid, sir, that they've slipped a long way."

As he gripped the railing, the palms of his hands were wet, moistened by the clammy tension inside an ambitious man who is suddenly conscious that his job is in jeopardy. He was able to visualize only two gleams of a silver lining around the dark cloud before him.

First, realizing the gravity of the situation in the 918th, Pritchard might agree to letting him send Frank Savage down here to take over, in spite of the fact that the job was beneath a brigadier general's rank. And second, if Savage assumed command and whipped the outfit back into shape, a catastrophe would surely be avoided.

But Savage would be getting a thankless, almost hopeless, task. Any commander who inherited the mess at the 918th could easily fall on his face. And if that happened, Henderson felt that he would be rid of a competitor, who was breathing down on his neck.

Either way, he told himself, its an even swap to me. Except for one thing. How did I ever get myself into a spot where I have to pull a reverse switch on these two guys? In peacetime, I had to send Davenport down to relieve Savage.

Squirming under the irony of his reflections, Henderson looked up in time to see a cluster of specks in the distance. And soon the specks swelled into a formation of B-17s.

"I count eight", said Pritchard.

Henderson, clenching and unclenching his fists, turned pale around his nostrils. "Must be a few cripples down on other airfields", he said.

"I hope so", responded Pritchard, gravely. "Seven would be the worst loss we've ever taken out of one Group. Check with the other stations and see if they've got a preliminary count yet."

"Yes, sir."

Henderson went below to a telephone and returned after a few minutes.

"Twenty out of twenty-one are in the landing pattern at the 901st, sir", he said. "And the 902nd is reporting nineteen out of twenty-one returned." "Thank goodness for that", said Pritchard.

He remained silent while the eight survivors of the 918th roared over the field and broke off, one by one, into their landing approaches. Then he started for the stairs with a stiff, determined stride.

"We'll go meet Davenport", he said, setting his jaw, so that Henderson could see the muscles stand out.

The staff car pulled away from the control tower, past a long line of spectators, resembling the sidelines of a football game. Bleary-eyed mechanics, headquarters clerks, cooks wearing their white chef's caps, and every face stricken, like the faces of mourners at a funeral.

But none more so than that of Harvey Stovall, sitting beside the driver. His throat having become so choked that he gave up trying to speak to the man behind the wheel, and gave him directions to Colonel Davenport's hard-stand with hand motions.

Presently a battered Flying Fortress, with jagged holes showing through the wings and fuselage, taxied up, swung its big tail around on the small circle of concrete and cut its engines off.

Pritchard got out of the car and waited patiently until an old man emerged from the waist hatch.

Keith Davenport's face was shocking, indistinguishable from that of a corpse, until he caught sight of the two generals. Then fury gleamed through the exhaustion in his eyes, as the pair walked forward to meet him.

"There, we proved it for you", he said. "Their flak is really good at nine thousand feet!" "How bad was it, Keith", Pritchard asked, gently?

Davenport couldn't help seeing the stricken concern in his superior's eyes. His voice lost a little of its edge.

"You see how many we've got left, sir", he responded? "That's all I had with me when we left the target area."

"All from flak", asked Pritchard? "Or from fighters too?"

"Flak", said Davenport. "I knew it would happen, General. I told Frank Savage so, last night." "It wasn't Savage, Keith. It was me. We had to try it."

Davenport made a great effort to keep silent, as Henderson placed his arm around his shoulders. "Come on, Keith, we'll give you a lift to Interrogation", he said.

Davenport and the two generals passed by Jesse Bishop and Heinz Zimmermann, who were shedding their flight gear near the nose of the aircraft. Bishop gave them a weary semblance of a salute, and a half smile, but Zimmermann purposefully looked the other way.

In the car, Pritchard held a light for Davenport's cigarette, as they drove toward the Interrogation hut.

"Did you hit the aiming point", asked Pritchard?

"I think we put a few in there", said Davenport. "We were late at the I.P., after our navigation got screwed up, so we didn't have time for a good run into the target."

"I'd like to hear more about that", said Pritchard. "Let's meet in your office after Interrogation. And bring along your Group navigator."

Heinz Zimmermann stood with a bowed head in Davenport's office, where the latter was concluding a critique of the mission, for the two generals.

"I believe, sir", continued Davenport, turning away from the wall map to which he had been referring, "that if the navigation had been better, we still could have made the rendezvous point on time. Then we wouldn't have caught all that flak alone. Their batteries would have been confused by the three Groups coming in simultaneously at different altitudes and on different courses, as according to the plan."

He glanced over at Zimmermann, who was still looking at the floor. "But the responsibility, of course, is mine."

Pritchard looked from Davenport to Zimmermann,

"We'd like to hear your version, Lieutenant", he said, gently.

The navigator raised his eyes to the general's. It was hard to tell whether the young man was sullen or brokenhearted.

"I did the best I could, General", he mumbled, in a low voice that sounded close to tears. "Honestly, I did. But I guess it was like the colonel says."

Henderson leaned forward, fixing his eyes on Zimmermann.

"Everybody makes mistakes", he said. "But it's unfortunate that those navigational errors this morning had to cost the lives of seventy men."

Zimmermann looked at Davenport with pleading eyes, begging for help from some of General Henderson's indictment. The colonel was about to speak, when General Pritchard stood up from the seat he had been occupying behind the desk.

"Colonel Davenport", he asked, "if your Group had gotten off on time, your navigator would have been able to fly the mission as briefed. Isn't that right?"

"Yes, sir. But we still could have . . . ."

"If I may interrupt, sir", said Henderson. "By the same token, Keith would have gotten off on time if there hadn't been a last minute change in the Field Order, for which my A-3 must assume responsibility."

"The other Groups", responded Pritchard, sharply, "got off on time. I don't want Lieutenant Zimmermann to leave this room feeling that he must shoulder the whole blame."

"Neither, do I feel that Colonel Davenport should take the blame for the errors of the navigator", replied Henderson.

Zimmermann winced and shuffled his feet, as Davenport faced Pritchard.

"I want to assure the general that it won't happen again", he said. "regardless of who was to blame." "The Group Commander, is always to blame", said Pritchard, quietly. "You need a rest Colonel, a long rest, badly,"

He then faced Henderson.

"General, you will relieve Colonel Davenport, and send someone down here as soon as possible to take over."

Davenport crumpled back into a chair, as though his legs had suddenly become filled with sand, leaned forward and buried his face in his hands. His shoulders shook, seemingly out of control, and tears ran through his fingers.

Henderson looked speechlessly at Pritchard. While Zimmermann, with a horrified expression on his face, stood there watching the instantaneous and complete collapse of his commander.

Pritchard was the first to transfer his attention from Davenport, who continued to sob silently, to Zimmermann. He walked over and guided the young lieutenant, by the arm, to the door.

"What has just happened in this room, is strictly between those who were present", he told Heinz. "I wish it could have been avoided in front of you." He patted him on the arm "And try not to feel so badly about it."

Zimmermann saluted the general, stiffly, then left the room and closed the door behind himself. As he slowly walked down the hall, thinking about what had just happened, he set his cap on his head, crookedly, went outside and mounted his bicycle, then slowly rode along the muddied concrete road to the combat- crew living site. He dismounted and, as he was passing by the corner of the first building, he encountered Major Stovall, whom he saluted.

The Adjutant passed him by without returning the salute, or showing any sign of recognition. As it was, Stovall was so preoccupied with his own troubles, aside from being so nearsighted without his glasses, that he wouldn't have even noticed Winston Churchill. But, to Zimmermann, it appeared to be an intentional slight on the major's part.

As the lieutenant neared his quarters, he passed an open doorway from which loud voices could be overheard, rehashing the mission. Zimmermann felt sure that he had heard his name mentioned and stopped, a few steps beyond the door, to listen.

"That knuckle-headed Kraut navigator sure screwed us up tight today", said a voice. "Yeah. He's a German ace. He can claim seven of our air- craft destroyed", said another. "Yeah, he's won himself the Iron Cross, with bar", said a third.

Zimmermann stood there, frozen, for a moment, then moved on. Immediately after he had left another voice spoke up.

"Aw, why don't you bastards quit your bitching. You haven't got a navigator in your whole damn squadron that can find the seat of his pants with both hands. I'll take Zimmermann any day."

But Zimmermann was already out of earshot. As he entered his quarters, he caught the invigorating scent of shaving lotion.

"You look like a man in a trance", said Jesse Bishop, who had changed into a fresh uniform and was knotting his tie in front of a mirror. "Where the hell have you been?"

"Over at Headquarters." "Doing what?"

"Listening to a general tell me my navigation cost us seven crews today."

"Nuts, How can anybody say it was your fault, when we took off so late that you had to change your data in flight?"

"Just the same, I'm a goddamn German ace, that's what I am."

"You're an over conscientious, stubborn, Dutchman, that's what you are. Why, the navigation was anybody's guess in that soup. The colonel was guessing right along with you. He told you to turn wrong when we hit the enemy coast."

"Maybe I misunderstood him."

"That ain't the way I heard it on the innerphone. Now, snap out of it. You've been needling me to pull a short mission to the Black Swan with you. Okay, I'll take you up on it right now. So, go throw on a clean shirt and we'll get going."

"That's not all", said Zimmermann. "I got the colonel fired. General Pritchard just relieved him for lousing up the mission."

"Fired!", Bishop whistled. "So the colonel carries out their mistakes to the letter. Then they fire him! Come on, Heinz, this really calls for the Black Swan."

"You go ahead, Jesse. I . . . I guess I'll hit the sack."

Bishop walked over and patted him on the back, but Zimmermann remained impassive.

"I'll tell you what, Heinz", said Jesse. "I've got to go over and borrow a few pounds from Major Stovall."

Zimmermann turned away and moved over to the window, where he stood, staring out at nothing. "When I get back", continued Bishop, "I want to find you looking pretty and smelling like a rose," He hurried out the door.

Heinz Zimmermann sat down, heavily, on the foot of his bed. "Seventy of our own guys", he said, aloud.

He waited until Bishop's footsteps had died away on the boardwalk. Then he drew his pearl- handled revolver out of its holster, cocked it, pressed the muzzle up against his right temple, pulled the trigger, and blew his brains out.

At Wycombe Abbey, twilight glimmered across the pond, whose glassy surface was ruffled here and there by the wakes of the wild ducks, and the gliding of the swans. G.I.s, walking arm in arm with W.A.A.F.s, strolled around the water's edge, tossing bits of bread to the birds.

Walking along in silence, Pritchard and Savage reached a old rustic bridge that spanned a brook running into the pond. As they stopped to lean on the railing, Pritchard tossed his cigar butt into the pond, then took out, and lit, a fresh Havana.

"When Ed told you that he'd relieved Davenport, just now, did he also mention that he'd recommended you as the only man qualified to take over", he asked?

"No, sir."

"Well, he did. And you are. But it's a step back for you right after a promotion. And it means you being exposed to combat again. On the other hand, we have a Group that couldn't answer a Field Order tomorrow, and the blunt truth is that an American fighting outfit has quit. If it spreads to the other Groups, and it can, or if the truth should get out now, we just might as well go home."

He flicked a cigar ash down to the water.

"And if we fold up here, where will it stop? It could be an irreparable blow to our side, at the very time that our allies are hanging on by a hair, absorbing terrible punishment, and counting on us to live up to our big promises. We are the only force in U.S. uniforms capable of hitting the number one enemy for a long time. But it's not just the bombing show, nor the prestige that's involved, so much as the spirit that wins wars."

He turned to look squarely at Savage, his eyes glistening.

"That's why I picked you to lead our first Group", he continued, in a husky voice. "That's why I've got to fish around in my hip pocket just once more, and come up with you. It's a bigger job than Ed Henderson's got. This time I'm giving you the big- gest job of this war."

He paused again.

"Frank, America is at stake."

Savage, looking at the thick overcast of fog beginning to drag through the high treetops near the Abbey, spoke for the first time.

"The weatherman", he said, "promises that everything will be closed down for at least a week. I'm going to need that time down at Archbury, General."

CHAPTER FOUR

SHAMBLES

Late in the afternoon, a fine drizzle was sifting down from soggy skies upon the airfield at Archbury. It was glistening on the rounded roofs of the Nissen huts, on the runways, and on the many different bombs stacked under thickets of dripping green leaves used for concealment.

Keith Davenport had departed, two days previously, leaving behind a shambles of despair.

Whatever bond there had been to cement the men in unity - centered upon the symbol of the Group and the fatherly personality of its commander - was now dissol- ved.

Battered by the cumulative losses of friends killed in combat, by the shock of Zimmermann's tragic suicide, and by the crowning blow of Davenport's collapse and dismissal, the 918th lay prostrate.

And psychologically defenseless against the inroads of indifference, discouragement and resentment.

General Savage, riding up to the south gate into Archbury Field, in the staff car that had brought him from PINETREE, knew the severity of the situation, both instinctively and from combat experience. He was well aware that he was about to step out on a stage, before an audience in which every member would hate him on sight.

Every act of his, and every word, would automatically be wrong, particularly so coming from a general officer. The Group would expect sympathy from him, and it would be prepared to reject that sympathy. However, Frank Savage had a plan.

Purpose showed in the hard set of his mouth, and in the hot intensity of his eyes, as he stared straight ahead through the rain smeared windshield. But, those that knew Savage well would have noted a telltale hint that alleviated the relentless expression in his eyes. The keen anticipation of a flier who loves to fly, of a leader who was born to lead, and of a fighting man waiting for the bell and knows how to fight.

A B-17 passed low over the car - low enough so that Savage could feel the vibrations from the engines cutting through him - and skimmed toward the runway. Savage's granite eyes glowed and his heart beat faster.

When the staff car reached the gate, a rain-coated, dispirited-looking, M.P., standing in an upended crate that served as a sen- try shack, tossed away a cigarette and, without saluting or com- ing to attention, waved his hand to motion the car on. Savage halted the driver and jumped out.

"Do you know me, Sergeant", he demanded of the sentry? "No, sir."

"Then why are you admitting me onto this station?" "I seen it was a staff car, sir."

The sentry was standing at attention now.

"Goering could have been inside it. Don't your orders require you to check all identifications?" "Yes, sir."

Pulling out his wallet from his uniform tunic, Savage gave the sentry his I.D. "Here's my A.O.G. card."

The sergeant examined it, handed it back and saluted.

"This is a military base, Sergeant", concluded Savage, "not a public zoo. You will check all visitors' identifications according- ly."

"Very well, General."

Looking badly abused, the sentry could only glare down the road after the car.

Half way to the administration site, Savage's slow moving car came upon two G.I.s walking in the opposite direction. Both of the men stared directly at him in the rear seat, but neither one saluted.

Again Savage stopped his driver and had him back up to the walking soldiers. He sprang out and halted them.

"Are you men in the United States Army", he asked?

"Yes, sir", replied both men, in unison.

Coming to attention, the two belatedly rendered their salutes, which Savage returned with a whiplash motion.

"Take a good look at me", he told them. "I'm going to be here for a while. And even if you're a block away, heaven help you if you ever pass me up again without saluting! You might want to spread that around."

Through the rear view mirror, as his car proceeded on, Savage could see the pair looking back at intervals, gesturing and turning their heads toward each other in vigorous conversation.

At the headquarters building, after directing the driver to drop his baggage off at the C.O.'s quarters, Savage dismissed him.

"You won't be seeing me back at PINETREE for some time", he said. "Good luck to you, Sergeant."

"Good luck to you, sir", said the sergeant, in an awed tone.

Savage walked down the hallway to the Adjutant's office, where the only person in sight was sitting at a typewriter in long-sleeved G.I. underwear, his uniform shirt draped over the back of his chair.

"How do I address you", asked the general?

The man stood up in confusion, groping for his shirt.

"I don't rightly understand the general", he responded.

"Are you a civilian? Or an Italian general? Or a rear admiral? How am I supposed to know?" "Sergeant McIllhenny, sir", he said, flaming with embarrass- ment. "U.S. Army Air Forces." "You're Private McIllhenny now", said Savage. "Where's the Air Exec?'

"Colonel Gately's not on the station, sir." "How long has he been gone?"

The ex-sergeant hesitated. "Two days, sir."

"Where can I reach him?"

"He didn't leave any number, sir."

"Where's the Ground Exec?" "Still in the hospital, sir." "And the Adjutant?"

"Over at the Officers' Club, sir."

"Get yourself dressed. Then go find the Adjutant and tell him to report to me in the Ops room." "Yes, sir!"

Savage left and moved swiftly down another hallway until he found the Operations room. It also was deserted, save for a tech-sergeant who was correcting the list of combat crews on the big blackboard. Savage's eyes scanned around the room, observing the litter of cigarette butts, crumpled candy wrappers, and miscellaneous trash on the floor.

Ignoring the sergeant, whose back was still turned to him, he stepped back into the hall, reached for and grabbed a fire hose nozzle from its rack, twisted a water valve on the pipe above it, and re-entered the Operations room, dragging slack hose after him. In a quick moment, the hose stiffened under the water press-ure and a gushing stream shot across the concrete floor, splashing up against the ankles of the sergeant, who whirled around as if he had been stabbed.

"HEY!", he yelled. "What the goddamn hell do you . . . ."

He stopped in mid-sentence, his jaw dropping at the sight of a brigadier general striding about the room, busily hosing down the floor. And Savage made a thorough job of it, directing the water stream under the chairs, in corners and under desks, until he had swept all of the rubbish, like driftwood, out into the hall. Then he switched off the valve and replaced the nozzle on its rack.

"Looks a little cleaner in here now, doesn't it, Sergeant?"

Gaping at Savage as though undecided whether or not he had a madman on his hands, Sergeant Coulter gulped and nodded.

"If I'd known that the general was coming . . ."

"Never mind that, I'm here now. But I don't suppose the Operations officer is." "Major Holloman had to go to town, sir."

"What for", asked Savage?

"I believe he's getting a haircut in London, sir."

"You mean he's shacked up with a babe in Thetford!"

The sergeant was dumbfounded both by the directness and the accuracy of the general's shot in the dark. But was it a shot in the dark, the sergeant asked himself? Hesitating in a state of indecision, he finally decided not to take a chance. "Yes, sir", he admitted.

"And the Squadron Commanders . . . . are any of them on the station?" "Major Cobb is here, sir. Over at the Officers' Club, I would think." "And where are the others?"

"If the general will pardon the expression", said the sergeant, resignedly. "I believe they are shacked up somewhere too."

"I think we're getting to understand each other, Sergeant", said Savage.

He sat down on one of the desks, dug into the musette bag hung over his shoulder and hauled out a box of crackers, a tin of Nes Cafe, and a can of Spam.

"Missed my lunch", he continued, as he opened the can of Spam. "Do you appreciate good coffee, Sergeant?"

"Yes, sir."

"Fine", said Savage, tossing him the Nes Cafe. "Whip up some good coffee for the both of us." The sergeant took the can over to the hot plate and set some water on to boil.

"I take it you're the Operations chief clerk", said Savage, as he munched on some crackers and Spam.

"Yes, sir, Sergeant Coulter."

"Glad to meet you, Coulter. My name is Savage. I'm taking over the Group." He went over and shook hands with the ser- geant.

While the sergeant was groping for an appropriate reply, Harvey Stovall entered the room, stopping just inside the door in a puddle of water, with his arm raised in a rigid salute. His eyes were bloodshot and raindrops sparkled on his nose. He was out of breath, having sprinted all the way from the club as soon as McIllhenny had told him: "There's a crazy general who wants you over in the Ops room right away."

Savage returned the salute.

"Major Stovall reporting as ordered, sir", he said, glancing up and down between the water and the general.

As Savage walked over to shake his hand, Sergeant Coulter came to the rescue. "This is our new commander, Major. General Savage."

"Very glad to meet you, General", managed Stovall, shaking Savage's hand. "We weren't notified that you were arriving today, sir, or . . ."

He stumbled like a schoolboy losing his place in a recitation, then recovered on a new tack. "The 918th", he said, with forced brightness, "never hoped for a general."

Realizing that what he just said didn't sound quite right, he lapsed into a painful silence. "Been drinking, Major", asked Savage, who could smell Stovall's breath?

"Yes, sir, I . . . I never had a drink in my life, until three days ago." Savage turned to Sergeant Coulter.

"Make another cup of coffee", he said. "Strong." Then he turned back to Stovall.

"I've got two jobs for you, Major, as soon as you've had your coffee", he told him.

"Number one, cancel all leaves and passes, and make sure that the Squadron Commanders are back here tonight. Then send the M.P.s out after the Air Exec and bring him in to me under arrest. Number two, set up a meeting for all combat crews in the Briefing room tomorrow at 0800 hours."

"The general wishes Colonel Gately under actual arrest?"

Savage recognized a hint of profound satisfaction in Stovall's tone. "Exactly", he responded.

The Adjutant saluted, executed a clumsy about-face, and was starting through the door, when Savage called him back.

"Your coffee, Major", he said, taking a cup from Coulter and handing it to Stovall.

"Yes, sir", said Stovall. "Of course, thank you, sir."

While the Adjutant was sipping his steaming coffee, Savage went over to the Order of Battle blackboard and began studying the chalked names and figures, which summarized the Group's operational status. Stovall, his eyes looking at the soaking wet floor, seized the opportunity to question Sergeant Coulter.

"What the hell is all this water doing in here, Sergeant", he asked, in a loud whisper? "And that mess out in the hall?"

Coulter lowered his voice.

"The general did it."

Annoyed, Stovall stared at the sergeant in complete disbelief.

"I asked you a serious question, Coulter", he said, a bit louder than he intended. Savage turned around.

"The sergeant isn't kidding, Major", he said. "And neither was I." He turned back and resumed his scrutiny of the blackboard.

Back in his new office a little over an hour later, after taking advantage of the fading afternoon light to drive around the airbase, where he familiarized himself with its layout and insured that the aircraft guards were on the job at their widely dispersed hardstands, Savage was attending to a number of papers that required his immediate signature. His mind had already become crammed with matters that would have to be taken up with Ed Henderson, such as valuable equipment and supplies that he had just seen being stored in the open, exposed to the weather, not enough bomb trailers, and a score of other items.

He was still wearing his trench coat, which was spotted from the rain, giving the impression to Stovall, who had just stepped through the doorway, that the walls of this office would see the new commander only on the run.

"Colonel Gately is outside, sir", said the Adjutant. "Send him in", order Savage.

"Yes, sir", said Stovall, as he disappeared.

Lieutenant Colonel Ben Gately's face displayed no consciousness of guilt, as he approached the general's desk, followed by two M.P.s. On the contrary, there was disdain in his eyes as he raised his hand in a salute.

He was still smarting from the indignity of having been arrested in front of Pamela Mallory, at Desborough Hall, where he had stopped for a drink on his return from a spree in London. Savage noted the slight trembling in the Air Exec's fingers, attributing it to a severe hangover.

Ignoring Gately's salute, the general dismissed the M.P.s with a nod of his head and then pressed a buzzer, summoning Stovall.

"Major, bring me Gately's Sixty-six dash One file", he said. "Also those of the Squadron Commanders."

While Stovall was getting the records, Gately lowered his right arm, unobtrusively, to his side. The disdainfulness in his eyes becoming intensified.

Continuing to disregard Gately, the general went on signing papers, until the Adjutant returned with the 66-1s. Savage lifted the top form off the pile and settled back in his chair, studying the compact personal entries. Two minutes passed.

Gately cleared his throat.

"General", he asked, "may I inquire as to why I was brought here under arrest?" "No!"

The word went through him like it was a bullet.

Savage proceeded to examine the records before him. Finally Gately's eyes wandered up to the clock on the wall behind the general. Five minutes had passed.

Gately began to assume a relaxed position, with his hands on his hips, and cleared his throat again. "May I sit down, sir", he asked?

"No", said Savage, sharply. "And stand at attention!"

The colonel snapped to and remained at attention. Another five minutes crawled by. Gately craved a cigarette. Cold sweat beaded on his forehead. Occasionally, slight shudders shook his body, in mute evidence of the scope of his previous night's excessive indulgence When, at last, Savage glanced up and nailed Gately with his eyes, the latter had the distinct feeling that he was looking into the face of a tiger. Actually there was, at times, something leo- nine about him, not in Savage's close- cropped head, but in his eyes and facial expression.

"You're the son of Lieutenant General Tom Gately, aren't you", he asked?

"Yes, sir."

"Fine officer, none better", said Savage. "Thank you, sir", replied the colonel. Gately began to look somewhat relieved.

"You, too", he continued, "are a graduate of the United States Military Academy. You have nine years of service and you were acting commander of this station as soon as Colonel Davenport left."

"Yes, sir. And I can explain . . ."

"Don't interrupt. Just listen. And answer my questions. You have led only two missions with this Group, is that correct?"

"Yes, sir, not including recalls and aborts."

"And you have more four-engine time, and more bombardment experience, than anyone else in the 918th."

Savage stood up, walked around and sat down on the front of his desk, never taking his eyes off Gately. When he spoke again, his voice was charged with contempt and his eyes revealed unmistakable hatred.

"Gately", he said, speaking slowly, "you've made yourself an enemy. The most bitter enemy you'll ever have as long as you live."

Savage hit his own chest with his forefinger.

"ME", he said! "As far as I'm concerned, you're a lousy yell- ow dog. You're a traitor to your country, to West Point, to the uniform that I hate to share with vermin like you, to the 918th, and to your father."

The Air Exec turned the color of wet ashes. Drops of sweat rolled down from his temples. His fists contracted into knots. He started to say something, but Savage cut him short.

"It would be easy for me to just transfer you out", he continued. "And saddle some unsuspecting guy with a trained professional soldier who has been willing to let a bunch of civilian school boys carry the brunt of the fighting, instead of giving them the leadership they deserved - and needed."

He then began to pace the floor, while still riveting his eyes to Gately's, who now, occasionally, looked away.

"That's what you want, isn't it? A cozy berth where you can sit out the war, preferably with a combat unit so that you can steal fake glory. But I'm not going to pass this buck."

He stopped directly in front of Gately.

"You are going to stay right here. Where I can show you how much worse I hate you than the goddamn Nazis - because you're supposed to be on our side. I'm going to burn your butt! I'm going to make you lay square eggs! I'm going to hold your head down in the mud and trample it! And I'm going to make you wish that you had never been born!"

Spotty color was returning to Gately's face, and he was shaking all over. Never in his life had anyone talked to him remotely like this, nor had he ever experienced the scalding sensation produced by the venom in each of Savage's words.

But Savage wasn't through, although he returned to his desk and sat down.

"Meanwhile, Gately", he continued, "you're going to do a lot of flying. You're going to make every mission, until further notice. You're an airplane commander now, not the Air Exec. I'm going to give you an aircraft and I want you to have this name painted on the nose . . .

THE LEPER COLONY

And I'm going to hand-pick a special crew for you. Men who have shown a predisposition for head colds and earaches. You're going to get a co-pilot who's all thumbs, a bombardier who can't hit his plate with his fork, and a navigator who can't find his own navel."

Savage paused for a moment.

"Have you anything to say?"

"Yes, sir", Gately said, in a strangled voice. General Savage, I have the right to a trail. And I have a right to prefer charges against you, sir, for personal abuse and exceeding your lawful authority."

Savage sprang to his feet. "Major Stovall", he called out!

Twelve O'clock High

There was a bang, from a chair being overturned, and then the Adjutant opened the door.

"Get me General Pritchard on the phone."

"Yes, sir", said Stovall, then he quickly withdrew.

"Rights, Gately", said Savage, his voice shaking! "Rights? You've got a right to cable your father. He'll be goddamn proud of you. I'd like to kill you with my bare hands. But I'm going to give you a break. I'm going to let you explain to General Pritch- ard just where you've been since Tuesday. To explain desertion of your post at a time when a Field Order could have come down!"

The alarm which had transformed Gately's face at Savage's mention of Pritchard, now began to resemble panic. The ex-Air Exec struggled, within himself, for several moments, then came to a decision.

"General Savage", he said, "I retract my statement." The general stared at Gately for a few minutes. "Stovall", he called out again, "cancel that call." Then he said, "That's all Gately."

Gately saluted, did an about-face, and left.

Savage felt weak, almost physically ill, after Gately had gone. Reaction to the violent emotions which had gripped him now left him trembling.

He had always hated to humiliate a man, and dreaded having to fire a subordinate. But against Gately, and all the Gatelys, he felt the ferocity of an anger that had been accumulating for many months.

But, upon this one man he had felt compelled to vent his personal war against complacency in the midst of what he believed to be a fight to the death, in the most liberal sense of the words.

Stovall walked in with some more papers.

"Would the general like something to eat brought over", he asked? "No thanks, Major", said Savage, still trying to calm himself down. "I think I'll drop by the Officers' Club for a beer, though. How about you?"

"A lot of new stuff just came in, sir", Stovall replied. "Maybe I can get over later. Er . . . . excuse me, General, but the insignia must have come loose on your trench coat."

Savage looked down at his shoulders, bare of rank insignia.

"To tell you the truth", he said, "I haven't got enough pairs of stars to go around. Put that on your shopping list, won't you? The next time you're in London."

"Certainly, sir", said Stovall. "If they'll sell stars to a major." "Hell, Harvey, you look more like a general than I do."

"A little older, anyway", replied the Adjutant, tactfully. Savage smiled, then picked up one of the 66-1 files.

"Cut an order tonight, relieving Colonel Gately as Air Exec", said Savage. "Very well, sir."

"There won't be any immediate replacement, though, until I've had more time to go over these reports."

Savage studied the 66-1 he held in his hand.

"He isn't the senior Squadron Commander, but Major Cobb's got the most impressive record here." He tapped the forms.

"He's flown the most missions, has the most decorations, and has the best efficiency reports." "He's a strong officer, sir", commented Stovall.

"I want the most aggressive we've got. How does he stack up in that respect?" "Major Cobb is certainly aggressive, General."

Savage studied the Adjutant for a moment.

"You seem to have some reservations about him", he said.

"Well, sir", began Stovall, scratching his head. He has just one fault - that you ought to know about. He goes out of his way to pick fights when he's had a drink, or two. It's gotten so everybody's afraid to go near him in the club. He's a big bruiser."

"Is that so", asked Savage, tapping his fingers on the desk? "And, how long has this been going on?"

"Just recently, sir. It started this last month, I'd say."

Savage rose and prepared to leave. "Thanks, Major. I'll think it over."

Outside, the rain had stopped and a full moon bathed the driveway in cold light, when Savage stepped through the door. A smartly uniformed solder stepped from the shadows and saluted.

"General Savage", he asked? "Yes."

"I've been assigned as your driver, sir", he motioned toward a sedan. "Fine", said Savage.

Suddenly the general looked a little more closely at the man, whose sleeves, bare of rank chevrons, proclaimed that he was a buck private.

"Say, aren't you the clerk I met in the Adjutant's office this afternoon?" "Yes, sir. Private McIllhenny."

Savage, struck by Major Stovall's skillfulness at devising this stratagem, smiled, in spite of himself.

"McIllhenny", he said, "I can't have a plain dogface private driving me around. Put those stripes back on in the morning."

"YES, SIR", declared McIllhenny, smiling broadly.

"I'll walk over to the Officers' Club, Sergeant. You can follow me there in a little while." "Very good, sir."

He set off without asking for directions, as Archbury Airfield had an arrangement of buildings identical to that of Savage's old station at Middle Heath. As he walked along he had a warm feeling of being back on his home grounds.

Entering the club, he folded his uniform hat, thrust it into his trench-coat pocket, and walked to the lounge. He was standing at the entrance of a low roofed, poorly lit room, that smelled of the coal burning in a stove, sitting in the center, and ugly with overstuffed, leather covered chairs, that were lopsided, hollowed and misshapen by the backs of many men.

A half dozen men were sprawled in a semicircle of easy chairs about the stove, and nearly every part of the room was crowded, except for the bar, where the only customer at the moment was a tall Major, built like a fullback football player. As he walked over to the bar, Savage was conscious of heads swiveling around, of faces looking up, and of eyes concentrating upon him.

Savage felt terribly alone. The word, he thought, had spread. I know what they're thinking, he said to himself, ... Davenport ... Zimmermann ... those damn generals ... brass hats who can- cel leaves. No one approached him. No one offered him a drink.

He reached the bar and ordered a beer. The major standing near him stared into his highball without glancing up. Savage noticed at once that the officer wore a black eye and a name tag on his leather jacket stenciled - J. R. Cobb.

Savage had finished half his beer by the time Cobb finally looked over at him. It was obvious that the highball he had been drinking wasn't his first.

"Have a drink", said Cobb, gruffly, brushing a cowlick of hair out of his eyes. "Thanks", said Savage, mildly, "but I've got one."

"Beer", complained Cobb, as he made a sour face. "English beer. Pour it back in the cow and have a real drink."

"The beer's okay with me."

"Have a scotch on me", said Cobb, his enunciation sounding a little thicker when he raised his voice.

Savage resolved to give the officer unlimited rope.

"I'm doing all right", he told Cobb. "Save your money." "You think I can't pay for a drink?"

"Sure, I know you can."

"Well, look at this", bellowed Cobb, as he pulled a wad of, crumpled, white five-pound notes from his pocket. "I can buy and sell you. Have a drink."

"I'll finish my own drink, if you don't mind."

"I do mind", he said, his face darkening with belligerence. "You don't like me, do you", he added? "Sure, bub. You're okay."

"Well, I don't like you!"

He finished off his highball in one gulp. "And don't call me bub."

For the first time Cobb noticed the absence of a rank insignia on Savage's shoulders. "What are you? A major?"

"No", replied Savage.

"A captain?" "No."

"Well, you're a pretty old looking lieutenant then. You must be awfully goddamn dumb."

As a score of spectators started edging toward the bar, Savage finished his beer and set the glass down, without comment.

"What's it take to insult you, anyhow", demanded Cobb? "I s'pose if I spit in your face you'd think it was raining . . . You yellow?"

"Nope", responded Savage. "You wanna fight?"

Savage smiled, faintly, and his eyes were flickering.

"You've got yourself a playmate, Major", he said. "There's plenty of light outside."

He strode to the door, followed eagerly by Cobb and every other man in the lounge. Most of them realized that Savage was their new commander, but no one made a move to interfere as he and Cobb headed to a clear space in the car parking area outside.

"Better take off that trench coat", said Cobb. "Just start swinging", said Savage.

Cobb took the general at his word and, evidently, tried to take his opponent's head off with his first hard swing. But Savage's left pushed him on the chest just hard enough to spoil Cobb's aim.

Then Savage stepped in closer, driving both fists into Cobb's face in two, nearly simultaneous, punches that traveled barely ten inches. Cobb toppled back. And no one who was there would ever forget how quickly Savage managed to spring forward and grab him by a handful of jacket, holding up Cobb's heavy, sagg- ing body by the sheer strength of one hand, to prevent his face from striking the concrete. The contest was over in six seconds.

The general pulled Cobb back upright, dazed, the fight gone out of him. Then he guided the groggy major over to his car, where McIllhenny jumped out and opened the door.

"Get in there and wait until I come back", Savage told Cobb.

As he walked back into the club, the crowd of officers quickly parted, then followed him inside. He went over to the radio, picked up the Green Toby and carried it to the mantelpiece. Then he turned around, facing the roomful of officers.

"Give me your attention", he called out. The murmur of voices hushed.

"This station is alerted from now until our next mission. That means hit the sack. The bar is closed until further notice."

He then walked to the door and outside, without glancing left or right, went over to his car and climbed into the back seat with Major Cobb, who was rubbing his jaw.

"One of the guys just tipped me off, General", said Cobb, ruefully. "I'm awfully sorry, sir. I guess I'm just a damn fool when I've had a couple of drinks." "That's right", said Savage. "You are."

Cobb smoothed his hair back.

"Two thousand guys on this station", he groaned, "and I had to go and pick on a general. Well, . . . that's the way my luck's been running. I'm glad I saved my second lieutenant's bars. But I hate the idea of leaving the Group."

"You think you've got a pretty fair Group here?"

"We've got the best goddamn Group in England, General! I know we have a black eye up at Bomber Command, but all we need is half a chance . . . And I've poured mine down the drain."

"Who said anything about busting you, or transferring you out? Are you trying to run my Group for me?"

"No, sir, but . . ."

"I'll admit that you made an horse's ass of yourself, but your Sixty-six dash One says you're the best Squadron Commander in the 918th. So, effective tomorrow, you're the new Air Exec of this Group."

"Gee", stammered Cobb. "Gee, sir, I don't know what to say."

"There's not a damn thing for you to say. Just cut out your drinking, entirely. You can't handle it. And save your fighting for the Germans."

At five minutes till eight, the next morning, the Briefing room was packed with the men of the combat crews. The place buzzed with conversation, most of it about Savage and most of it uncom- plimentary.

"Why did they have to send a general down here." "Who the hell does this guy think he is? Superman?" "Stand by, men, for a good old-fashioned fight talk."

The predominant feelings of the crews were that Davenport had been relieved, unfairly, for complaining too loudly and too often, on their behalf, to superiors who weren't interested in his complaints.

Chaplain Twombley, who had taken the liberty of attending, uninvited, sat expectantly in a front row seat while, near the rear door, the Flight Surgeon sat next to Harvey Stovall, who was waiting anxiously to call everyone to attention as soon as the general appeared. Stovall was nervous, as he had heard about Savage's unconventional encounter at the Officers' Club with Major Cobb, an event which had both impressed and puzzled the witnesses.

Most felt that Cobb had it coming to him for a long time, and were glad to see somebody step up and oblige. But Stovall knew that the men were too far gone to be won over so quickly by any spectacular act on the part of the new commander, even if he was a general. He prayed that Savage would have the discretion to handle these hard-boiled crews, whose sentiments were dangerously close to mutiny, with a sensitive tact.

At one minute to eight, Savage entered. "Ten-SHUN", called out Stovall.

The men rose raggedly to their feet.

"Rest", said Savage, as he walked forward to the platform. The crews sagged back into their chairs.

Savage appeared to be fresh, although he had been up and going all night, looking into every nook and cranny of the station and poring over reports that X-rayed the 918th's status. Over in his quarters, his bags were still unpacked.

Savage waited until the shuffling of feet and chairs had died down. Then, in a clear voice that carried well, he said.

"I'm General Savage. Your new C.O."

His eyes swept the room slowly, giving each man the impression that the general was looking directly at him.

"The local weather is going to be okay today. At eleven hundred hours there will be a briefing for a practice mission."

He paused until a scattering of coughs ceased.

"I was sent down here", he resumed, "to take over what has come to be known as a Hard Luck Group."

He paused again.

"Well, I don't believe in hard luck."

Savage was reaching deep inside himself to find the words to express his feelings. It was immediately apparent to the crews that he had not prepared any pat speech in advance.

"Hard luck doesn't win battles", he continued. "It doesn't get bombs on the target." A pause.

"I'll tell you one reason why you've had hard luck. I could see it on your faces . . . at the club last night. I can see it there now. You feel sorry for yourselves."

Stovall winced. A faint murmur passed over the assemblage.

"Why should you be the fall guys, you're asking yourselves. Well, who the hell else is there? We're it. This is the front line in the dirtiest, bloodiest war in history. We're fighting the most powerful air force and the greatest land army of all time. And the most fanatical enemy. In that kind of a fight, somebody's go- ing to get hurt. Us . . . you . . . me."

An electrified silence gripped the room.

"Hitler is going to whip us unless someone goes out and beats him. If we fail to beat him, then we are turning over our wives, and our children, to rot in Nazi concentration camps, just as sure as hell. That's what has already happened to those people who have failed to beat him.

Unless a man amongst you is willing to have that happen in America, how can he be sorry that he is sitting in this room, this morning? How can he think that his own life is that important?" Savage stopped concentrating on his next words "Fear is normal", he continued. "Go ahead and be afraid. But remember that the difference between being afraid to die, and quitting, is surrender. And I'm not going to surrender while I'm C.O. of the 918th. Forget about doing twenty-five missions . . . and going home.

Consider yourselves already dead.

If any man here wants to save his hide, then he'd better make up his mind right now. Because I don't want him in this Group. He can come and see me in my office. I'll be there in five min- utes."

Savage jumped from the platform and started down the center aisle, his head up and his eyes looking straight ahead. Ordinar- ily someone should have called everyone to attention, but the men were frozen in their seats, transfixed by a mass reaction of furious resentment, not only for the mortifying implications of Savage's words, but for the deliberately antagonistic manner in which he had said them.

As the general reached the door, a voice rang out, "I'LL TAKE COLONEL DAVENPORT."

There was an instantaneous roar of assent, which echoed and burned in Savage's ears, as he stepped outside and walked away.

Harvey Stovall was the first to rise. He had the feeling that he had better hurry over to his office before the line started forming at the door marked - C.O.

CHAPTER FIVE

RALLY POINT

When the Adjutant entered his office, he could see Savage already at his desk, signing papers with a fierce concentration. Stovall sat down and went to work on the Morning Report, trying to check it in his usual methodical manner, but every few minutes his mind would wander and he found himself glancing apprehen- sively out the window.

Except for Sergeant McIllhenny, industriously polishing the general's car, and the passing of an occasional bicycle or jeep, there was little activity in front of headquarters. No aircrew members had appeared, and Stovall began to breathe a little easi- er as he carried the Morning Report into Savage, who gave him a searching look.

"What are you sweating about. Harvey", Savage asked? "For awhile, sir", said Stovall, "I expected trouble."

Savage merely snorted, then began going over the Morning Report. As Stovall returned to his desk, he was reconsidering his estimate of Savage's psychological approach to the combat crews.

Apparently, he mused, a splash of ice water in the face has its uses - like the effect of a slap on an hysterical person. Then he heard footsteps coming down the hall. Lieutenant Jesse Bishop knocked, then entered.

"I'd like to see General Savage", he said, firmly. "How about me", asked Stovall. "Won't I do?"

"The general said that he'd be in his office", replied Bishop, pointedly.

The Adjutant leaned back in his chair and looked the young man over for a moment.

"You, Jesse", he said, sadly?

Stovall fiddled with his pen, screwing and unscrewing the cap. Then he swiveled his chair around, toward the window behind his desk and, without turning back, told Bishop to go on in.

Bishop entered Savage's office, walked up to his desk and saluted. "Lieutenant Bishop, sir."

"Shoot, Bishop, what's on your mind."

"Sir, . . . the airplane commanders picked me as their spokesman. They all want a transfer. The whole lot."

Savage's expression hardened. He gave Bishop a long stare. He had been primed to throw the book at a few malcontents, if necessary, but this was different. This was worse than anything he had foreseen. This was a total emergency.

Bishop stared right back at him.

"One of my final acts", he said, "before I left PINETREE, was to forward a recommendation for your Congressional Medal of Honor - for the mission your pilot was killed on."

Perhaps more than anyone in the world, Savage had been fully qualified to understand the magnitude of the deed described in the masterfully understated official language of Bishop's citation. Never had he been more moved by the act of another human being.

"I can understand why they chose you to come here, Bishop", he continued. "Maybe the recommendation did have something to do with it, sir."

He could have truthfully added, except that he was unaware if the fact, that he was also the most popular man in the Group.

"We're not quitters, General Savage. We just want transfers." Savage drummed his fingers on his desk blotter.

"So, I wasted my breath this morning", he said, firmly. "You think I was talking a lot of hot air." "We've all heard better fight talks from football coaches", re- sponded the lieutenant.

Savage stood up, his eyes glaring.

"All right, go back and tell them to put their requests through their squadron channels", said Savage. "And tell them this, too. Until those requests are acted on, one way or another, all of you are still on combat duty. You all fly."

"Yes, sir. We understand that." "Is there anything else?"

"No, sir."

"That's all, then."

Bishop saluted, and then left the room. Savage, his forehead creased, stood and slowly walked into the Adjutant's office, sit- ting down on a corner of Stovall's desk.

"There is trouble, Harvey", he said.

"I couldn't help overhearing", said Stovall.

"That's fine, I'm glad you did", replied Savage, "because your reaction is important to me. I want to know how you feel about this situation - where your sympathies are?"

Stovall considered carefully before answering. He removed his glasses and began polishing the lenses with his handkerchief.

"My sympathies", he professed, at length, "are where they've always been, and always will be. With the 918th Bomb Group."

He finished polishing his glasses and set them on his desk.

"I'm just a civilian", he continued. "A lawyer, by trade, sir. I took on my biggest case when I came over here to England. The 918th is my client. And I aim to see my client win its case."

His usually mild eyes showed slow fire.

"But, in any event, my sympathies don't really matter! They sent you down here! And you can count on me as long as you're in command."

Stovall noted, with some surprise, the relief that began show- ing in the general's face. It had never occurred to him that such an impregnably, self-confident type, as Frank Savage, should question the automatic loyalty of his gray-haired Adjutant, no matter how disturbed Savage might be about the young men of the combat crews.

He began to realize how deeply the general must have been shaken by Lieutenant Bishop's visit.

"In any case, Harvey", said Savage, "we'll get down to cases, as you put it. Winning cases. A tough case takes a little time, doesn't it?" "Yes, sir."

"This one will take at least a week for preparation. Maybe a little more. And I'll need some legal assistance."

"That's my specialty, General."

"All right, then. How long will it take the Squadron Adjutants to submit all those requests for transfers?"

"It's a lot of paper work, sir. Two or three days, at least."

"And after the requests have reached you, how long before they'll be ready for my signature?" Stovall's eyes crinkled in a shrewd look.

"Well, let's see, General", he said. "I've got a stack of Monthly Reports due about now. And I believe in thorough, method- ical work - taking things in order. Why, it might be three days before I could even get around to all those requests."

He began filling his pipe.

"A couple of days more to check them over, thoroughly. You know, those Squadron Adjutants most always make mistakes. And we don't want any papers going out from this headquarters that aren't in the proper form. That would be a bad reflection on the Group. My guess is that all those requests will have to go back to the squadrons to be done over."

"How long, then", asked Savage, with a faint smile, "before you can have them ready for my signature?"

"Roughly, about ten days, sir", replied Stovall.

"That", stated Savage, "is a hell of a way to run a railroad. You red-tape Adjutants are all alike." "Yes, sir", said Stovall, with a bit of a grin.

He stood up and started back to his office. "But, why should I buck the system?"

There was a twinkle in Stovall's eye as he reached for a memorandum to the four squadrons of the 918th, which he had just drafted, stipulating that all official communications were to be acted upon within twenty-four hours. He was tossing the memorandum into his HOLD basket, instead of the OUT basket, when majors Cobb and Kaiser appeared.

Stovall ushered them into Savage's office and introduced the Flight Surgeon to the general, then he withdrew back to his office.

"Good morning, Doc", greeted Savage. "How healthy are we this morning? Any casualties besides Major Cobb, here?"

The new Air Exec looked sheepish, as an overnight shiner had bloomed to match the blue and yellow discoloration beneath his other eye. But Major Kaiser seemed to fine nothing amusing in the general's question.

"Psychologically, General, the command is far from healthy", said Kaiser, frowning earnestly. He hesitated before adding: "As I dare say the general will agree."

Savage nodded.

"Do you know of any pills that might help", he asked?

"At the moment", said Kaiser, "I am somewhat too far out of my depth to venture a prognosis. But I shall observe the effect of the general's recent shock treatment with close interest." Savage considered this for a moment.

"How do we stand physically", he asked?

"Nothing unusual to report, sir. We have thirty-two cases of mild inflammation of the upper respiratory tract."

"You mean thirty-two colds."

"Well", Kaiser coughed gently, "yes, sir. Then there's Lieutenant Colonel Brown, the Ground Exec, sir. I believe we had better ship him home. He has a lung condition that won't respond to any of our treatments."

"Okay, Doc, see to it. And see what you can do to clean out the hospital. In general, if a man is strong enough to blink his eyes, I want him returned to duty. Understand?"

"Yes, sir."

Kaiser's face brightened

"And before any flying personnel are grounded, I want you to bring each case to my personal attention."

"Very well, sir."

Kaiser noticed that Major Cobb was boiling with impatience. "I'll be getting along, sir", he added, saluting the general.

He left, hurriedly, like a man with an immediate purpose.

"General", blurted Cobb, flushing with suppressed anger, "I did my best to cool off those hotheads after you left. I tried to stop Bishop."

"Bishop spoke only of the airplane commanders", interrupted Savage. "How about the Squadron Commanders?"

"They were in on it too, sir. The damn fools ought to be busted down to privates." "I want no talk of busting anybody. For the time being, we'll just sit tight."

"All right, sir", said Cobb.

But he continued to radiate indignation.

"The chumps", he continued. "I told them that you didn't get that Silver Star of yours out of a Crackerjacks box, but for leading the first Bomb Group over Europe. But, it was a waste of my time."

"Let me do the worrying here, Joe", said Savage, soothingly. "That's what I get paid for." He forced a smile, got up and walked with Cobb toward the door.

"I'll join you in Ops in a few minutes. Go ahead and get the practice mission set up, and put me in the lead ship with Gately. You do the briefing - I'll just be a spectator."

"Yes, sir", said Cobb.

Halfway through the door the Air Exec stopped and turned around.

"Oh, I forget to tell you about Gately", he said. "He walked out of the meeting, Washed his hands of what was going on."

"Okay", said Savage, a little impatiently, as he continued on into Stovall's office. Turning to his Adjutant, he said: "Harvey, I haven't met all of the Group Staff yet. Call them in here at ten-hundred for a short meeting."

"Yes, sir."

Stovall summoned a clerk and instructed him to broadcast the order over the Tannoy system.

"Oh, and Major, there's one other thing that needs attention right away", continued Savage. "I'll be needing a new Adjutant."

Stovall looked at him like a ham actor giving an exaggerated double-take.

"You have any ideas for the right man?"

"Well, sir", said Stovall, groping for something to say as though he had been clubbed on the head, "there's Captain Snodgrass. He's the best of the Squadron Adjutants. I think he could swing the job."

He peered at Savage's poker face in stricken bewilderment. "Fine! Cut an order assigning Snodgrass as Group Adjutant."

"Yes, sir."

"And cut another order relieving Colonel Brown as Ground Exec. I'm sending him home. Replace him with the next senior officer."

"But", managed Stovall, seeing the light, and weak with relief, "but, that's me, sir." "I can't help that", said Savage.

He reached out and shook hands with his new Ground Exec.

"Now listen, Harvey", he said, seriously, "Air discipline begins on the ground. That's going to be your ball game. I want ground discipline on this station, until someone upstairs tells me the rules have been changed. You're going to answer to me for a strictly military organization at Archbury Field, composed of soldiers - not sad sacks."

"Very well, sir", responded Stovall, grinning and involuntarily sucking in his gut.

THE LEPER COLONY stood out, in freshly painted red letters on the nose of the B-17, squatting on Ben Gately's hard-stand.

While waiting for Savage to show up, Gately was performing a final visual check of the aircraft. He twirled the turbo wheels of the four superchargers under the wings, testing the rim of each wheel with his fingertip for any unevenness of rotation.

He examined the landing gear tires for cracks, thrust his right hand against the landing gear strut, measuring the oleo piston for proper clearance, grabbed each propeller and shook it to check for any play in the engine mounts, and inspected the control sur- faces.

He had already checked everything inside the aircraft - guns, bomb bay, oxygen system, radio, fuel, ammunition. And double checked the previous final inspection of the co-pilot.

Finally satisfied, he called the crew together under the nose.

"Well, fellows", began Gately, "we're a fine looking collection, aren't we?"

To the sullen combat men who faced him, it was clear that Gately was a changed man, from the handsome, debonair, Air Exec to whom they were accustomed. He was still handsome, but there was nothing debonair in his expression. Baxter, the co-pilot, who knew him best, recognized that Gately had been suffering, but he had no means of gauging the intensity of the white heat which had consumed Gately since his interview with Savage the evening before.

Baxter noticed an unnatural quiver in Gately's voice. "Are you wondering what this is all about?"

"We sure are", said a gunner, amidst a general chorus of assent.

"I can't tell you more than this", stated Gately, "because I don't know myself. We're the 918th's new leper colony - just like it says on the nose. We're all considered deadbeats."

The nine faces of the men around him stared with breathless curiosity.

"Each one of you was assigned to me on the assumption that you didn't know your jobs. Or that, if you did know them, you hadn't been cutting the mustard."

There was more of a shake in Gately's voice now, gripped as it was with bitter emotion. "How do you like it."

Nobody answered.

"Well, I don't like it", he continued, after a pause. "And you won't either - the first mistake you make with me. General Savage is all set to climb on our backs and ride us with a pair of spurs. There's only one way to beat that kind of a deal, and The Leper Colony isn't going to give him a chance. Understand? We're going to keep that blowtorch turned the other way."

He looked slowly at each man, at nine different expressions, all of which, however, told him that there was no need for any-thing more to be said.

As he left the group and walked to the edge of the hard-stand for a smoke, Gately's mind was filled with the things he had not said. His fear was that he was playing right into Savage's hands. What more could Savage ask than that he, Gately, should try to "show him"?

The thought had tortured him through half of a sleepless night, but where was the alternative? The trap was tight. For the first time in his life, Gately was obsessed with an ambition that blotted out all else - an ambition to get even with Savage, to contrive a terrible revenge.

Everything must be sacrificed to that end, even if, on the sur- face, it should appear that Savage had succeeded, perfectly, in jacking up a weak officer. But, Gately had sworn to himself, this thing was going further than Savage had ever calculated. He would fight this upstart general with his own weapons, with a spotlessly clean record, with superior performance in combat. Waiting. Always waiting for the day to come when he could strike back. It was the only way.

At exactly one minute before time for "Stations", a staff car drove up and Frank Savage emerged. He was wearing a flight cap and a flight suit, opened at the throat and with the sleeves rolled up above his tanned forearms.

Taking his flight gear from Sergeant McIllhenny, Savage walked up to Gately. Both men's faces were expressionless.

"Everything set", ask Savage?

"Yes, sir", shot back Gately, with a little more than military sharpness.

"You fly this morning", said Savage. "I'll ride behind the seats or up in the top turret, where I can see."

"Radio", called out Gately. A sergeant sprang forward.

"Rig up an extension cord to the top turret so the general can talk on the Command Set." "Yes, sir."

The man hurried into the aircraft, followed by the rest of the crew. As Savage walked forward from the waist to the flight deck, his eyes took in everything.

Gately and Baxter were seated in the cockpit when the general assumed his position behind them. Savage was glancing at his wrist watch, from time to time, until it was twenty seconds before "Start Engines" time.

"Energize one", ordered Gately.

Baxter pressed a switch and out on the right wing an inertia starter whined. Savage watched his sweep second hand.

"Five seconds", said Gately, "four seconds, three. . . two . . . hit three!"

The Fort shook as the number three engine's propeller spun and the engine caught.

In quick succession, Gately ordered: "Hit four . . . Hit two . . . Hit one!" The B-17 came alive, its four props pulling at the air.

A little impressed by the smooth teamwork between pilot and co-pilot, and by the dexterity with the switches and throttles of the co-pilot, whom Major Cobb had guaranteed to be all thumbs, Savage leaned forward toward Baxter's ear.

"Been practicing", he asked?

"Yes, sir", said Baxter, blushing in spite of himself.

How, he wondered, did the general know that he and Gately had put in a half hour of cockpit drill after the Briefing?

The rumble of twenty-one Flying Forts, breaking into thunder directly above Archbury, brought Master Sergeant Tony Nero out of the Aircraft Repair Hanger at a lumbering trot. Swarthy, built down close to the ground, along the lines of Mister Five-by-Five, and clutching a spanner wrench in one hand, Nero shaded his eyes with the other hand.

He frowned, critically, as he watched the three boxes of the staggered formation, in which many of the B-17s were far out of position, until the 918th Group was out of sight.

"Lousy", he said, aloud, spitting a stream of tobacco juice on the concrete!

Then he turned toward the hanger to resume supervising the removal of a wing tip assembly from the current Hanger Queen, which he was cannibalizing to keep other aircraft operational. But Nero's dissatisfaction with the stragglers, who had made the Group formation look so ragged, was tempered with personal pride that all twenty-one aircraft had gotten off the ground without any mechanical trouble.

Give me a little more of this bad weather, he told himself, and I'll have enough aircraft flyable to keep this new general off my neck. Two hours later, while helping with an engine change out on one of the hard-stands, Sergeant Nero, again, looked up to see the Group returning directly over the airfield from its practice mission, He rubbed his eyes.

"Hey you guys, look at that", he cried out to the other mechanics, as he watched the spectacle of every plane drawn up tight in position, even in the difficult third element of the high squad- ron. "Well, what do you know", he added, with an ear-to-ear grin. "The layoff must've done 'em some good."

"More then likely", said a crew chief, who had been one of the two men Savage had confronted for not saluting on the road to the gate, "that iron-assed general has been chewing their tails up there."

The weather broke the following afternoon. And as Frank Savage was sitting in the bathtub in his quarters, with water swirling around his hunched-up knees, a shaft of red sunlight broke through the clouds in the west, Shortly afterwards, a jeep skidded to a halt outside the build- ing and Major Cobb hurried in. Savage, wiping himself down with a towel, met Cobb in the bedroom.

"We're alerted, sir", said Cobb.

Savage's reaction was instantaneous, as though Cobb had abruptly presented him with one million dollars. As if a surge of electricity seemed to pass through him, illuminating his eyes.

He held up his thumb and forefinger, as though he were measuring a one inch shot of whisky. "Jest right, Joe", he said, "jest right! Start everything rolling. I'll be right over."

"Roger."

Cobb hustled out to his jeep and drove off. And, by the time Savage was leaving his quarters, Cobb had already gotten the 918th's machinery in motion.

Men at the bomb dumps, at the fuel trucks, in the kitchens, at the transportation section, of the military police, at the armament section, in engineering, at the control tower, in the intelligence and operations sections, were setting about their tasks with a will.

Even Chaplain Twombley was affected, as he made his usual arrangements to call in a prist for early morning Mass.

On his way to the Ops room, Savage stopped by the Officers' Club to set the Green Toby on the mantel. The room was filled with fliers, in spite of the closed bar.

And as he walked through the lounge, and back to the door, past men reading, writing letters, and playing checkers or cards, he encountered no smiles of recognition, no sign of softening of the stubborn animosity in their faces, which glanced up or looked away. Nor had he seen any reaction of excitement to his signal that the 918th was once again alerted for a mission, "So what", their faces seem to say!

After Savage left the lounge, Jesse Bishop turned to Baxter, with whom he had been discussing the Group's second practice mission that morning. "Speaking of the devil", remarked Baxter.

"The weather would have to break", said Bishop, "before we had time to transfer out from under that hot rock."

"Our requests went up from the Squadron today", Baxter told him. "Don't hold your breath till they're approved", advised Bishop. The pair fell silent.

"I wonder", continued Bishop, "if Savage thinks he invented formation flying?"

"Stick your wing tip in the other fellow's cockpit", quoted Baxter, sarcastically. "Why doesn't he try it himself for a few hours at twenty-five thousand feet, instead of riding in the top turret?"

Baxter and the rest of Gately's crew had spared no effort in spreading the word that Savage had proved to be a non-flying general.

"Why did we have to get a guy who won't even shoot a landing on a practice mission", asked Bishop?

A thin mist hovered above the runways just before dawn the next morning, as Savage rode from hard-stand to hard-stand, where the tense crews huddled around small fires in empty 55 gallon drums, blowing on their hands.

To each pilot he said substantially the same thing: "I want all twenty-one ships to drop their bombs on those sub pens at La Pallice today. It's likely we'll get fighters going in and every straggler they pick off means fewer bombs on the target. So show me how close you can stack yourself in there."

One pilot unwittingly summed it up for the rest when he turn- ed to his co-pilot, as Savage drove off, and said: "I'll stick it in there, all right. But not for General Savage. How much of this mission is he going to see, anyway, hiding out in the radio com- partment?"

Savage's last stop was at Jesse Bishop's B-17, which had been assigned to lead the Group. It was shortly before time to "Take Stations" and the crew were already on board. Bishop was in the pilot's seat, when Savage approached the waist door, noting the words painted above it.

WHERE ANGELS AND GENERALS FEAR TO TREAD

He squinted at the legend with a wry smile, then climbed in and made his way forward to the cockpit. When he got there he tapped Bishop on the shoulder.

"Move over Bishop", he said. "That's my seat."

There was no real necessity for Harvey Stovall to attend the mission critique that took place in the Briefing room, four days later, but wild horses couldn't have kept him away. He occupied his usual seat near the rear, keeping his eyes toward the door for Savage's arrival.

"Ten-SHUN!"

The voice was not Stovall's, for a pilot sitting closer to the door had beaten him to it. As one man, the crews stood up and came to attention.

Then, there was an immediate silence that was only broken, briefly, when everyone resumed seating while the general mounted the platform.

"Give me your attention", said Savage. "I'm sorry that we haven't been able to hold a critique after every mission. But, with missions three days in a row, like we've just had, we'll just have to lump them together into one." He paused. "And in case any of you guys are getting sleepy, you'll be glad to know that we're standing down tomorrow - everything's socked in from here to Denmark. So, tonight the bar is open again."

He stopped once again, waiting until a prolonged murmur of approval had died down.

"A word, first, about these critiques. I want them to be bitching sessions", he continued. "This is the place to bitch about anything that concerns the success of a mission, whether it's your aircraft, your equipment, the tactics, what somebody else did or didn't do, or whether you think I screwed up in the way I've been leading these missions.

Everything's to be forgotten when we leave this room. Your beefs won't do any good over in your quarters. Get them off your chests here - and anything goes. Then, maybe something useful can be done about them."

He paused, as he waited for someone to say something.

"Okay, then", he resumed. "The La Pallice mission first. I haven't got much to say about that one. The bombing was good. All ships reached the target. No losses. Very little battle dam- age."

He paused again.

"You know why? Because the formation looked like the picture book. Those FWs passed us up and went after those three other Groups that were strung out.

They took one look at the 918th and they weren't buying any. So, let's keep it that way. Of course", he added, as an afterthought, "that's tough on you gunners. You didn't get a chance for many claims that day, did you?"

There was a flutter of dry laughter from the enlisted men. "Okay, the Lille mission. Not so hot."

He waited until a contagious cough, spreading to several other suffers of colds, subsided. Harvey Stovall leaned forward attent- ively.

"Bombing, . . just fair. And we didn't lose any aircraft. But we picked up a lot of battle damage from fighters, when the high squadron lagged half a mile behind the Group, entering the target area."

He paused.

"Pettingill", he called out!

"Yes, sir", a chubby-faced captain stood up.

"You were leading the high Squadron. Explain what happen- ed."

"You see, General", said Pettingill, "Bishop lost his number four engine when the FWs hit us near the I.P. He couldn't keep up with his element, so I dropped back to his speed to cover him."

"In other words", said Savage, "you jeopardized the whole Group for one airplane. You violated Group Integrity for the sake of a buddy. To save ten men, you endangered all the rest.

What I mean by Group Integrity is that every gun on every aircraft is needed for the defensive fire power of the formation. We didn't dream up the staggered formation because it looks pretty, but because it places every aircraft in a position where it is needed to defend the Group.

Crippled airplanes are expendable. Let them go. Let the Ger- mans shoot down your own brother, if need be. The thing that's never expendable is your obligation to get bombs on the target.

From past mission reports, I've discovered that there had been too much of this buddy stuff, before I came here. Maybe you people think of it as commendable. Heroic, even. I think it's un- forgivable." Savage stopped to blow his nose.

"Ordinarily", he resumed, "I'll give a man a second chance. But not when Group Integrity is involved. Pettingill, I'm reliev- ing you of command of your Squadron, as of right now. And I'll take action, on the spot, against any other man who puts his bud- dies, or his Squadron, ahead of this Group.

We're going to operate this Group as one big Squadron." Pettingill, red in the face, slowly sat down.

"Who is Colonel Gately's co-pilot", called Savage? "Here, sir. Lieutenant Baxter."

"Baxter, you're promoted out of the Leper Colony. Pettingill, you're busted down to be Gately's co-pilot."

Amidst the buzz of comments that arose, Gately sat motionless, his eyes fixed straight ahead. This was the first time that Savage had singled him out in public. But Gately felt no humiliation. Only a deepening of the anger that glowed within him, day and night.

He had been waiting for Savage to lay it on, carrying out his threat, implementing the words - "I'll hold your head down in the mud and trample it!".

Now he felt vaguely relieved by the manner in which the whiplash had come. He couldn't catch me off base on my job, thought Gately, so the dirty skunk had to hit me this way - from behind.

"Getting back to the mission", said Savage, as he picked up a pointer and indicated a spot on a map behind him. "the high Squadron mistook the Brest Peninsula for Land's End and started letting down into a lot of enemy flak. Luckily you all got home, but not without excessive, and unnecessary, flak damage. So now we've got seven men in the hospital having shrapnel pulled out of their butts with flak clippers.

I'll admit that the weather was thick. But if you'd kept up with the rest of the Group, that navigation error could have been avoided. Whoever the navigator was, he gets another chance, this time. But next time, Gately will have a new navigator for the Leper Colony."

He looked toward the back of the room. "Is the Ground Exec here", he asked? Major Stovall stood up.

"Harvey", said Savage, "the Lille mission concerns you, too. Have the Billeting Officer work up a complete reassignment of quarters. I want everybody to get a new roommate - somebody who isn't their pal.

That ought to help each man here to get used to the idea that he has only one loyalty. And that's to this Group."

"Very well, sir."

Then Stovall sat back down.

"All right. Today's mission. St. Nazaire. Bombing good. No losses. Battle damage slight. Same story as La Pallice.

Our formation was tight so the fighters passed us by and concentrated on the other Groups. Any comments? Any questions?"

No one spoke up.

"Well, I have", continued Savage. "Bombardier trouble. Hathaway! The strike photos show that you've been toggling late three missions in a row. Your bombs have been way over, plow- ing up fields, instead of landing in the target area. What about that?"

Lieutenant Hathaway got up slowly, scratching his head. Embarrassed and badly flustered, be stared at Savage for a moment.

Could I see the general about it after the critique", he asked, finally? "What's wrong with now?"

The man looked at the floor, still scratching his head, then faced the general with a trace of defiance.

"Well, General", he said, "it's those civilians that are around the targets - and most of them aren't German, either. General . . . I don't like killing civilians and smashing cathedrals."

A silence followed the young bombardier's confession, and more than one other bombardier, who secretly felt the same way, waited for Savage's reaction.

"I'll say this for you, Hathaway", responded Savage, "you're honest. But you're also a goddamn fool. A hundred and forty million Americans, back home, are working twenty-four hours a day to manufacture bombs and bombers. Nine men risk their lives riding with you for the sole purpose of putting those bombs on enemy installations. And men who have spent their whole lives in the Air Force, have selected those installations for attack. Then you have the gall to nullify the whole thing by electing yourself as a committee of one, to select a corn field. Who gave you that right? Nobody did! Do you think of yourself as being a humanitarian? If everybody in the Eighth Air Force was your kind of humanitarian, we could save lots of time by turning the world over to those humanitarians in Berlin.

. . . Gately?"

Gately stood up, but without answering. "Here's a new bombardier for you."

Gately hesitated for a moment and then sat down, still without answering. "Now, does anybody have something to bring up?"

There was nothing but silence.

"All right, but next time I want there to be plenty of squawks. A real bitching session. Okay, then, that's all."

Savage gave Stovall and Cobb a lift in his car, after leaving the critique, for the Air and Ground Execs occupied adjoining quarters in the C.O.'s block. Stovall was the first to speak, as they drove through the rain.

"I've been waiting for the chance to tell you some news, sir", he said. Savage, lost in thought, seemed to jerk his attention to Stovall.

"About those requests for transfers I sent back to the Squadrons for correction, yesterday." "They're back on your desk again", asked Savage, quickly?

"Well, no, sir", smiled the Ground Exec. "Two of the Adjutants have notified me that several of the requests have been with- drawn."

Savage broke into the widest grin that Stovall had seen the general permit himself, since coming to Archbury. Then Savage reached over and slapped Cobb on the shoulder. "How're we doing, Joe", he asked, with delight? "How're we doing?" Cobb grinned back. Then, with his usual bluntness, he said.

"I wouldn't exactly say you're getting popular, General. But three missions without a loss, sure doesn't hurt."

"I'll be happier yet", said Savage, "when everybody around here stops being so loss conscious and they start getting more bombing conscious."

Stovall thought to himself: I'll be happier when they all start admiring this guy, instead of just giving him grudging respect.

He knew, from bull sessions at the club, that the crews had attributed the successes of the first two missions to luck. But there had been no mistaking their changing attitude in the Brief- ing room, after today's mission. He glanced over at Savage, who looked ten years younger than on the day that he arrived at the station. He appeared intensely alive.

The phone was ringing when the three men entered Savage's quarters. Stovall answered it, then turned, reluctantly, to Savage.

"I spoke a little to soon, sir", he said. "One request for trans- fer just came back. Only one." "Whose", asked Savage?

"Jesse Bishop's."

The general's exuberance evaporated. Some moodiness set in as he poured three drinks and handed one to Stovall and to Cobb.

"See if you can get hold of Bishop", he said. "I'll see him here."

When Lieutenant Bishop appeared fifteen minutes later, Cobb and Stovall were just leaving. Bishop, completely at ease, his eyes watching Savage, calmly stood waiting.

"Have a drink", asked Savage? "No, thank you, sir."

"Have a seat, then", said Savage.

Bishop sank into a chair, rather unwillingly.

"Your request for transfer just came back up to headquarters. And as several of the other officers have withdrawn theirs, it occurred to me that yours might have slipped through by mis- take."

"There was no mistake, sir."

Savage tossed a few lumps of coal on the grate and stirred up the fire. "Is it personal", he asked? "Something you've got against me?"

"No, sir."

The general waited for the young man to amplify his state- ment. But he began to see that it would be like pulling teeth to get Bishop to loosen up.

"What do you expect to gain", asked Savage? "A pilot with your record ought to have a good future with this outfit. Why change to another? It's all the same business."

"That's right, sir", replied Bishop. "The same racket. That's why I want out. Not just to another Group. They can put me in a tank, or a foxhole. Just so I'm out of the Air Force." "You want to quit flying", demanded Savage?

"Yes, sir."

Savage took a sip of his drink and stared at the fire for a few seconds. "What's so good about the ground forces", he asked?

"When they fight, they fight Germans. Or Japs."

"Now, wait a minute", said Savage. "Don't tell me you're going to start talking like that bombardier - Hathaway."

"He's got something", responded Bishop. "I don't like bombing French civilians, either. My mother is French. Born in Lille. And I've bombed it twice. But that's not the point."

"What is the point?"

The young lieutenant tensed up.

"What's the use in my trying to tell a general?" "You don't like generals, do you?"

"No, sir, I don't."

"Did it ever occur to you that there are different kinds of generals? Or that I was once a lieutenant, like you?"

He took off his uniform jacket and threw it on a table.

"There aren't any stars on me now", he continued. "So forget I'm a general and tell me what's eating you."

"All right", said Bishop. "I'm not afraid of flying, or combat, or generals. But, if I'm going to get killed, I want a good reason. I don't believe the generals over here know what they're doing."

"How do you mean?"

"Take today. What good did we do? We bounced a bunch of bombs off the roof of some sub pens without hardly denting them. The crews know we're not penetrating twelve feet of con- crete. Why can't these generals figure that out too?"

"I'm beginning to see what you mean", said Savage. "How many of you feel this way?"

"I'd say everyone. Officers and enlisted men. We came over here to bomb Germany. We'd like to know why we're not doing it? Instead of piddling around making phony headlines."

Twelve O'clock High

Savage got up and passed a cigar to Bishop, which he declined, lighting a cigarette instead.

"So, you want to bomb Germany", he said. "I'll bet you don't want to half as much as I do. That day won't come soon enough to suit me."

He scratched the back of his head.

"But, let me ask you this. How many of our small formations, do you think, would get to the target? When we don't have any fighter escorts, yet, to go all the way in with us? And how many, do you think, would get back?

Don't you see, Bishop, we've got to walk before we can run? Shallow penetrations into France are teaching us to walk. And we are hurting the enemy, too. Why else would they put up their best fighters, and move in so many extra flak guns to try and stop us?"

Savage rose and stood before the fire.

"I'll grant you that the sup pens are hard to hit. So we can't penetrate the concrete. Still, we're learning what kinds of bombs it will take. And, we're doing plenty of damage to their machine shops and other installations around the pens.

Any damage we do reduces the ship sinkings on the Atlantic. If the subs win, England will be starved in two weeks, and we'll be fresh out of aviation gasoline. Then where are we? Crimey, Bishop, give those dumb generals a little time."

"Well, why haven't we gotten enough crews and aircraft to go in deeper", shot back Bishop? "Because we're fighting all over the world. Because there just isn't enough of everything to go around. And, because every theater commander thinks that the boil on the back of his own neck is the biggest."

Savage walked over and laid his hand on Bishop's shoulder.

"String along with me", he said, his voice actually pleading. "You've done me a lot of good. I need to know how you feel. I need you in this outfit."

He paused.

"Won't you string along with us?"

Bishop looked away. He seemed about to say something, but then remained silent, staring at his knees.

"Look, Bishop", said Savage. "Soon - sooner than you think, we're going to be putting up a hundred B-17s for every ten we've got now. Then three times that. And we'll be going to Germany. To Berlin, and every part of the Third Reich.

Before this war is over, you are going to look up and see the sky black with American bombers. A solid overcast of them."

He moved away, towards his chair, then swung around.

"That's a promise", he said. "From me to you. And don't ever forget that I told you." Bishop suddenly rose to his feet.

"My mind's made up, General", he said. "I'm not going to go for any more promises. There have been too many made already. All I want is a transfer."

Savage looked sadly over at him.

"Let's be practical about this, Bishop", responded Savage. "Even if I sent your request to higher authorities, there wouldn't be a chance of it's approval. They're not going to spend thirty thousand dollars training a aircraft commander, only to ship him off to the infantry.

If you transfer, it's bound to be just to another Group."

"That's no good", exclaimed Bishop! "I'll have to request to be grounded." Savage made an effort to control himself.

"Damnit", he said, almost shouting, "don't you know where that would get you? You'd meet a Flying Evaluation Board and a Medical Board, and they'd find nothing wrong with you. So you'd wind up right back here for disciplinary action. And that's an ugly, nasty business. A Congressional Medal of Honor man winding up with a Dishonorable Discharge."

Bishop reached for his cap and started to leave. He stopped at the door, and said. "If that's the only solution, sir, then I'll take it."

After Bishop disappeared into the rain-swept darkness, the general stood for a long minute at the open door. His eyes were troubled, but in his mind he was not yet discouraged. There was still an ace- in-the-hole, Bishop's crew. Just wait, he told himself, until you try to face that crew of yours, Jesse!

Savage then closed the door and returned to the warmth of the fire.

Jesse Bishop confided his decision to no one, least of all to his new co-pilot, Baxter, or, as Savage had guessed, to the members of his crew. Nor, had he been able to make himself go and interview with the Flight Surgeon.

The simplest thing, he thought to himself, will be to just not show up for the next mission. And let matters take their course.

Two days later the issue faced him squarely, at four o'clock in the morning, in the form of Baxter's flashlight shining in his face.

"Shake the lead out of your butt", said Baxter. "Breakfast in fifteen minutes."

Bishop, who had been only half asleep, struggled up onto his elbows. Now, he thought! He'd better tell him now, and get it over with. But the words wouldn't come.

"Roger", he said, yawning.

Baxter lingered near the door, insuring that Bishop didn't drop back off to sleep.

"Damn him", Bishop cursed, to himself. "Why doesn't he go away and leave me alone!" But Baxter just winked his flashlight at him.

"Hit the deck, Jesse", he said. "Plant both feet on the floor."

Bishop swung his legs out of bed and sat up, whereupon Baxter disappeared. Having failed to make his decision known, Bishop now felt himself to be lost in a maze. There must be some way to postpone the inevitable a little longer. Suddenly he thought of a compromise.

Occasionally, when he hadn't been sleeping well, he had gone to Briefings even though he wasn't scheduled to fly. Okay, so, he'd get dressed, eat breakfast with the crew, sit in at the Brief- ing, and get himself excused afterwards. That would postpone having to tell Baxter for awhile.

In the combat mess, drinking coffee and eating eggs with the other crew members, Bishop's mind focused more sharply on his problem. He'd skip the Briefing. It would be much less painful.

He tried to shut out of his mind the fact that Baxter would have to take over with a strange co-pilot. And Baxter was fairly new in the Group, still a bit green. What about that?

And the rest of the crew? They all believed that he, Jesse Bishop, could fly them safely back to base with four engines shot out.

Bishop was bucking what Flight Surgeons would come to recognize, during the war, as an American trait, which the Germans most grossly underestimated, or failed entirely to anticipate in their analysis of the "decadent, undisciplined democracy".

The trait was not courage, nor patriotism, nor mechanical know-how. It was the extraordinary, nearly incredible lengths, demonstrated time after time, which Americans would do something or go somewhere rather than fail the other members of their team. Whether it was a combat crew, or called by some other name.

Torn with indecision, Bishop finished his breakfast and then followed the others out to the trucks, waiting in the darkness to transport the crews to the Briefing room. Quit vacillating, he told himself.

And then, purposely separating himself from Baxter in the confusion around the trucks, he set out, on foot, for his quarters. With each step he felt relief, now that his choice was irrevocably taken.

He stretched out on his bunk and tried to slow down the fast thumping of his heart. In spite of what he had done, he looked at the luminous dial of his wrist watch. It read 4:56. Four minutes until Briefing.

Presently, he looked again, feeling that ten minutes must have passed. But the minute hand had moved only two minutes. Why, he thought, couldn't it already be an hour from now? Five hours? Tomorrow? The next time he looked, the hand was pointing straight up. The Briefing had begun Abruptly, Bishop sprang from his bed, made a frantic grab for his flight gear and rushed through the door. He jumped on a bi- cycle that was outside and pedaled madly through the darkness.

Dismounting from the bike, he hurried into the hall outside the Briefing room, where he could hear Savage's voice calling the roll of airplane commanders. "Hammet?"

"Here, sir!" "Todd?" "Here, sir!" "Wieback?" "Here, sir!"

Jesse knew that the general was getting near his name in the roll call. He hesitated, just outside the door, panting from his exertion. He was still in time.

But, for some reason, he couldn't move. His mind raced back and forth like an alternating current, between the pull of panicky emotion, which had catapulted him out of his quarters, and the pull of his convictions, of his mental resolve.

"Cottrell?" "Here, sir!" "Bishop?"

After a moment he heard Savage call out more sharply. "BISHOP!"

There was another pause. Bishop still stood paralyzed, his heart rising up into his throat. The sound of his name, and the timbre of Savage's voice, burned him like a hot iron.

"Is Bishop's co-pilot here?" "Here, sir", said Baxter. "Where's Bishop?"

"He's a little late, sir."

At Baxter's next words, Bishop felt something explode inside him. "I know he'll be here in a minute, sir."

"Cobb", said Savage, "have a standby ready, just in case."

But Jesse's hand was already on the doorknob. Then, after he turned it and stepped inside, he scanned the room with his eyes for the bench where his crew usually sat. Spotting Baxter, he walked down the side aisle and, as he slid into his seat, Savage caught his eye for a brief moment.

To Bishop, the general's eyes said, as plainly as if Savage had shouted: "Thank Goodness!" But the rest of the crews only heard Savage say, with an uncharacteristic crack in his voice.

"Cancel the standby for Bishop." "Lambert?"

"Here, sir!"

The Red Cross girls knew that something, unprecedented, was taking place, after the mission, when they began handing out doughnuts, coffee, and cigarettes to the boisterous combat crews that were trooping into the Interrogation Room. The men were slapping each other on the back and shouting to one another between interrogation tables. So much so, that several Intelligence officers, grinning broadly, threw up their hands and temporarily postponed further questions.

They had been halfway across the English Channel, outward bound, with thick clouds forcing the bomber stream from base altitude down to only four thousand feet. And, they had heard the Recall order from higher headquarters.

They had watched as the four other Groups turn around and set course for their home bases. And they had seen General Savage, in the lead B-17 of the 918th, continue on, leading them towards the enemy coast and apparently ignoring the Recall.

They had seen the cloud ceiling lift, until Savage eventually climbed them back up to twenty-one thousand feet, in time for the bombing run over the railway marshaling yards at Liege. The target had opened up.

They had seen their bomb bursts mushroom all around the aiming point. And then they had all come safely home.

The 918th, all alone, had gotten through to the target.

Amidst all the jubilation, Savage was speaking on the telephone to the Operations officer at Bomber Command, giving him a flash report on the mission. He was leaning with his back against the wall, his hat tilted back on his head. His face was weary, but happy, and in his hand he held a drying print if the target strike photograph, which the Photo officer had just rushed over to him from the darkroom.

"From the first strike photo", Savage was saying, "it looks like we clobbered the M.P.I. . . . Yeah, about six tenths cloud cover. Five minutes later would have been too late."

He listened to a question from the other end.

"No, . . only half a dozen fighters, . . Me-109s. The soup was too thick for them, I guess." He said "yes" several times, then hung up.

"Ten-SHUN!"

The clamor in the room died away as General Ed Henderson walked in. "Carry on", he called out, then he went over to where Savage was.

The men who had been milling around near Savage drew back a bit. However, the noise did not resume its previous level.

Twelve O'clock High

"Well, Frank", said Henderson, in a voice that could be overheard, "I see you've got a picture there already."

He eagerly examined the strike photo, which Savage had handed over to him.

"Beautiful", he said. "Just beautiful. But for crying out loud, Frank, you shortened my life ten years! Didn't you hear the Re- call?"

Savage looked Henderson straight in the eye without blinking. "No, Ed", he said, "I didn't hear any Recall."

"Were you guarding Channel 'B'?"

"Sure. And all I got was gibberish the whole way. My radio operator had trouble, too, on the Liaison set. Bad tube."

Overhearing this, Savage's radio operator-gunner recalled, with a bit of a smile, how the general had opened the receiver cabinet right after they landed and had accidentally, on purpose, broken a tube with his fist. Henderson glanced about the room.

"Did anybody here hear the Recall", he asked in the direction of the men standing nearest to him? "No, sir", answered several fliers, simultaneously, and shak- ing their heads. All of them regarding Henderson with wide-eyed innocence.

Then Lieutenant Colonel Ben Gately stepped forward.

"I heard the Recall, General", he said. "Clear as a bell." "What position were you flying?"

"Deputy Leader, sir. On General Savage's wing."

"Couldn't you relay the message, Gately? Or attract his attention?"

"I tried to, sir, several times. But I could never get any re- sponse."

During the conversation, Gately, purposely, avoided meeting Savage's stare, which was aimed at him like gun barrels. Jesse Bishop, who was witnessing the scene from the background, realized that his coffee mug was shaking, when the hot liquid spilled over and stung the back of his hand.

"Well, Colonel Gately", said Henderson, dropping his tone of interrogation, "I guess it's just one of those things."

He installed a beaming smile on his face, like a man putting on a hat, and confronted the sea of faces in the room.

"Congratulations to all of you", he said. "Fine job today." Then, turning back to Savage, he said.

"Can I give you a lift back to your office?"

Savage followed Henderson from the Interrogation room, looking back, when he reached the door, to casually wave to the crews. Most waved back with gleeful gestures, some clasping both hands above their heads. Savage could see overt proof that his deliberate gamble to ignore the Recall had paid off. Psychologically, the 918th had turned the corner.

Thirty minutes later, as he was approaching the Officers' Club on his bicycle, Bishop changed his direction and rode across the Admin site to the headquarters building. Harvey Stovall greeted him outside the general's office with a hearty handshake.

"What a day, Jesse", he cried! "A real red-letter day in the history of the 918th, and the Eighth Air Force. Cripes, will those other Groups be burned up. I guess we showed them how to put this business on a paying basis!" He continued to pump Bishop's hand, then said. "Great going there, boy!"

Bishop responded to the warmth in Stovall's congratulations, but his smile had reservations in it. "Is the general busy", he asked?

"Can't you hear", responded Stovall?

Even through the closed door to Savage's office, Henderson's raised voice was plainly audible. "Goddamnit, Frank", he was angrily saying. "You might have lost the whole Group. Aside from that, what am I supposed to tell the other Group Commanders? They obeyed their orders. Then you made them look like chumps, while the 918th became heroes. General Pritchard called me four times from London - half out of his mind!"

Stovall and Bishop, exchanged glances, as they continued to eavesdrop from the outer office.

"I can't be expected to run a big show", continued Henderson, "if my commands are ignored by a grandstand artist."

There was a considerable pause. Then Savage spoke.

"You have my official statement", he said, "that I didn't hear the Recall. And I'm getting tired of repeating it. But you might as well know this. Any time my judgment tells me that I can get through to a target, I'm going on through, Recall or no Recall."

There was another long pause.

"Very interesting, Frank", remarked Henderson, at last in a lower voice. "We'll see about that", he coughed, to himself. "And one more thing", he continued. "What sort of a screwy ass deal is this that you've been giving Colonel Gately?"

"Did he call you up", asked Savage, sharply?

"No", said Henderson. "My Air Inspector reported to me that you're carrying a regular Army lieutenant colonel in an airplane commander's job."

"Your Air Inspector has no kick coming", said Savage, "as long as the Group, as a whole, has no overages in grade. If I want to get technical about it, I can carry him as temporarily un- assigned."

"Your treatment of an officer of Colonel Gately's rank and background, strikes me as being shortsighted. You know his father's in a key position. There could be serious repercussions over it. We need aircraft! And, to get them, we need friends in Washington! Not enemies!"

"I'm responsible to you for results, am I not", snapped Savage? "And as long as I give you results, my methods used in this Group are my own responsibility. You know that as well as I do."

"I can use Gately up at my headquarters, if you'll approve a transfer", persisted Henderson. "Gately is not available to fly a desk. He's got a job to do in this Group."

The phone on the Ground Exec's desk rang and, while Stovall talked, Bishop was unable to hear the conclusion of the conver- sation in the next room. But, a minute later, he watched as Henderson came striding out of the office and down the hall in, what seemed to be, extreme displeasure.

Without interrupting his phone conversation, Stovall motioned Bishop towards the general's office. When Bishop knocked, Savage looked up from his desk with a swift transition, from the scowl on his face, to a quizzical look of eager anticipation.

"What're you waiting on", he called?

Bishop approached the desk, self-consciously, and saluted.

"General Savage", he said, "would you mind, very much, if I asked you to kick me in the tail?"

With deliberation, he turned around and bent over. Savage immediately got up, moved around behind Bishop, swung his boot back and lightly touched him squarely on the seat of his pants. Bishop straightened up, turned around and faced Savage, with a flushed smile.

"Sir", said Bishop, "I'm awfully hard to convince. I'll never know why it took until today for you to convince me, and the rest of the guys. But, from now on, you can tell me black is white - and I'll believe it."

"Okay, Jesse", Savage told him, "let's start now. I want you to be the one guy in the Group that doesn't believe I'm a general. That door is always opened to you. Any time you think that I'm not doing so hot, come in and tell me. Let me know what the others are thinking, too. I need you plenty, and I'll count on you to keep me straightened out. All right?"

"All right, sir."

At PINETREE, the Chief of Staff handed Henderson a teletype message, which read in part: ". . . and convey my commendation to the Commander, and all members of the 918th Bombardment Group, for a superb display of leadership, tenacity, and skill, in surmounting extremely adverse conditions, to reach and bomb today's target. Signed, Pritchard."

"Shall I add the usual congratulations from us", asked the Chief of Staff? "Just forward it marked 'noted'", said Henderson.

When the officer had withdrawn, Henderson read the message once more. Then, he crumpled it up and threw it into the waste- basket.

CHAPTER SIX

PAMELA

When Captain Snodgrass, the new Adjutant, ushered two new-ly assigned Red Cross women in to meet Savage, he observed that the general looked rested and chipper. Savage chatted with the two women for several minutes, welcoming them to the station, and agreeing with them that their first concern should be the welfare of the enlisted men, rather than with the romantically inclined officers.

One of the girls was rather pretty, the other definitely homely, but as his visitors were leaving, Savage noticed that the homely girl had kind of interesting legs. Suddenly he remembered that, for an infinity, he had not once thought about a female.

It was a rediscovery of a vital part of himself, that had been numbed into oblivion by the pressure of his job. A thrill, almost like a twinge of pain, shot through him, and he felt a spark of gratitude toward the homely girl with the interesting legs, for reminding him that there were still women in the world.

Later that morning, after Savage had made a dent in the stack of paperwork in his IN basket, that betrayed his recent neglect of an office routine, Harvey Stovall stepped into the room from his new Ground Exec's sanctum.

"A flight leftenant is here to see you, sir", he said. "I'm busy as hell, Harvey. You take care of it."

"If the general insists", said Stovall, blandly, "but . . . ."

"I do insist", said Savage, trying not to interrupt his concentration on a new list of lead navigators. "Very well, sir, I'll try to put her off."

Savage picked up his pencil to resume his work, then slammed it down. "Did you say her", he called to the retreating Stovall?

"Yes, sir. Flight Leftenant Pamela Mallory."

"Well, for goodness' sake", snapped Savage, "don't just stand there! Show her in!" He stood up, briskly, straightening his tie, then added.

"No. Hold it. I'll be right there."

He hurried to Stovall's office, cordiality sticking out all over him. When he entered the room, Pamela Mallory met him with a formal salute, which he returned. Then they shook hands.

"Come right in", he said, pleasantly. "It's good to see you again, Flight Leftenant." "Thank you, Colonel", she said, smiling faintly.

"Don't tell me", he continued, as he showed her to a chair, "why you're here. I'm way ahead of you. Enemy fighter react- ions. Or, do you want a true copy of Roosevelt's directive to General Marshall? And by the way, it's General Savage now."

He noticed that Stovall was still lingering at the other corner of the desk, openly admiring the woman's unmistakably aristocratic, English features, and intrigued by the suave change which had come over the general. The guy, Stovall was thinking, knows how to turn on the charm like a floodlight. I should have known.

"Major", said Savage, "I'll ring for you if I need you." Stovall nodded his head to Pamela, and strode to his desk.

"Actually, General Savage", she said, "I've come here for quite a different matter. But, since you mentioned it, I have been wondering if you ever did anything about the subject of our last conversation?"

"Sure I did. I got General Henderson to put out a feeler to the Air Ministry the next day . . . ." "And nothing came of it", she asked?

"Well, . . . you know how it is. They shipped me down here to the sticks, so I've been kind of out of touch."

He offered her a cigarette, in order to change the subject.

"I feel as guilty as hell", he apologized, "for not yet having called at Desborough Hall. If you would, please explain to Lord and Lady Desborough that, and convey my regrets."

"They understand perfectly", said Pamela. "We know you haven't had a spare minute. And when you get a breather, they'll be delighted to see you. And so will I . . . . I often get home on weekends."

There was a pause, and a tinge of blush in her face.

"We've had masses of your chaps", she continued, "from the 918th dropping in. And we're really quite fond of all of them."

"They're not a bad bunch", said Savage. "By the way, I understand that this airfield is on your estate. Major Stovall tells me that your father had rubble carted here, all the way from Coven- try, to help make our runways. I think that's great of him."

"Father's not a bad type", she agreed.

"I'm convinced of that", he said, pointedly. She cocked an eyebrow at him.

"The runway", he added, hastily, "is kind of a poetic touch. No, . . I guess symbolic is a better word. I'm really looking forward to meeting your father."

He lit up the cigar that had gone out on his ashtray.

"Tell him that I'll think of Coventry every time I shoot a land- ing."

He thought he could detect that Pamela was moved by what he told her. And he was correct, but he didn't know that the town of Coventry also held an additional significance for her. For, on the night of that air raid, she had lost her boyfriend Eric, a Beaufighter pilot.

While Savage had been talking, it had occurred to her that, not since Eric's death had ended their brief romance, had she been so conscious of such a powerful attraction to any man.

"I'm glad that you appreciate my father's gesture to you Americans", she told him. Then, adopting a more businesslike tone, she continued.

"Quite apart from the social amenities, I came to see you on an official matter." Pamela noticed the familiar look of skepticism appear in the general's eyes.

"First",. he said, laying a pack of American cigarettes on her lap, "I want you to accept these. And no arguments."

"Really, I shouldn't", she protested. "Bunk", replied Savage.

"I shan't row about it", she said. "I quite understand that you are a forceful type."

Savage's eyes clouded for the first time during the interview, as the Gately incident crossed his mind.

"I'd best get on with it", she continued. "What I came to see you about is rather a delicate matter." "Okay", he said. "I don't bruise easily."

Pamela hesitated for a few seconds.

"Unfortunately", she went on, "your ruddy American sergeants are much too persuasive. I sometimes think that we would be better off if we'd had the damn Germans." He shook a finger at her.

"Watch that stuff", he grinned. "We send guys home on the next boat for goosing out British allies."

Pamela's eyes opened wide at the remark.

"What an extraordinary expression", she exclaimed! "You know", explained Savage. "It means needling." "Try me again", she said.

"Ribbing."

"One more chance?" "Riding."

"It's no use", she admitted, smiling in spite of herself. "But you're putting me off. There is one of your bodies I wish they'd sent home a long time ago. Before . .. . you see . . . one of my corporals is in serious trouble."

She regarded Savage expectantly, as though he should help her out. But he merely gazed at her, politely.

"A sergeant of yours is responsible for her being P.W.O.P.", she stated.

Savage gaped at her.

"What in hell is P.W.O.P.", he asked?

"It's an R.A.F. abbreviation", she countered, coloring a trifle, in spite of her air of being matter of fact, "for Pregnant Without Official Permission."

The general struggled to suppress a laugh, but failed.

"You're kidding", he said. "You don't mean there actually is such a regulation."

"Of course there is", she said, frostily. "And we don't think there is anything humorous about it, General. Our married W.A.A.Fs. are required to apply for official permission before they can.... increase their families."

Savage pondered this information for a moment. "Does this case involve a married woman?"

"No. And that's the bind. Corporal Lambeth is not married."

"Then", said Savage, "I can't see how this F.O.B. regulation, or whatever you call it, applies." Pamela stiffened.

"It's P.W.O.P.", she corrected him. Savage laughed again.

"That beats me", he said.

"Pregnancy", she said, bridling, "is not a laughing matter, sir. The regulation, of course, applies whether she's married or single."

"Okay, Flight Leftenant."

Then, turning official in his own tone, he said:

"On which of my sergeants has this Lambeth woman put the finger on?" "I beg your pardon", said Pamela, coldly, nonplused.

"Who's the guilty sergeant", amended Savage?

"An orangutan", she said, bitingly, "named McIllhenny."

"Well, I'll be damned", remarked Savage, a bit startled, then added, half to himself: "how does the guy find the time?"

Pamela bit her lip.

"General Savage", she demanded, "the child may arrive any time. I would have taken this matter up months ago, had I known the father's identity. All I want is for you to do something about it."

"From what you've told me", said Savage, pokerfaced, "there appears to have been too much done about it already."

Now, it was Pamela's turn to smother a smile. Savage's eyes twinkled at her. "Just what do you expect me to do", he asked?

"I think you should order him to marry her."

"H'mm", said Savage, looking at his fingernails. "Tell me, Flight Leftenant, was there any force involved in this case.... that a court-martial could construe as rape?"

Pamela avoided his eyes.

"On the contrary", she replied, clearing her throat, "I gather that this wretched girl is very much in love with him."

"And Sergeant McIllhenny?"

"He appears to be a bit shy. That's why I believe you should use your authority."

"Let's be realistic here", said Savage. "I can order a man to go out and possibly get killed. But, I can't order a man to marry anyone. Don't you think that's carrying obedience too far?"

"I do not", said Pamela, a little hostile. "You sound as though you consider marriage a dreadful thing, General. Don't you believe in marriage?"

"I'll go with you halfway on that", he said. "It's okay for you women."

It was hard for Savage to judge, from her expression, whether Pamela was merely annoyed, or slightly baffled. He, was enjoy- ing himself intensely, his pulse was quickening with anticipation. This young woman was going to make an exciting quarry.

"I take it the general is not married", she said, after a pause. "You would be correct", he said.

"Never?"

"Never", he answered.

She looked at him with genuine curiosity.

"Haven't you ever been in love", she asked?

Now it was Savage's turn to feel disconcerted by the suddenness with which his lady visitor had strayed from the main topic, and by the personal nature of the question.

"Love", he finally said? "What is it, anyway? I wouldn't be able to tell you. Frankly, I'm a very enthusiastic admirer of the female sex. But I believe that ninety-five percent of the human race would never fall in love, if they hadn't heard so damn much about it."

"How clever of you", she said. "You haven't been reading Thoreau, by any chance?" "I've done my own research", said Savage.

Pamela stood up.

"This has been most instructive, General Savage", she told him. "But a bit beside the point. So, you refuse to intervene with Sergeant McIllhenny?"

"It strikes me that you're taking too dim a view, as you English put it, about this case", said Savage. "Thousands of people are being killed every day in this war. And thousands of babies are being born. Frankly, I just don't think a mutually agreeable roll in the hay is all that important."

Inwardly, Pamela recoiled at his words. All of the emotions which had been attracting her towards Savage, all of the inner excitement of anticipation that some wonderful thing might come of their meeting, had deserted her in an instant.

Keen disappointment replaced those feelings - disappointment that Savage, whose personal impact had given her a brand new experience, was just another one-night stander.

"Is that your official attitude", she asked? He caught the change in her voice.

"Official and personal attitudes are hard to separate, sometimes", he told her.

He stood there, troubled, feeling as though a warm fireplace had suddenly been doused with cold water.

"Of course", he added, uncertainly, "I can bust McIllhenny, for an unseemly contribution to Anglo- American relations. That's my best offer."

"A fine lot that would do", she said, "Although he richly deserves it. Now I must be getting along. Good day, General."

Savage accompanied her to her car, noticing that she was not quite as tall as he.

"When am I going to see you again", he asked, opening the car door and helping her in.

"The 918th is always welcome at Desborough Hall, any time", she answered. "Mother is always there."

Savage stared at her car as she drove away, then returned to find Stovall placing some fresh paperwork on his desk. The major looked up, and regarded him with a quizzical expression.

"May I borrow a phrase from the British, sir? And remark that . . . you've had it", he said. "You an eavesdropper, Harvey?"

"That door isn't soundproof, General."

"You're right. As of the moment, I've had it", said Savage. "But, I still think I'd find a lot of company in the position I took."

"That's the trouble", said Stovall. "She's not interested in the ordinary." He lifted some papers from Savage's OUT basket.

"You picked the wrong girl to try to convince", he concluded, "that a roll in the hay isn't important."

"Come in, Sergeant", said Savage.

McIllhenny, who in addition to his driving duties had resumed his clerical work in the Adjutant's office, had been summoned to the general's office by Stovall.

"I've had an official complaint lodged against you from the Royal Air Force, Sergeant ", said Savage.

McIllhenny stood there and looked blank.

"Did you, or did you not", asked the general, "knock up a W.A.A.F.?"

"I'm afraid I did, sir", replied McIllhenny, without hesitation, "But it was months ago, sir. Before I was transferred to this Group."

"You should have transferred to Hawaii", said Savage. "But, before I forget it, McIllhenny, I want to thank you for the eggs you scrounged for my breakfast this morning."

"Did the general find them fresh?" "Right out of the hen."

"I'm pleased that the general enjoyed them."

"Thanks. Now, to get back to this business. Your offense is serious. Anything that causes friction with our Allies is serious."

"Yes, sir."

"So, tell Captain Snodgrass to cut an order this morning, reducing you to private." "First Class, sir."

"You heard me. Private!"

"Yes, sir. I'll type the order for the captain immediately, sir. Will there be anything else, sir?" "No."

"Very well, sir."

"Persons decorated, join the reviewing party". called out General Pritchard!

Simultaneously, Harvey Stovall, facing the ranks of the 918th drawn up in parade formation on the ramp area, in front of the Aircraft Repair Hanger, shouted the command.

"918th Bomb Group, pass in review!"

Jesse Bishop, wearing the Congressional Medal of Honor around his neck, was the first to join the reviewing party, consisting of Generals Pritchard and Henderson and a pair of high ranking R.A.F. officers. Pamela Mallory and her family stood with a delegation from the village, composed of the mayor and other local dignitaries.

Next, Savage, who had just received an Oak Leaf Cluster to his Silver Star, took his place to Bishop's left. He was followed by Major Cobb and three other officers, who had all received the Distinguished Flying Cross, and several gunners who had received D.F.Cs., Purple Hearts, and Air Medals.

The marching band made it's blaring circuit past the reviewing party, and Savage's heart beat hard as the four Squadrons marched smartly past. Harvey Stovall, he reflected, had done a good job of organizing a decoration ceremony on quick notice.

Whatever the men of the 918th lacked in the matter of creased slacks, they compensated for it in the snap and precision which arose from their collective pride in having a Medal Of Honor recipient in their midst. They also took pride in the Silver Star that had been bestowed on their commander, for the mission on which the 918th had been the only Group to reach the target When the ceremony was over, Henderson was the first to rush over to Savage and shake his hand, just ahead of Pritchard.

"Keep it up, Frank", said Henderson, with an edged smile on his sallow face. "Just keep it up and you'll be the most decorated man in the Eighth Air Force."

Savage smiled back at him with a cool, detached expression, that said to Henderson: Thanks for the snide crack. After accepting Pritchard's congratulations, Savage regarded Henderson through narrowed eyelids.

"By the way, Ed", he said. "We must be nearly ready for that first strike into Germany." Henderson glanced at Pritchard, who took the cue and said.

"That's right, Frank. Very soon, I think."

"In any case", said Savage, to Henderson, "I want your permission, in advance, to fly that one." Pritchard glanced from Savage over to Henderson, who saw at once that his superior was puzzled. "Something Frank and I have discussed on the phone", Hen- derson explained, hastily, with a disarming smile. "I've become increasingly aware, General, of my responsibility to . . . shall we say . . . protect General Savage from himself."

Pritchard studied his two subordinates, alternately, for a mo- ment.

"Are you saying that Frank isn't allowed to lead missions without your permission", he asked? "Well, sir", said Henderson, smoothly, "you might say I be- lieve it's time to put him on a ration.

He won't be doing us any good as a P.o.W. in Luftstalag Three."

"Perhaps that's wise", said Pritchard, then turning to Savage. "You can't make every mission, you know."

"Naturally, sir", replied Savage. "Matter of fact, I've skipped the last two or three. But I've got to be free to go when I think I should."

"The two of you ought to be able to thresh this out", said Pritchard. "I'm sure Ed won't tie your hands, Frank. But he has a good point."

Savage felt somewhat relieved, but not entirely. He had hoped that Pritchard would give clearer evidence that he knew a fighting outfit couldn't be led from behind a desk. Henderson, stroking the side of his cleanly shaved chin with his fingertip, said nothing. Savage stared at him.

"Well", he asked? "How about Germany?"

While Henderson hesitated, Pritchard slapped a hand on the Bomber Commander's shoulder.

"Hell, Ed", he said, jovially, "we both know that Frank ought to lead the Air Force on that first one to Germany."

"No argument about that, sir", said Henderson, promptly.

As the group of three generals broke up, Pamela Mallory walked over to Savage, smiling rather shyly.

"Congratulations, General", she said. "Thanks", he responded. Pamela touched the red, white, and blue ribbon.

"Beautiful", she murmured. "And it really means something. Something we can both agree is important."

She was looking straight into his eyes. But, before he could think of an answer, she said, "Cheerio", gave him a little salute, and was gone.

Driving toward the Officers' Mess for lunch, Savage passed a cyclist whom he recognized, through his rear window, as Jesse Bishop. He told Private McIllhenny to stop and then he got out and stood at rigid attention, in the middle of the road. His right hand was raised in a salute, appropriate even from a four-star general to the lowest ranking private, if that private wore a pale blue ribbon with white stars on it.

Bishop had thrust his Medal of Honor into a pocket of his uniform jacket, but as he approached the general, it was obvious that he was as self-conscious about it as if he had been wearing a blinking neon sign.

When he rode up to Savage, Bishop raised his right hand from the handlebars to return the salute, his face smiling, but red from embarrassment. Savage maintained a perfectly straight face, as Bishop pedaled hastily by, almost losing control of his teetering mount.

Feeling refreshed after a long, deep sleep, Savage got up at dawn, slipped into his bathrobe, and strolled down the hall, of the C.O.'s living quarters, to the common bathroom. As he passed by it, he peered into the small bedroom assigned to Private McIllhenny, but found the his driver was already up and gone.

The general shaved leisurely, dressed quickly and, having heard Major Cobb stirring in his own room, tapped on his door.

"Coming right up", said Cobb.

A minute later the two of them, preferring some exercise to taking the staff car, set out on foot for the quarter-mile walk to the

Officers' Mess. A cold, butter-colored sun hit them level in the face as they strode along, gulping in the frosty Fall air, which hinted of snow.

"Maybe we'll rate a white Christmas", said Cobb, surprising Savage into remembering that Christmas was only about two months away.

"Sergeant Nero would rather have a green one", he answered, thinking of the maintenance crews who had to work in the freezing weather, out in the open.

As they walked along in step, and in silence, Savage felt his blood coursing faster from the exertion, and his spirits warmed. He felt relaxed, strangely at peace, as a boxer might find precar- ious but, nonetheless, welcome peace in the time-out between rounds.

The Group, he told himself, although still shaky, was at least up on it's knees. And, Stovall and Cobb, neither of them afraid of work or responsibility, had the makings of satisfactory deput- ties, in the air and on the ground.

Presently, Cobb broke the silence.

"Sorry I spoiled your record yesterday", he said.

Cobb had lost two airplanes, leading the Group, on a day that Savage had remained behind. It was the third mission which the general had not accompanied. Jesse Bishop, having been promoted to a Squadron Operations officer, had led one of the other missions, from which one aircraft had not returned.

"I know, Joe", he said, a bit consolingly. "But what the hell, in that kind of flak, I would have lost them too. Nobody can do anything about the flak on a bombing run, sitting there straight and level."

"That's not what the men think", said Cobb. "You've gotten yourself a reputation . . . all over the Eighth Air Force."

He glanced sideways at Savage, a little bashful. "You're supposed to be invincible", he added.

This was so forceful an admission, from the laconic Air Exec, that Savage flushed with pleasure; then he frowned, his thoughts instantly taking a more somber turn. This invincibility business could be a two edged sword.

You had to put your championship on the line, every time. One bad mission, with heavy losses, which could happen to anyone, might shatter the myth, in this case into more fragments than the reviving 918th could well withstand.

"Invincible", he repeated, partly to himself? "I wish you hadn't put it that way, Joe."

Cobb waited. Savage, unconsciously, slowed his walking. He wondered if Cobb even vaguely suspected how vulnerable he really felt sometimes, sitting up there in that lead ship.

The one thing Savage was confident of, however, was that he would never spare himself. That was the measure of his strength.

"Did you ever stop to think, Joe, that the Germans are already converting more from bomber production to fighters", he asked? That our Intelligence shows they're moving fighters from other fronts, to bolster the fighter belt in Western Europe, against us?"

"Yeah", said Cobb, casually. "I guess we've been irritatin' 'em."

"Plenty", said Savage. "And maybe tomorrow we'll head into Germany. Just think how those bastards are going to react. Fatso Goering has promised them that no bombs will ever fall on the soil of the Third Reich.

When those German fighter boys come up at us, they're going to be reacting the same way our guys would, if enemy bombers approached Pittsburgh, or Washington, D.C., or Los Angles.

They're going to smack into us like maniacs." He paused, then said.

"They won't stop us. But not I, nor anybody, is invincible to a twenty-millimeter shell."

As the two continued walking, he returned the salute of a lone soldier, who smiled and looked straight into his eyes as he went past, reminding Savage of the changes that had come over everyone at Archbury, from privates to officers, who would match him for drinks at the club.

"Over Germany", he continued, "we can't afford to have any indispensable men. That's where you, the squadron commanders, Jesse Bishop, and the others come in."

He was thinking about the big question mark that always hovered above that lonesome figure, sitting in the lead ship of each large formation. Wingmen and flight leaders could be expected to cling to the formation, if only for self-preservation.

They would follow where the Group leader took them. Thus, the success of the whole venture would depend upon the tenacity of a few key men, who could press on through any amount of fighters and flak, to reach heavily defended targets.

Neither Germany, during the Battle of Britain, nor the Japs, had produced enough such leaders. So, their bomber formations had been turned back many times, by air opposition.

Savage knew that he must develop other men, in the 918th, who would never turn back. "You guys", he added, "are going to be the Group leaders."

When he next spoke, Cobb's voice sounded worried. "General", he asked, "you aren't thinking of leaving us?"

Immediately, Savage thought about Henderson. How long would it be, he wondered, before that political smart-ass star- gazer would start trying to sell General Pritchard on the idea of a new assignment for a competitor, who was in a position to collect too many medals and headlines?

"I wouldn't worry too much about that, Joe", he said. "The big job is still ahead, and I aim to stick around awhile."

The Air Exec looked far from satisfied.

"I hope the brass upstairs don't pull any fast ones", replied Cobb. "We're kind of getting used to you down here."

Savage remained silent. During the next dozen, or so, paces, Cobb seemed to be trying to make up his mind about something. Finally, he screwed up his courage to ask a question that had troubled him for several days, ever since he had assigned Ben Gately, and his Leper Colony, to the lead of a mission. Savage had studied the crew list carefully that day, but offered no objection. Then Gately aborted in mid-Channel with a bad turbo, and a runaway prop, leaving Bishop, flying as his deputy, to take over the lead.

And, although Gately had done a smooth job of returning to base on only two engines, no mean feat, Savage was furious.

"Just what I might have expected", was his comment.

"Sir", said Cobb, "I'd like to try letting Gately lead another mission, soon." "Why", asked Savage, making the word sound like an epithet?

"Well, you see, sir", struggled Cobb, painfully aware that the general was freezing up on him, "his own plane was down for an engine change that last time. And he had to rely on a spare ship that went sour on him."

When Savage merely compressed his lips, saying nothing, the Air Exec was encouraged to continue. "General", he said, "Gately's changed to beat all hell since you got here. I think he'll turn out okay."

"Assign Gately to missions as you see fit", Savage told him, coldly. "But don't make excuses for him, to me. I don't care to discuss him", he added, "even with you."

With Cobb smarting under the rebuff, the two men continued on, passing near the edge of the perimeter track, where a B-17 was parked. It's sturdy tail rising gracefully from the dorsal fin along its spine. As always, the rugged, clean lines of the Fortress reassured Savage. Here was a reliable tool. A powerful weapon to grasp in your hands.

He noted that the airfield appeared nearly deserted, in the early morning light, as the 918th was sleeping late this day. And then he heard spasmodic bursts of machine gun fire.

Curious, the pair changed directions and walked toward the sound, until they sighted a small group in the vicinity of a high mound of earth, which served as a target butte. Gunners, thought Savage, bore-sighting their fifty calipers. However, as soon as he was close enough, he recognized a strange cast of characters.

Chaplain Twombly and the Flight Surgeon were sitting a little apart from the others, on a blanket, field stripping their pieces. Sergeant Nero was explaining second-position stoppages to Harvey Stovall. A little distance away, Sergeant Coulter, Private

McIllhenny, and an armorer, whom Savage didn't recall, were firing short bursts at a target.

As Savage approached, the men stopped, came to attention and saluted. "What's going on here, Harvey", he asked?

Major Stovall seemed a little perplexed.

"Morning, General", he said, wiping his brow. "I guess you might call this part of the Airfield Defense Plan you asked me to draw up. I figured that all of us ground-pounders ought to know which end of a machine gun the bullet comes out - in case of an emergency."

The others, especially Private McIllhenny, appeared to be relieved by the Ground Exec's reply. Savage had a vague feeling that there was something fishy about their expressions, as though they had been caught in some illicit act, but he merely said, "Fine, fine", and proceeded on to the Officers' Mess.

There, he and Cobb would enjoyed a feast of three fresh eggs each, which the mess sergeant presented with the compliments of Private McIllhenny.

Halfway back to his office, Savage and Cobb were intercepted by the Ground Exec, who leaped out of his jeep in a state of uncharacteristic excitement, and handed the general an envelope.

"From PINETREE, sir. By motorcycle courier", said Stovall. "I couldn't locate you right away, so I opened it and signed for it."

Savage was seized with foreboding as he opened the letter. He had never seen Stovall so upset. The letter read:

SUBJECT: O.T.U. training in the Continental United States, Zone of the Interior.

TO: Commanding Officer, 918th Bombardment Group (H)

1. Effective immediately, you will refrain from further partici-pation in any combat action (missions) without specific prior authorization from this Headquarters.
2. The Commanding General, United States Army Air Forces, Eighth U.S. Army Air Force, has been requested to return a suitable General Officer, qualified by outstanding experience in combat, to the United States, Zone of the

Interior, for urgently important duties in connection with the training of heavy bombardment groups for combat. You are here- by advised that in the opinion of this Headquarters, no officer, other than yourself, can meet these subject require- ments.

3. Pursuant to para. 2, above, you will consider yourself in readiness for re-assignment to this important duty, to which you will be ordered as soon as practicable. Meanwhile, you will take appropriate action relative to termination of your present duties at a reasonably early date, of which you will be advised in due course.

SIGNED: Henderson, Brigadier General, U.S.A.A.F.

Headquarters, Eighth U.S. Army Air Force Savage read through it twice, then handed it back to Stovall. He turned to Cobb. "You go with Harvey", he said, grimly. "I'll be over soon."

When the jeep had driven away, Savage proceeded at a slow and heavy pace toward the headquarters site. His eyes burned straight ahead, his teeth were clenched and, from time to time, his lips moved inaudibly. Gradually his pace quickened, and by the time he reached the headquarters, he was striding almost at a run.

He saw his car outside and, approaching an open window of the Adjutant's office, he shouted . . . "McIllhenny!"

He had already climbed onto the back seat when his driver arrived. "PINETREE", he said. "And bend that throttle."

Savage found Henderson in his quarters at Wycombe Abbey. The latter had just emerged from his bathroom in a green silk dressing gown, rubbing shaving lather from his neck with a hand towel, and greeted Savage with an apologetic smile.

"I had to work late last night", he explained. "What's new, Frank?"

"Nothing's new", responded Savage. "I got your letter. The same ancient bottle of two-star Henderson."

Henderson reduced his smile, but continued in his manner to ignore Savage's dangerous expression. "You're a lucky guy, Savage", he said. "Wish I could fill the bill for that assignment back in the

States. It means command of the Second Air Force, probably in sunny Colorado."

"Don't fling that stuff at me", snapped Savage.

Henderson eyed him, calmly, but no longer smiling, the towel dangling in his hand.

"Your manner is un-military", said Henderson, "and I might add, insubordinate. But, you've made quite a hobby of it lately."

"First of all, I want to place this discussion on a personal, not an official, basis", said Savage. "You've made it clear that we have no personal relationship. I prefer to talk to you officially. We're both Army officers."

"Correct. And I have no apologies for my record as a soldier. However you care to construe it, this conversation is strictly personal with me."

"What do you want", asked Henderson?

"I want you to find someone else to fly that desk at Colorado Springs. And I want you to take that letter and shove it. This is no time to try and railroad me."

Henderson dropped his hand towel on the floor and moved a little closer to Savage.

"I don't get this", he said, furiously.

"Then I'll spell it out for you. I have no military ambitions that threaten you - now, or after the war, and I couldn't be less interested in another star. My job at Archbury isn't finished, and I aim to finish it."

Henderson moved still closer, until he was looking up at the taller man, from only a foot away. "This is ridiculous", he said. "I don't follow you at all. I have to comply with a directive from Washington, and it says outstanding combat qualifications. That's you, and I'm sure General Pritchard will agree."

"I can't believe that General Pritchard would pull me out of the 918th now", said Savage. "You're a fast talker, Henderson, but not that fast."

"Apparently you've hypnotized yourself with the notion that I'd stoop to anything to get you out of my hair. But I refuse to lower myself, to argue such a point with you."

Savage grabbed Henderson by the lapels of his dressing gown with two well-muscled fists. "Okay", he said, through his clenched teeth. "We won't argue. Just forget that you wrote me that letter! I'm busy, see. And I've got a job of fighting to do with the 918th!"

"Take your hands off of me", snapped Henderson! Slowly, Savage released him and stepped back.

"All right", he said, his voice ringing with conviction. "But I'm giving you fair warning, here and now, on a purely personal basis."

His eyes bored into Henderson.

"Don't mess around with me. Just keep the goddamn to hell out of my road!"

Henderson had turned pale with anger and was trembling. The expression in Savage's eyes had become literally murderous.

"Go ahead", he breathed. "Go ahead, Savage, and get yourself killed! But never say I didn't try to stop you!"

"There, that's better", said Savage. "A big improvement on your letter." He turned quickly and walked out.

While driving Savage back to Archbury, Private McIllhenny was eager to unburden himself, to the general, of a matter in the forefront of his mind. But the scowling, preoccupied figure in the back seat discouraged him, until they were close to the base, when McIllhenny observed, through the rearview mirror, that Savage seemed to have shaken off whatever had been obsessing him.

Maybe, thought McIllhenny, now is the time. He had been tipped off by Sergeant Nero that an irate family in the village was gunning for him. Because, the day before, a local daughter had given birth to twins, for which she considered, a certain, Private McIllhenny responsible.

Weighing the alternatives of marrying a girl who already had twins, or a W.A.A.F. corporal who presumably would present him with only one offspring, McIllhenny hadn't wasted much thought in choosing the lesser evil.

"General", he said, "may I bring up a personal matter?" "What is it, McIllhenny?"

"You see, sir, I've been wrestling with myself over something." "Yeah! And who won?"

"Well, sir, it's just that", he stammered a little, "I . . . I'd like to ask your permission to get married."

"Now wait a minute", said Savage. "Maybe I had to bust you down, but don't get the idea that anybody's trying to coerce you into a shotgun wedding."

"Oh no, sir, it's not that", he responded. "I've decided that I'm in love with Corporal Lambeth, and I want to marry her. That's all."

The general whistled to himself. Then he thought of Pamela. This was wonderful. Perfect. He smiled broadly.

"In that case", said Savage, "I wish you all the luck in the world, McIllhenny. You have my blessing."

"Thank you, sir", said McIllhenny, as much relieved as Savage.

They pulled up in front of the headquarters block and as Savage got out, his mind already racing at the prospect of an early call on Pamela, to break the good news, McIllhenny faced him.

"I shall do my best, sir", he said, "to make ends meet on my current pay." Savage burst out laughing.

"All right, all right", he said. "You win. Put those stripes back on." "Thank you, sir."

"Sergeant" McIllhenny saluted solemnly and hurried into the Adjutant's office, where he immediately inserted a sheet of paper into his typewriter.

CHAPTER SEVEN

ACHTUNG!

"Desborough Hall", said Savage, as he entered his car. "Very well, sir", replied Sergeant McIllhenny.

Both the staff car and its passenger were immaculate. The sergeant had seen to the car and the general had chosen his newest uniform slacks and jacket, and his shiniest shoes.

After a short drive through the Sunday afternoon sunshine, they turned onto a winding driveway that passed between magnificent oak trees. As they drove between the trees, they caught occasional glimpses of the ancient family home of Desboroughs, complete with Tudor style architecture, tennis court, croquet lawn, boxwood hedges and flower gardens, now mostly convert- ed to vegetables. Likewise, what formerly had been a manicured green velvet lawn, was now plowed up to the last square foot on behalf of England's impoverished citizenry.

A hundred yards from the mansion, an armed British soldier stepped out onto the road with a red flag and stopped the car. Savage's impatience with this delay was short lived, for almost at once a tremendous explosion filled the air from nearby. Then the soldier waved the car on.

A fusillade of machine gun fire rattled off not far from them, followed by streams of tracer bullets overhead.

What is this, Sergeant", exclaimed Savage! "The Fourth of July?"

But, before his driver could answer, both men jumped in their seats as a covey of small rockets smoked into the sky with a great WHOOSH!

Then suddenly, appearing out of nowhere, a company of middleaged Home Guardsmen, with perspiration steaming down their beefy red faces, charged out into the open with fixed bayo- nets, and sprawled on their stomachs along each side of the road, ahead of the car. McIllhenny stepped on the brakes, but the pre- caution was unnecessary. Because, before he could stop, the Guardsmen had leaped to their feet, in response to a shrill whistle from their captain, and stampeded out of sight into the woods.

"Near as I can tell, sir", said McIllhenny, as they started off again, "it's the invasion of England." "Or the wrong place", remarked Savage, as they drove on to the front door.

But then, Savage saw Pamela approaching, casually, from the tennis court on the far side of the house. She carried a racket and was wearing a thick white sweater, as a concession to the chilly whether. At the sight of the girl, a shot of adrenaline tingled into Savage's bloodstream, akin to his reaction to emergencies in the air.

To himself he said: Steady, Frank. Steady there, ole boy. For in her tennis outfit she was a vision.

She waved to him, and it seemed to Savage that her smile was barely polite. He wasn't close enough to see that the corners of her smile were unsteady.

Savage and McIllhenny had just gotten out of the car when the ground shook with the loudest explosion yet. Both of them jumped, but Pamela didn't seem to have noticed, as she and the general shook hands.

"How are you, General Savage", she asked?

"Scared stiff", grinned Savage. "Let me out of this flak!" "Oh, that", she said.

"Would you mind telling me what that is?"

"A land mine, I should think", she answered, somewhat indifferently. "Don't you know?"

Pamela looked apologetic, as they started walking towards the tennis court.

"I forgot that you haven't been here before", she said. "They have turned our place into a proving ground, of sorts. Unexploded enemy bombs and mines are brought here for disposal. They also test new rockets, and Lord knows what else. Very hush, hush - top secret, and all that."

"Nice", commented Savage, "Very soothing." "Well, we've gotten rather used to it", she said.

They took a few paces in silence, broken only by sporadic gun fire. "I have some good news for you", said Savage, at length.

"Really?"

"About Sergeant McIllhenny and your W.A.A.F. I've got it all fixed up. He's decided that he's going to marry Corporal Lambeth."

"Thank you", she said, "very much."

Savage was somewhat disappointed at her lack of enthusiasm. And as they neared the tennis court, he noticed, for the first time, that the 918th was present in force.

Major Cobb and Jesse Bishop were on one side of the net, with Ben Gately on the other side, rallying with his opponents while waiting for Pamela to return, It was obvious that Gately was very good.

Lord and Lady Desporough were already coming down the gravel path to welcome the general.

Lord Desborough had a homely face, big of nose and wrinkled with such character, that Savage had to search, in vain, to find a resemblance to Pamela. But, he saw the answer, instantly, in Lady Desborough, whose lovely expression and classic features proclaimed that she must have been a famous beauty at one time.

During the exchange of greetings, Lord Desborough gripped Savage's hand like a former Cambridge oarsman, which he was. And Savage got the impression that Pamela's father possessed a deceptive charm and ability, behind his rugged Saint Bernard dog like features, and his melancholy eyes.

Cobb and Bishop stopped what they were doing and walked over to the sidelines to say hello to Savage. Leaning against the net post, bouncing a ball up and down, Gately met Savage's eyes for an instant. He nodded impersonally, merely saying, "After- noon, sir".

"Take my place, won't you, General", urged Pamela? "Not today, thanks", said Savage. "You all go ahead."

"If you don't mind", said Pamela. "The boys say that they have to get back to the station after this set. Just a few more points. Besides, father and mother would love to monopolize you, anyway."

She rejoined Gately and play resumed. Pamela was clearly a competitor, heedless, in her concentration, of whether or not she was being graceful. To Savage, it seemed that her efforts to re- turn even the hardest smashes, that came off of Cobb's racket, made her much more attractive than some self-conscious lady performers he had watched.

Bishop and Cobb played recklessly and loudly, but Gately stroked the ball back with precision, and in silence, until he and Pamela had come from behind to win the set. Savage begrudged the flashing smile she gave Gately, and her words: "Good show, Ben". Gately ignored Savage, during the brief chatter, before the three junior officers thanked their hosts and left for the airfield.

After some further polite conversation, Frank and Pamela shook off the older couple, and found themselves in front of a fire in the library. The Desborough's butler appeared

"Tea", asked Pamela, appraising Savage through her wide, violet eyes? "Tea is fine", replied Savage, not too convincingly.

"Bring two gin and tonics, please, Benson", she told the butler. Seeing Savage's appreciative smile, she added . . .

"Better?"

"My favorite brand of tea", said Savage.

"Now that we are away from your office", she said, "I want to talk to you about Ben Gately." She paused, noting the general's reluctant expression.

"Do you mind", she asked him?

He studied her for a moment, then finally said. "What about Gately?"

"Why don't you like him?" "Not my type, I guess."

Savage hoped to stay clear of the subject of Gately's official record. "Is it important", he asked?"

He guessed, from her expression, that she must have taken Gately's attentions fairly seriously.

"It's just that I'm a bit puzzled", she parried. "The fact that you relieved him of his old job is none of my business. But I do wonder if you understand him?"

"I believe I do", said Savage, noncommittally.

"For instance", she said, "do you know that he's always hated the Army? That he never wanted to go to your West Point? That he hated being forced into his family's military tradition? And that he dislikes flying, except for the higher pay?"

"What about it", asked Savage, guardedly?

At that moment the butler entered with their drinks and a platter of cucumber sandwiches. Savage touched Pamela's glass.

"Cheers", she said. "Cheers", repeated Savage.

As Benson left the room, she hastened to continued.

"It's just that we're all so fond of Ben. And he's out of place in this war. He's like a square peg in a round hole, and he's so terribly sensitive. But we think he's a good type . . . if given the right chance."

Savage stared into his glass, then into the fireplace.

"He's getting his chance", he said, putting a conclusive period on the subject matter by the tone of his voice.

Pamela sipped her drink, then set it down. She then stretched back her arms, in a yawn, and smiled across at him.

Savage felt at a loss, devoid of any ideas for the proper approach to this young woman. Helpless to prevent the precious minutes with her from slipping away, wasted.

Pamela, too, was experiencing a peculiar sense of frustration. They weren't getting anywhere, she felt, but what worried her more was that she wanted them to get somewhere. Why, she asked herself?

Here was a man that seemed so callous, something almost inhuman about him. He's not my type, she told herself. And yet, in spite of that, she was moved by an urge to impress him - to arouse his interest.

"You seem a bit tired", she said, finally. "I feel fine."

Relishing the surprise that she had in store for him, she asked.

"In spite of that bad show? Over Villecoublay last Friday, at twenty-two thousand feet? At 1413 hours?"

She saw at once, by Savage's expression, that she had scored. While leading the 918th home from a target, he had had a vicious encounter with two Staffeln of FW-190s, under the exact circumstances which she had just cited. He held his glass, unsipped, staring at her in astonishment.

"Been talking to the guys?"

"No", she said, smiling mysteriously. "But, even if I had, I doubt that they could have told me that those FWs came all the way from Denmark, and refueled at Woensdrecht, before they intercepted you."

Savage set his glass down with a clink.

"What is your racket, anyway, Pamela", he asked?

Then, realizing he had used her first name, he corrected himself. "I mean, Flight Leftenant."

"Pamela is better", she told him. "If I may call you Frank, General." "Okay, Pamela", he said. "Now, where did you get that infor- mation?" "I'm afraid it's Top Secret."

"You're talking to an Allied general aren't you?"

"Yes! A red-tape general who ought to know about it already, through channels. Although it is no secret that the Air Ministry does sometimes wonder if you Americans don't talk too much."

Savage showed that he was getting provoked.

"Security's a shell game", he told her. "Once I signed my life away for a Top Secret communication from the Air Ministry, with envelopes inside of envelopes, and all it did was inform me that document number so-and-so was no longer classified as Secret."

Pamela laughed.

"Isn't it priceless", she said, sympathetically? She nibbled at a cucumber sandwich.

"I think I shall take a chance on you."

She paused, as she finished her sandwich, then looked at him in the eyes. "Have you never heard of RT-Intercepts?"

"Sounds vaguely unfamiliar", he said.

"I'll tell you what", she continued. "If you actually are interested, my show is on the coast, near Lowestoft. We're a radio monitoring station. You can drop over for a visit, if you like. And I think you'll find it interesting . . . and maybe even helpful in your line of work."

"The Group's standing down again tomorrow because of the weather", he said. "How about it?" "Tomorrow, then", she said. "Any time . . . we work around the clock. With any luck you may hear the guttural voice of a particular friend of yours. Herr Adolph Galland."

"Am I supposed to know the gent?"

"You should. He made two head-on passes at you, last Tuesday, south of Abbeville. He nearly rammed your plane."

Savage, completely bowled over from what she just told him, stared at her. "I'm changing my brand of whisky", he muttered.

Pamela had another jolt ready for him.

"He doesn't like you at all", she told him. "Called you a swine . . . a scweinhund . . . when one of your gunners chipped the corner off his windscreen." She stood up.

"Well, I afraid I'm going to be late."

Savage got up, temporarily deprived of any further light conversation. England, he thought to himself, knows what it's doing since they've found that they can trust their women with some of the damnedest jobs of the war.

Together they walked down the hall, and were descending the front steps when they encountered Pamela's father, who drew the general to one side.

"As long as you are in England, General Savage", he said, "I want you to consider this house your home. Whenever you feel like it, just pack your bag and walk in.

And another thing, sir. I went to school with Charles Portal, and so if I can ever be of help to you in any matter involving the Air Ministry, I'd be only too happy."

Savage graciously thanked his host, then continued down the steps. Pamela was waiting by his car, where McIllhenny had just stepped out and was shaking hands with her.

"Corporal Lambath", Savage was surprised to hear her saying, "is a much better choice than that girl in the village with twins. I wish you both much luck."

"Thank you, ma'am", said McIllhenny, blushing.

Savage experienced a bad moment of embarrassing recollection. Why in hell, he asked himself, did he have to go and tell her that he had fixed it?

Pretending not to have overheard what she had said to McIllhenny, he tried to maintain a normal expression as he shook her hand. Her eyes flashed at him in a merry smile and as he looked back into her eyes, he tried to bluff it out for a couple of seconds, then broke into a grin.

"A fellow can try, can't he?"

Two days later Savage attended a conference, of all the Group Commanders, at WIDEWING. The code name for Major General Pritchard's headquarters in London.

Detailed plans of tactical procedures for an imminent strike into Germany were at the top of the agenda. Toward the end of the long session, Savage took the floor.

"General Pritchard", he said, "I think there is one more thing that ought to be brought up at this meeting."

He paused for a few seconds.

"With General Henderson's permission", he continued, "since it does lie in the province of Bomber Command, rather than the Group Commanders." "Go ahead, Frank", said Henderson.

"We are wasting a lot of gasoline on the mistaken assumption that we're drawing up enemy fighters and diverting them on a wild-goose chase."

He paused again and looked around the room.

"We're probably just fooling ourselves, but we're not fooling the Germans. Not any longer. Worse still, we tip our hand that the main effort is directed elsewhere."

Henderson bristled, but Pritchard asked the first question.

"What makes you think so, Frank?"

"Because the R.A.F. has a wealth of information available to us, but which we have never asked for, which proves it. I visited one of the R.A.F. radio stations on the coast yesterday, that monitors all Luftwaffe voice communications, twenty-four hours a day.

They have German speaking W.A.A.Fs. who have been at it so long that they know the German fighter controllers, their com- manders, and their pilots by their voices, and they know their names.

They record, in minute detail, how, why, and where the German fighters maneuver to meet our penetrations. And they know when and why we outguess the Germans, and when the Germans outguess us."

His eyes swept around the room again, noting that Pritchard was not the only one hanging on his words. Henderson, on the other hand, was nervously biting a pencil.

"Our diversions are a case in point", he continued. "Those W.A.A.Fs. who listen in, monitoring RT-Intercepts as they call it, are laughing at us. And so are the Germans." "Why", interrupted Henderson, no longer able to contain him- self?

"Because, when we send out our bombers on diversionary missions, we usually don't send their fighter escorts. The minute the enemy radar shows a formation without fighter support, they know at once it's a decoy."

Amidst the buzz of comments that arose, Henderson was alone in his silence. He looked as though he wanted to sink through the floor, when Pritchard directed his gaze toward him.

"Ed" said Pritchard, "is your R.A.F. Liaison Officer here?"
"Yes, sir. Group Captain Heeley."

He motioned toward a beribboned R.A.F. pilot, who stood up.

"Group Captain", asked Pritchard, "can your people arrange to let us have these RT-Intercepts on G.A.F. fighter reaction?"

"I don't see why not, General Pritchard. Top Secret stuff, but of no use sitting in a filing cabinet. You see, sir, we may have overlooked that this intelligence can be more useful to your units in daylight operations, than it is to us in night bombing, since we seldom run into larger fighter concentrations at night." "Thank you, Group Captain", said Pritchard.

Then turning back to Henderson.

"Ed, fix it up. And assign a member of your staff, full time, to study this information and plot the enemy fighter reactions, after every mission. I realize that we're bumping into a hundred new twists every day in this business, but I'm afraid we shouldn't have fumbled the ball on this one."

After the meeting broke up, Savage spent the long drive back to Archbury deep in thought. He had added fuel to the animosity which Henderson felt towards him.

He had not done so deliberately, but out of necessity. For he had understood at once, on his visit to Pamela's station, that her work with the RT-Intercepts was of immediate importance to the Americans. And that, in spite of it's secrecy, Henderson's staff should have been enough on its toes to ferret it out.

By bringing up the matter at Pritchard's conference, he had counted on quick action, at the expense of going through normal channels, and he was right. But now, it was going to be harder than ever to get along with Henderson.

Gradually his mind lapsed into the warm luxury of retrospection, about the day he had spent with Pamela. He had been professionally impressed by her intelligence and knowledge of her job, and had been fascinated by her intimate familiarity with the enemy personalities.

The Jagdfuhrer responsible for fighter defense in the Holland area was her personal foe. And her pet hate was that credit hogging German fighter ace, Adolph Galland, who specialized in shooting down crippled Fortresses.

But, the memory that warmed Savage the most, about his day at Lowestoft, was simply Pamela, herself. Many women had aroused his desires and affections over the years, but no woman had ever so completely won his respect.

It wasn't merely that, in her own field, she knew as much about fighting as he did in his - a concession which he would have made to few, if any, men. But, that her integrity seemed like a rock.

You could sense, he reflected, that her personal compass always pointed, undeviating, to True North. There would never be but one man in her life. And he, Frank Savage? Could he ever settle for one woman?

The cumulative philosophy of his mature years told him no. To himself, he said: to hell with all women. Then, deliberately, he transferred his thoughts to his more familiar problems within the 918th.

Major Stovall brought a letter into Savage's office, but instead of laying it in his IN basket, he placed it on the desk in front of the general, who picked it up and read it thoroughly. The letter was from a fellow Group Commander, and read as follows:

My heartiest congratulations to the 918th Bomb Group for a superb display of leadership on the mission of the 29th.

Your Group Leader, Lt. Colonel Benjamin Gately, was faced with a difficult decision, when the Wing Leader, whose Group Colonel Gately was following out of the target area turned off course.

Colonel Gately, failed to convince the Wing Leader, by radio, of his navigational error, and knowing that enemy fighters would concentrate on any Group straying from the main bomber stream, elected to maintain Wing integrity by following his Wing Leader.

Had Colonel Gately not brought his defensive firepower to the support of the solitary Group, flying off course, it is probable that the latter would have been annihilated, when intense fighter attacks were subsequently encountered.

Please convey my compliments to Colonel Gately for his fine example of air discipline on this mission.

Savage finished reading the letter, swiveled his chair around, and stared out the window, lost in thought. Finally, Stovall spoke up.

"Would the general like to prepare his own indorsement to Colonel Gately", he asked?

Savage still hesitated. He had been disturbed by the extent of the battle damage sustained by the Group, as a result of Gately's judgment. But it was hard to criticize Gately for following the military's axiom: try to persuade your leader of an error, but follow him, right or wrong.

"I want to consider this a little, Harvey", he said.

Stovall left the office, as Savage resumed his scrutiny of the bleak view beyond the windowpanes. As he was doing so, Jesse Bishop entered, without knocking, walked up and sat down by the desk.

"Hi, Jesse", said Savage, relaxing into a smile as he turned his chair back around. "What have you got?"

Before Bishop could answer, the phone buzzed. "Excuse me, Jesse", he said.

While Savage was talking on the phone, Bishop pulled open one of the desk drawers, reached into a box of cigars, grabbed one and lit it up.

"Have a cigar, Jesse", said Savage, as he was hanging up. "Roger that", replied Bishop, blowing out a puff.

"How'm I doing", continued Savage? "I can tell that you came in here to rack me back for something."

"Yes, sir, I did."

He took a deep breath.

"The guys think that you're being too tough on Colonel Gately." Savage frowned after hearing this.

"Don't try me too far, Jesse", he warned. "We made a deal, didn't we, sir?"

"Okay. Go ahead."

"Well, sir. As Major Cobb will verify, that Leper Colony of Colonel Gately's has turned into a regular factory for lead navigators and lead bombardiers. His gunners have the most claims, too. So, the men would think more of you, if you eased up on him."

"I don't care what the men think of me, personally", said Savage, "so long as they do their jobs. And you can tell them to mind their own business."

"Yes, sir", said Bishop, looking a little crestfallen. "But don't go off mad", amended Savage.

Realizing how busy the general was, Bishop chatted a little longer, thanked him for the cigar, saluted, and left.

Savage called in McIllhenny.

"Take a First Indorsement", he said.

"Yes, sir", said McIllhenny, as he picked up a pencil and scratch pad from the desk.

"To Lieutenant Colonel Benjamin Gately. Subject: Commendation. Paragraph One: It is always a matter of satisfaction to me to receive from another organization, a communication of this kind, reflecting favorably upon a member of the 918th Bombardment Group." He paused. "For my signature, Sergeant."

It was early evening and the general was still working at his desk, in a feverish concentration, when he heard a knock on the door. Looking up, he saw Gately standing, ramrod stiff, in the doorway.

It was the first time that Gately had set foot in the office, since the day of Savage's arrival. He was holding a sheet of paper in his left hand.

"What is it", asked Savage, distantly? Gately saluted.

"May I speak with the general?"

"Of course", said Savage, without warmth. "Come in."

He allowed Gately to stand in front of him, instead of offering him a chair.

"I just received the general's commendation", he said, with a barely audible tremor in his voice. "And, I came to thank you, sir."

"You have yourself to thank, Gately." Savage's manner was still cold.

"Your work will receive the same recognition from me as anyone else's in the Group."

He took a puff of his cigar.

"You've been doing all right, Gately."

Gately mistook these words for an overture from Savage. Conflicting emotions, springing from lingering hatred, and growing respect, welled up within him.

He still remembered, word for word, burned into his brain, what Savage had once told him. But, as he stood there, he could not repress an inconsistent desire for the general to get up, come around the desk, and shake his hand, burying the hatchet.

His emotional stress had brought him to a crossroads. And Savage continued to regard him through inscrutable eyes.

"But", he concluded, "there's still a long way to go."

Gately bit his lip, reluctant to leave the office on so inconclusive a note. Then his jaw slowly set into a harder line. He raised his right hand in a salute.

"Yes, sir", he said, in a choked voice, then he turned quickly and departed Later that evening, the Green Toby leered out over a lounge that was deserted, save for a few ground officers.

Savage, wearing his flight suit with the sleeves rolled up above his elbows, stood before the crews in the Briefing room.

"Give me your attention!"

What little noise there had been, was quickly hushed. Each face in the room was curious, and tense, for the men had come to know that, whenever Frank Savage appeared in flying clothes, they could expect some bad news.

Savage now only led the rugged missions. But his mere presence also reassured them. That's because the general had never failed to bring every ship back to base.

"First of all", he called out, in a penetrating voice, "I want to introduce our commander, General Henderson. He is paying us the honor of coming along with us, on today's mission."

There was polite applause as Henderson, bundled up in winter flight gear, stood up and waved his hand.

"Would you care to say anything to the crews, sir", asked Savage, politely?

"No, thanks", replied Henderson, flashing a personality smile back towards the combat men. "I'm just a crew member today."

And then he sat back down.

A ball-turret gunner nudged a tail gunner sitting next to him.

"If he's just a crew member", he whispered. "What does that make us?"

"Gentlemen", resumed Savage. "Business is picking up. As I told Major Cobb earlier, the Germans are converting more and more from bomber production to fighters. And our Intelligence shows that they're moving in fighter units from other fronts, to bolster the fighter belt in Western Europe, against us.

"Sounds like they've heard about the 918th", he said, smiling.

His words met with laughter and applause. Then he paused, while his eyes pierced to the back of the room.

"This morning", he told them, "for the first time, our Intelligence Officer will swing his pointer toward a target on German soil - Wilhelmshaven!"

A deep throated cheer, lasting for many seconds, shook the room. Finally, he held up his hands, until quiet was restored.

"I thought you'd like it", he said, with some pride in his voice. "The 918th will lead the Eighth Air Force today. I'll lead the Group. Major Cobb will lead the high squadron, and General Henderson will ride with him. Colonel Gately will lead the low squadron.

I have only one more thing to say, before the briefing officer takes over. The Germans have been dishing it out for a long time, now. Let's go find out, today, just how much they like tak- ing it!"

He motioned to the Intelligence officer, stepped down from the platform, and took his seat beside Henderson.

Three hours later, at Savage's hard-stand, after the last of the B-17's four engines had barked to life, Sergeant McIllhenny quickly backed the general's car into the slipstream, behind the tail, and out of sight of the cockpit. He jumped out, rushed to the car's trunk, yanked out a kit bag crammed with flying equipment, sprinted around the tail of the aircraft to the rear door and, assisted by a waist gunner, clambered aboard.

"Achtung! Feindliche Flugzeuge!" (Warning! Hostile aircraft!)

At Lowestoft, Pamela pressed the headphones closer to her ears as she listened to the crackling warning of ground observers, to the Jagdfuhrer (Fighter controller), Northwest Europe. Actually, she was just kibitzing, because her supervisory duties did not require her to act as an operator.

For half an hour she listened to the chatter of the German fighters, taking off and forming up to intercept the American bomber force. And then she heard the first of the Messerschmitt Groups make contact with the B-17s.

"Achtung! Diekeautos, Amerikanische!" (Warning! American heavy bombers!)

Her body seemed to become rigid, as her mind raced forward hundreds of miles to the east. To the frozen upper levels, plumed with vapor trails, where, at that instant, Frank Savage must be squinting through his windshield, at the black specks hurtling toward him, head-on, out of the sun - from . . .

TWELVE O'CLOCK HIGH.

Reception became so poor that she was unable to judge how the battle was progressing. But occasional guttural ejaculations of glee told her that several Flying Fortresses had gone down in flames. Presently, she tuned in the American bomber channel, listening for some minutes in vain, The B-17 pilots were maintaining excellent radio silence.

Suddenly she heard a faint call.

"Wheelbarrow leader to Yellowjacket leader, over."

And then she recognized Savage's voice clearly, in reply. "Go ahead, Wheelbarrow."

"Give me a check with reference to course, right or left."

There was a pause of a few seconds. Then she heard Savage's calm voice, again. "Yellowjacket to Wheelbarrow. Seven miles right."

"Roger, Yellowjacket."

Then there was continued silence. Pamela removed her headphones, lighted a cigarette with trembling fingers, and walked to the window, where she stood, staring out into the curling fog.

Straining their eyes upward, from the twenty-one hard-stands, around the perimeter track at Archbury Field, all the crew chiefs made a fast count of the formation of Fortresses thundering over- head. Some had props feathered, while others had tattered wing- tips and holes big enough to be spotted at their one-thousand foot altitude, from the ground.

"Twenty", rose from scores of lips. "One missing."

For several roaring minutes, the B-17s milled about, over the field, dropping one by one onto the runway, half of them firing double red flares on the final approach, as they glided swiftly to earth with wounded aboard. Gradually, the din subsided, as engines clanked into silence on each of their hard- stands.

The maintenance crew at Gately's empty hard-stand continued to gaze into the sky, long after the last propeller had jerked to a stop. They shaded their eyes with their hands, searching the horizon for some sign of the Leper Colony, as peaceful silence once more enveloped the airfield.

In the waist of Savage's B-17, McIllhenny was racing against time. It was his plan to shed his bulky flying gear and change into his regular uniform, in order to return to the staff car before the general could emerge from the cockpit, by his usual exit, out though the nose hatch. But, this time, Savage came back through the aircraft to the rear door, and caught McIllhenny, literally, with his pants down.

"Who authorized you to go along on this mission, Sergeant", he asked?

His voice was weary, and McIllhenny could see that Savage was in no joking mood. The general's nerves were on edge from the severe stress of what had proved to be a bloody struggle in to and out from the target.

"No one, sir", said McIllhenny, apprehensively.

"You jeopardized the safety of this aircraft", snapped Savage.

"Well, sir, I've checked out okay as a gunner, and I hated to miss this big one."

"You overreached yourself, McIllhenny. From now on, you stay out of the airplanes. And take those stripes off. You're reduced to private, and so help me, that's what you're going to stay!"

"Yes, sir", said McIllhenny, despondently.

Upper most on Savage's mind was the missing aircraft, and Gately. Badly shot up, the Leper Colony had hung on with three engines until the Group was starting back across the Channel, with enemy fighters still in the vicinity.

Then it lost another engine and had been forced to drop out of formation. Savage had watched, with some alarm, as the rest of the low squadron started lagging behind, to cover the crippled aircraft.

With his thumb reaching for the mike button, he prepared to blast an order at the low squadron. But Savage heard Gately beat him to it.

"Baker Two", Gately had called out! "Take over the Squadron! And close up on the Group! . . . GODDAMNIT, CLOSE IT UP!"

The low squadron had quickly re-formed on the lead squadron and Savage had watched as Gately dived down to wave top level, dropping further and further behind, until he was lost from view. The Intelligence officer met Savage at the door of the Interrogation room.

"What about Gately's crew", asked Savage, at once?

"They ditched in the Channel, sir. And all of them were safely picked up by British Air Sea Rescue. They ought to be back at the airfield tonight."

Savage nodded without comment, and walked on through the chattering crews, only stopping to accept a cup of coffee and a doughnut from a Red Cross girl. Henderson, jubilant, his manner suggesting the swagger of a combat veteran, was already talking, excitedly, on the Ops phone, to Bomber Command, when Savage approached.

"Good show", he bubbled to Savage, in the R.A.F. vernacular, after hanging up. "Good show!"

Impulsively, he shook Savage's hand.

"How did the other Groups make out", asked Savage? "I counted three ships going down." "PINETREE says the final count is four", replied Henderson. "It could have been worse." "Yes", said Savage, dryly, "it could have been worse."

After getting rid of Henderson, who seemed to have temporarily forgotten all his personal grudges toward Savage, in the flush of his enthusiasm at having survived his first combat mis- sion.

Savage decided to look in at the office, before going over to the Officers' Club.

He wanted a drink, badly, to relieve the greatest reaction of fatigue he had yet experienced, after a mission. But, in his heart, he was happy. Because, his had been the first American bomber, in World War Two, to cross the German coast. And they had bombed the Fatherland, at last.

When he got to his office, Major Cobb was waiting for him. "Have you got a minute, sir?"

"Sure, Joe."

"You aren't going to like this, sir", said Cobb, cautiously. "Right this minute, nothing bothers me. So, now what?"

"You see, sir, I understand that you caught McIllhenny, and busted him for stowing away." "Yes. What about it?"

"If you'll pardon me, sir, that makes things kind of compli- cated."

"Why is that?"

"The precedent, sir. I mean, we'd have to bust Captain Twombley, too." "Holy crap", exclaimed Savage! "Don't tell me the Chaplain stowed away!"

"Yes, sir. I didn't find it out about it, until I heard him saying the Lord's Prayer over the innerphone. He was manning the left waist gun."

"Well, I quit", said Savage, as he reached for a cigar. "I'm afraid that's not all, sir."

Cobb hesitated.

"Keep talking", said Savage, a glint creeping into his eyes.

"I might as well give it to you all at once, sir. Damn near the whole Ground Echelon stowed away for this mission. The Flight Surgeon and Harvey Stovall were at the waist guns in Jesse Bishop's ship. Even Sergeant Nero went along - with Harbold."

Savage threw up his hands, walked over to the window and turned his back to Cobb, He didn't want the Air Exec to see the tears that were pressing up towards his eyes. But, he managed to hold back the tears, and face Cobb, again.

"Any of them get hurt?" "Not a scratch, sir." Savage rubbed his head.

"So that's what Stovall was getting at, with his cooked-up Airfield Defense Plan, at the target butts this morning."

He sat down again, puffing on his cigar.

"I'll let it go, this time, Joe", he went on. "However, I'm going to hold you responsible that there is no reoccurrence. It's too risky."

"Yes, sir."

"But I'm still sore at McIllhenny. I'll bet that he was at the bottom of it all. Maybe he ought to sweat it out as a private . . . for awhile, anyway."

"I wouldn't advise it, sir." "And why not?"

"On account of McIllhenny having just been officially credited with two FW-190s destroyed, and one probable. A natural born gunner."

Savage looked up, with a helpless expression, as Harvey Stovall appeared, looking distinctly sheepish and showing some inappropriate marks on his face, from the tight oxygen mask he had worn.

"Hell of a nerve you've got, Harvey", he said. "Showing your face in here. While you're at it, get ahold of McIllhenny."

Stovall went out and, after a moment, returned with Private McIllhenny, who was wearing a shirt with plain sleeves. He saluted Savage, imperturbably.

"McIllhenny", said Savage, "put 'em back on."

"Yes, sir. Thank you, sir."

"Now, all of you, leave me alone for a while. Give me some time to pull myself together."

The three men withdrew, and McIllhenny immediately walked over to his desk, where he opened a bottom drawer and pulled out a shirt with sergeant's stripes on it. He quickly changed, and thrust his plain sleeved shirt back into the drawer.

A moment later, Savage appeared behind him. "I suggest, McIllhenny, that you . . ."

He stopped, staring at McIllhenny's sleeves.

"Skip it, Sergeant", he said, grinning and laughing to himself. "I'm too late. I was going to suggest that you get yourself a set of stripes with zippers."

Still grinning, he walked across the hall to Stovall's office, where he offered to buy the Ground Exec a drink, effective immediately. The pair were soon outside, in the twilight, setting out on foot for the club.

"Did ya hit anything up there today, Harvey", asked Savage? "I think I got a piece of one", responded Stovall, proudly.

"Ours, or theirs", asked Savage? I'm surprised I haven't already gotten a complaint from our Spitfire escort."

"Lay off me, please, General", said Stovall, plaintively. "I think I'm suffering from what I can only describe as combat fatigue. But, since you mentioned it", he added, thoughtfully, "a Spitfire does resemble a Me-109, from head-on."

"Better get yourself some new glasses there, Major."

"I couldn't use 'em anyway, sir. They frosted up on me."

"Why, you nearsighted old goat. You couldn't have hit the side of a balloon hanger!" Stovall fumbled for his pipe.

"Seriously, Harvey, I'm plenty burned up with you. A gray headed old fud like you should have better sense. How do you think I'd feel having to send your wife an M.I.A. report on you? Besides, if I had to get a new Ground Exec, he might be even worse than you are."

Savage's tone was scolding, but he had placed a hand on the shoulder of his friend, and his eyes were affectionate.

"You don't seem to realize", said Stovall, "that none of us groundpounders would have gone along with you today, if we thought it was going to be dangerous!" "You're hopeless, Harvey", he said.

But again, as in the office when he learned about the stowaways, he was strangely moved.

As they were approaching the door to the Officers' Club, the general saw Chaplain Twombley walking up a side path on a collision course. He also observed that the chaplain was trying to avoid him, by stopping, turning around, and pretending to be looking at something in the distance.

"Twombley", called out Savage!

The chaplain jumped, almost dropping the cigarette he was trying to light. Then, with a guilty conscience written all over his face, he walked over and greeted Savage.

"Your business is fighting sin", said Savage, sternly. "From hereafter, you will concentrate on sin exclusively."

"I grasp the general's point", replied Twombley. "You are looking at a penitent and contrite man." "Then, we'll say no more about it", said Savage. "As a matter of fact, I wouldn't be surprised but what your prayers came in handy, more than once, this morning."

"Prayer", said the chaplain, "is a wonderful source of strength, General. And I have seen some powerful praying before the take-offs since I came to Archbury Field. That's why I had to make one mission, in order to find out what the praying was all about."

CHAPTER EIGHT

TO ALL MEN

Rolling dice for drinks, at the bar, with Stovall and Cobb, the general hummed, under his breath, in accompaniment to "I've Got Sixpence, Jolly, Jolly Sixpence", which the swarm of young officers surrounding Jesse Bishop, at the piano, were lustily sing- ing, their glasses held high. Cobb lost, and not too gracefully.

After critically examining the dice, he handed them back to their owner, Harvey Stovall. As Savage sipped his Scotch, gratefully, he was listening to the confident ring in the voices of the men working off their tension in song.

When several choruses of "Sixpence" were over, a request went up from various parts of the lounge, for Bishop to play the "Warsaw Concerto". A hush descended as Jesse began to play, filling the room with music that gripped the audience.

At the bar, Savage listened with one ear while conducting a low-voiced conversation with Cobb and Stovall.

"General Henderson gave us a long stand-down", he said. "At least three days." "You can thank me", grinned Cobb. "He had to ride with me today."

"What I was thinking", said Savage, "is that now is the time to pull a short mission on London. Harvey, fix up the maximum number of leaves and passes for the Group, will you?"

"Roger, Willco, and out", said Stovall, fervently.

Savage smiled at this proud display of technical lingo from the Ground Exec, in his newly acquired role of battle scarred airmen.

"Amen", said the chaplain, who was standing behind Savage, ordering a beer, and had overheard. Savage regarded the chaplain, thoughtfully. He then glanced over toward Bishop, at the piano, then brought his eyes to rest on Stovall.

"Harvey", he continued, "one thing about Jesse has been bothering me lately. He's all tensed up inside. Tied up in knots. And I was wondering if he doesn't need", - he caught himself out of deference to Twombley - "some relaxation?"

Stovall looked uncomfortable.

"If you mean blowing off steam on a wild tear", he observed, "well, that's just not Jesse's style." "What I'm trying to get at", said Savage, "is . . . . I've got to stick around here . . . so maybe it's up to you and Joe, to kind of take charge of Jesse, and really show him London. The whole works." "Sir", stated Stovall, "while I do appreciate the compliment, I'm just an old, dull, family man."

"You, are a horny old goat, Harvey", said Cobb, laughing rudely. "Tell us how many Atlantic City conventions you've lied to your wife about."

Stovall looked almost hurt. So, Savage intervened.

"Let's not get too personal here", he said. "I just want you two reprobates to see to it, that Jesse doesn't spend all his leave in meditation and prayer. Do you get my drift?"

"We'll do our best", said Stovall. "But I'll have to let Joe do the navigating."

"For shame, gentlemen", said Twombley. "Remember that you are your brother's keeper. Do not tempt Bishop too far from the paths of righteousness."

He sipped his beer, contemplatively.

"And yet", he continued, "excepting a man who has seen the follies of Piccadilly, perhaps he cannot be saved."

He set his, now empty, glass down.

Bishop finished playing, amidst a prolonged applause and cries for more. Then Savage left the bar and began circulating amongst the men, whereupon Chaplain Twombley turned to Stovall and Cobb.

"If I may change the subject entirely", he said, speaking seriously, "I have a suggestion. Harvey, you know the American cemetery outside of London, don't you? Well, there are a lot of 918th men buried there, and I'd like to hold a brief memorial service for them."

He sounded almost apologetic.

"Do you think it would be out of place to do it tomorrow? Or would it interfere with the men's leave? And, do you think there might be a dozen or so, who might be interested?"

"We can certainly find out, Chaplain", said Stovall. "I will post a notice and see what happens. Personally, I think there are quite a few men around here, who've been waiting for a chance to pay their respects. I know that I'd be there."

"So would I", said Cobb.

"Please", said Twombley, "don't feel that I'm thrusting this on anybody." "We'll see how many sign up", said Stovall.

At the American cemetery, Chaplain Twombley waited, prayer book in his hand, against a background of white crosses, intermittently illuminated by flashes of sunshine. Standing before the chaplain, his head bared, General Savage was in the center of a gathering of more then three hundred officers and enlisted men from Archbury Field.

The chaplain began by reading the twenty-third Psalms.

". . . .Yea, though I fly through the valley of death, I shall fear no evil . . ."

As he read on, the words registered in the minds of each man present, with realistic and immediate significance. He finished in tones of forceful simplicity, dropping the prayer book to his side, and looked out over the impassive expressions on the sad faces of his uniformed congregation.

"When death comes, as it must to all men", he continued, speaking with no advanced thought, "may we grant ourselves the courage to meet the unknown, as bravely as those fellow airmen who lie buried here."

As a bugler stepped forward and began sounding taps, Jesse Bishop felt a lump rising in his throat, as the bugle's notes descended, in utter finality, from the long, pleading high note.

Stovall, Cobb, and Bishop checked in at Claridge's, accompanied by a telephone number for a girl named Penelope. She was a photogenic ambulance driver who had been recommended to Cobb, by one of the guys in the Group.

Fortified by a stiff Scotch and soda, and impressed by the luxurious suite of two bedrooms, and a sitting room, done up in a soft beige, Penelope got busy on the phone and came up with dates for all hands. Two girls, who arrived in time for the second round of drinks, were extra attractive, though not quite as pretty as Penelope.

The party was soon going in high gear, with all talk of dinner temporarily in abeyance, after Stovall came up with a bottle of Scotch, which he had in his bag. Then, three other members of the 918th, whom Bishop had bumped into in the lobby, barged in, swelling the liquor supply and the feminine contingent still further.

Penelope, ignoring Cobb in favor of Bishop, was sitting on Jesse's lap, on a stuffed chair, and running her fingers slowly through his thick blond hair, while sipping her drink. Animated by the warm glow of the whisky inside of him, Jesse was accept- ing the girl's attentions with a flushed grin of pleasure, while Cobb, sitting on the couch, pretended to be satisfied with the bru- nette curled inside his arm.

Only Harvey Stovall, although making himself more agreeable to a chubby girl with a saucy nose, still clung to a semblance of detached dignity. He had resolved to have a good time, but within limits.

At length, Cobb left the brunette, got up and meandered over to Jesse and Penelope. "One side, Junior", he said, insultingly to Bishop. "Make way for a grown man." Penelope moved an arm around Jesse's shoulder, as Bishop stared up at Cobb.

"Beat it, Joe", he said, good-naturedly.

Cobb leaned down toward Penelope, and told her.

"You're wasting your time", he said, suggestively. "And your robbing the cradle. Come on, babe, let's you and me start getting serious."

There was nothing good-natured about Penelope's expression.

"You bore me", she said, acidly, "right off my feet. Now, would you mind going away?"

Cobb straightened up, swaying slightly on his feet. Then he forced a grin on his face. "There's no hurry, babe, I like 'em hard to get. I'll be back."

He returned to his own girl, without looking at Bishop. Some time later, Cobb followed Stovall into the bathroom and closed the door on the noisy hilarity outside.

"Harvey", he said, "I'm layin' off Penelope to give Jesse a clear field. But I'm damned if I'd do it for anybody else."

"That's mighty big of you, Joe", replied Stovall, who had seen Cobb's rebuff. "But he doesn't need any help from you, or anyone. He's all set."

"Which reminds me", said the Air Exec, "that it's time the ole Cobb man started getting set, too." He hurried out and rejoined his girl. However, so engrossed had everyone become, in their own drinking, arguing, and paw- ing, that Cobb was scarcely noticed as he maneuvered the blond into one of the bedrooms, and was gone for some time.

When he returned, the party had gotten bigger, louder and better. Stovall caught Cobb's eye and shook his head, reproachfully, but Joe smugly ignored him.

Cobb turned to accept a drink from Jesse, who had Penelope hanging from one arm, as she stared up at him with an adoring expression. Without being conspicuous about it, but making sure that Cobb was watching him, Bishop steered Penelope into the other bedroom, closed the door and locked it behind him.

"Too noisy out there", he said, looking self-consciously at Penelope.

"You're so right", replied Penelope, looking not in the least self-conscious, as she slid her arms around his neck and kissed him.

He turned his head slightly, so that the kiss landed more on his cheek than his mouth. She turned away and sat on the foot of the bed.

"Penelope", he said, sitting down in a chair and lighting a cigarette. "Would you . . . would you like to do me a big favor?"

"Like anything", she answered, smiling up at him, demurely. "How about staying with me for awhile? In here?"

"As long as you like, Jesse, darling", she said, unzipping her dress and letting it fall to the floor. "Why don't you take your shirt off, and we'll get nice and comfortable?"

Bishop looked embarrassed, in spite of the uninhibited complexion the evening had taken.

"Please don't get the wrong idea", he said.

She kicked off her shoes, laid back and nestled her head on a pillow.

"But I think your idea is fine", she told him. "Now you come right over here, darling, with me, and be sociable."

Bishop hesitated, then went over, sat on the edge of the bed and offered her a cigarette. "Not now, darling", she whispered.

"Look, Penelope", he said, uncomfortably. "I guess I must seem like a dope, but couldn't we just sit here and talk for a little while . . . maybe half an hour?"

"Why, what is there to talk about", she asked, studying him with a changed expression.

"Gee. It's hard to know just how to say it", he said. "I . . you see . . . I've never been with a girl, in my life."

Penelope shifted her head on the pillow, regarding him with tender eyes.

"Why, you sweet boy", she told him, slowly. "Perhaps I will have one of those cigarettes." After Jesse lit it for her, she continued.

"There's always a first time, though, isn't there Jesse?" "Sure", he said, "I guess there is. But can't we just talk?"

"Of course. I'm sorry I've been so bold. Throwing myself at you. But the war is a wonderful excuse . . . so little, and all that sort of rot."

"No, . . no", protested Bishop. "Please, don't think that. I think you're wonderful . . . a guy would be awfully lucky to get you."

"I believe that I'm beginning to get it", she said. "You don't want to your friends to think that you're a sissy. You think, that you've got to show them."

Bishop seemed to cringe.

"The truth is", he confessed, "those guys out there, and back at the Group, all kid the hell out of me - well, about not being a man."

"You look like plenty of man to me", she said. "What is there to be afraid of? Do I scare you?"

"No, hell no. I mean, just the opposite . . . or, what I really mean is, it's something else." "Another girl?"

"Yeah . . . yeah, that's it. We grew up together. Some day I'll get home . . . and I want to marry her."

Bishop had walked over to an ashtray to extinguish his cigarette. Penelope got up, too, moved over and kissed him lightly on the cheek.

"So, this is all window dressing", she said, softly. "To try to convince those chums of yours that you're a man."

She laughed gently, almost a giggle.

"How odd. It's really very funny. Do you know what kind of man you are, Jesse Bishop?"

He waited for her to answer her own question, showing, in his sensitive eyes, that her answer just might hurt him.

"You're the kind of man, every woman in the world would like to find", she told him. Suddenly, there was a vigorous knocking on the door, follow- ed by Cobb's muffled voice. "Hey, Bishop! We're all going out for dinner. Come on!"

Jesse exchanged glances with Penelope.

"What's the hurry, Joe", he called out. "I'm busy."

"I know goddamn well you're busy, you two-faced, horny little bastard. But, come on! Can't you take a little, and leave a little?"

Penelope put her dress back on and Bishop walked with her to the door, and opened it. As the door opened, she deliberately slid the zipper back up the side of her dress, in front of Cobb and the whole room.

"Really, Major", she said, confronting Cobb, "you are such a drunken, bloody nuisance." Then she turned her admiring eyes upward at Jesse.

"What a man", she sighed.

By the evening of the third day, the men of the 918th were straggling back to Archbury Field. Most were broke and hung over, but all were happy.

Savage sat in his quarters, drinking a nightcap with Stovall, Cobb, and Bishop, and listening, with vicarious enjoyment, to the exaggerated accounts of their adventures. Including the emergence of Jesse as a dark-horse winner in the battle of the sexes.

Savage noticed that Bishop was fidgeting with the ribbing, for he was inwardly chaffing as much under his new reputation, as he had been under his old one. Stovall and Cobb, both look- ing the worse for wear, excused themselves early to hit the sack, but Jesse, who seemed comparatively fresh, lingered behind.

"I'm glad you had a good time, Jesse", said Savage, when they were alone. "I wish I'd been along." "We sure missed you, General", responded Bishop, sliding into a chair, aimlessly, as though he couldn't make up his mind whether or not to stay.

Savage walked over to the hearth and stoked up the fire. Bishop sat and studied his fingernails, then fixed his eyes on the red and blue coals in the grate, seeming to find something interesting there.

"How's the weather look for tomorrow, sir", asked Bishop?

"So-so", said Savage. "Seven to eight-tenths cloud cover over most of the target areas, I'm afraid." After Savage returned to his chair, and his drink, there was another silence. Bishop still watched the fire.

"Stick around", said Savage, as Bishop made a halfhearted move to stand up. "What's the rush?" "Well, sir, no particular hurry, I guess", he said, as he relaxed back into his chair.

It was becoming clear, to Savage's observant eye, that Jesse's restlessness went far below the surface. The pre-weekend leave tension was still there, in the young man. Things, he reflected, must have failed to pan out for Bishop . . . wrong girl, maybe.

"Sweeten that drink for you, General", said Bishop, as he leaned forward, looking for an excuse to stand up?

"Haven't finished it yet, thanks." Savage took a sip.

"You know", he went on, in a conversational tone, "dames are funny. Sometimes they help get your mind off things . . . . help you blow off some steam. And sometimes they make you feel worse."

"Yeah", said Bishop, somewhat noncommittally.

"But I think you guys had the right idea. Hit the town, shack up, get it out of your system. Usually, you come back to the station feeling a lot better."

Bishop didn't answer right away.

"It all depends", he said, vaguely, "how you feel about things. It's okay for most guys, I guess." So, that was it. Savage perceived, in an intuitive flash, what must have happened. He studied Bishop through sympathetic eyes. "You got a girl back home, Jesse?"

"Yes, sir."

"Pretty nice girl, eh?"

"Yes, sir. She's really great."

He went over to the table and poured a small additional shot into his own glass.

"General", he asked, abruptly? "Do you think that I've got anything to apologize for, to the rest of these guys? Just because I want to keep myself for a girl back home."

"Jesse", said the general, as he stood back up, "you've got me on a spot there. I'm the wrong guy to ask for that kind of advice. Hell, I've been knocking around for so many years now, and taking my fun double-parked, that I'd completely forgotten that a guy could feel the way you do."

He turned and began a reconnaissance of the hearth, his eyes crinkle in some reminiscence. "Maybe I felt that way once, I guess. When I was somewhere around eighteen. Anyway, it's been too many years ago."

This revelation of Bishop's viewpoint - the honest conviction of a twenty-one year old young man - bothered him strangely.

He searched his mind for the source of the disturbance, but was unable to recognize that the source was Pamela.

"You don't think I'm . . . well, sort of a Christer, do you, General?" "Hell, no. If anything, you're just the opposite."

Bishop's eyes flashed.

"I don't give a damn what the guys think", he said. "If she can wait for me . . . I can wait for her." "Well", said Savage, "what do you say that we talk about something else? Before you get me all balled up with myself."

Bad weather continued to ground the bombers, and while returning from a visit to Wing Headquarters the next morning, the general was passing through the village of Archbury, when he saw Pamela, carrying a shopping bag, come out of a chemist's shop near the Black Swan. So he halted the car and jumped out "Hello there", called Pamela, cheerily, as he walked up to her.

Immediately he realized that he was trying to analyze her smile and her voice, trying to gauge whether they held only a normal cordiality, or a little more. He guessed, hopefully, that it was more.

"Hello, yourself", replied Savage. "What do you say to a 'arf pint in the Black Swan?" "Exactly what I need, my Cockney friend. I'm parched."

He led her into the gloomy interior of the ancient pub, where they seated themselves at a scared table, and ordered some beers.

"How's the Luftwaffe doing", asked Savage?

"Rather quiet lately. I'm sure they're grateful for the long rest your chaps have been giving them." "That works both ways", said Savage.

Their beers arrived, and they touched their beer mugs. He took out a cigar, then started feeling his pockets.

"I'm sorry I haven't any cigarettes on me", he said. "Excuse me, I'll be right back." "Please don't bother", she called out to him, as he hurried out to his car.

He returned with two packs.

"You're going to take these", he told her.

"In that case, I accept them", she said, smiling agreeably.

"That's progress. Real progress", he said. "The next step is, you're having lunch with me." "Thanks, awfully. But I'm meeting Ben Gately for lunch in half an hour."

Savage tried, not very successfully, to look unconcerned. A painful, unfamiliar emotion, so unfamiliar that he barely recognized it as jealousy, was disturbing him. For the first time, he became aware that he didn't like the idea of Gately, nor any other man, making time with this girl.

Again, he caught her scent of gardenia. He noticed the sparkling clarity of her eyes, her long, slender fingers, and the impression she always gave of immaculateness.

"I wish I'd known you were coming down in the middle of the week", he said, toying with his glass. "Couldn't we . . . well, couldn't you let me know?"

"You could ring me up."

"But, unless I rang you up every day, I might miss you."

"That's perfectly true."

Savage continued to toy with his drink, staring at it, thinking about Gately, and of Pamela's unspoken implication that if Ben Gately could take the time to phone her often, why couldn't he? Savage shrugged, and smiled at her.

"Just so long as it's somebody from the 918th", he said. "We own you, and you own us."

"How impersonal. You make me sound like a corporation. And actually, I have a very personal feeling toward you."

"Toward me?"

"Towards your Group. You see, I'm really a combat crew member." "I only wish you were", he remarked.

"But I am. I go along on every mission."

She accepted another pint of beer from the barmaid. "Yellowjacket to Wheelbarrow", she said, imitating his voice, without too much difficulty, for hers was low. "Goddamn it to hell, Joe, close it up!" Shaking his head, Savage blushed, and touched her beer mug.

"Roger, Yellowjacket", he said. "I promise to guard my language from now on. You are a full- fledged crew member, and I may even make you a Squadron Commander, if you work hard."

"Do you really think I'd have a future under you . . . . under your command?"

She saw that Savage had not missed her slip of the tongue. Blushing a trifle, she took out a compact from her gas mask bag and powered her nose.

"I'm ashamed of you", he said. "Cosmetics in gas mask bags are contrary to regulations." She gave him a quick, furtive smile.

"Please don't turn me in", she asked. "I have enough trouble already, disciplining my W.A.A.Fs. for doing the same thing."

Savage knocked a long ash from the end of his cigar, braced himself, and fastened his eyes on Pamela's.

"Look, Pamela", he said, tensely. "Let's stop this fooling around. There's been too much of it already, and it's my own damn fault."

Pamela returned his gaze, steadily, expectantly. He noticed the tiniest of tremors at the corner of her half smile, and plunged ahead.

"Whether you like it or not, and you better like it", he said. "It has suddenly occurred to me that, I'm in . . in love with you."

Pamela's reaction was the last one that he had been prepared for. She stared at his eyes so long, and so intently, that he felt as though the two of them were locked together in some kind of death struggle.

Slowly, her eyes filled with tears until they brimmed over, and then she quickly turned her head to partly shielded her face in her hand. Savage became conscious of the ticking of a small clock on the wall shelf above them, as the seconds ticked past.

He sat there, stricken and stunned, not only by Pamela's reaction to his words, but by the violence of the bomb that had exploded inside of him, blasting the words from his mouth. Words that he hadn't said for many years. Words which, even at that moment, he found difficult to believe he had spoken. But he knew, beyond any question, that they were true.

Helplessly, unable to remove his eyes from her averted head, and her slightly quivering shoulders, he slid has hand onto hers. She started to move her hand away, then gripped back hard with her fingers.

She then reached into her gas mask bag until she had found a handkerchief, then she dabbed at her eyes and nose. Finally, she turned and looked at him, from under damp eyelashes.

"Do I look dreadful", she asked?

"No. You look the way you always do. Beautiful. Only more so." "This is perfectly awful. Give me a cigarette, quickly."

He handed her a cigarette and then fumbled with the lighter so clumsily that, between them, it took three tries before she got her light.

"I'm horribly ashamed", she said. "Making such a fool of myself."

They were staring at each other in growing wonderment, in mutual disbelief. As their tense faces began to relax into shaky smiles.

"A man came up and hit me on the head, from behind", continued Savage. "What hit you?" "You!", she said, he voice sounding on the edge of hysteria. "Something you said. Something insane. Something I've been dreading ever since I met you."

"It wasn't insane. In fact, I'll repeat it. I said I loved you. Now tell me, what's dreadful about that?"

"Don't keep saying it", she pleaded. "Oh, damn it all, I don't know what I'm saying." "Relax, Pam", he said. "Just relax."

"If only you'd made passes at me. I could have brushed you off. That would have been the easy thing to do. But how can I brush off a man who breaks me down, right in front of my eyes? You've made things so abominably difficult."

"Okay then, let's make things still more difficult. I'm asking you to marry me." For a moment, he thought she was going to cry again.

"When, Frank", she asked, breathlessly?

The question was barely out, before she caught herself.

"What in the world am I saying? I must be delirious. You too. We're both absolutely crazy." "I like the way you start that speech, better."

"Let's face up to it, Frank. We'd be a miserable combination . . . we wouldn't have a chance. We mustn't even talk about it."

"We've got to."

"But we don't believe in the same things. Love. Marriage."

"I admit, I don't believe in love. But damnit, I'm in love. And it's the first time in years that I've said it."

"But it's too quick . . . . much too quick, Frank."

"Yes! But, lightning strikes quick, too. And for keeps."

"But you'd make a wretched husband. The other woman and all that. I couldn't bear it." "You are the other woman."

He squeezed her fingers tightly.

"All the other women. Wrapped up in one package."

They sat there for a few moments, catching their breaths and just looking at each other, as though for the first time.

"How does a girl know", she asked? "Until it's too late." "You'll find out. After we've been married sixty years."

There was rare beauty in her eyes, as she watched his face closely. She saw the jaw muscles moving under his skin.

"This job I've got won't last forever. They'll give me some new assignment eventually . . . where I can offer you something better than a Nissen hut."

"Frank, you've got to stop talking that way. It's all simply out of the question." Savage slowly twisted his beer mug, around and around, be- tween his fingers

"Damn that Bishop", he muttered, as though he was talking to his beer mug. "He got me into this. It's all Bishop's fault."

Pamela frowned.

"What on earth does Jesse Bishop have to do with us?"

"Sorry", he said. "I'm just rambling. I couldn't explain it . . . even to myself."

Suddenly, Savage became aware of Sergeant McIllhenny motioning to him from the doorway, and beyond McIllhenny, a jeep from the 918th.

"I'm afraid that man is here again, Pam", he said, rising. "I'm A.W.O.L. Never can tell what this weather's going to do."

He reached for his hat.

"And I have to go back to Lowestoft this afternoon", she said. "Damnit. Anyway, I'll call you from the field."

"Perhaps you won't have to, dear", she told him. "Since we are getting a little better acquainted, would you think me too forward if I were to ring you up?"

For that answer, he seized her arm and guided her towards the door, stopping at a large phone booth, hidden away in the privacy of a dark corner, beneath a staircase. He backed her into the booth and closed the door behind them.

Instantly, their lips crushed together. And he held her tightly for a long time. "You're hurting me, Frank", she said, finally.

He continued to hold her. "You're really hurting me."

At last, he released her, stepped back, and held up his thumb and forefinger a half inch apart. "Just right", he said! "And remember, Pamela. No cold feet. No backsliding."

"But, Frank . . . wait . . . I didn't really . . . nothing's settled."

"Everything's settled. You and I are going on through to the target. There isn't any turning back." He slapped his hat on his head and headed to the door.

Savage walked about the Ops room, feeling like a stranger, as he helped lay on the next day's mission. The blackboard was strange. Joe Cobb was strange. The whole room was strange.

For several minutes, lost in concentration, he would regain his old self. Then Pamela would flash across his mind, like a white light, filling his insides with an indescribable warmth.

He was summoned to the phone in his office. It was Pamela.

"I have to leave right off", she said, and the sound of her voice pierced through his heart like a rapier. "Say something to me, Frank. Talk to me."

"When can I see you?" "When can you come?"

"Will you be home for the weekend?"

"It's never certain. Could you come to Lowestoft?" "If we get a stand-down. Even if I have to crawl." "Flying is faster."

"Then I'll fly."

There was a paused, as both of their minds raced. "Well", she asked?

"Well . . . what about the cold feet? How are they doing?"

"Come up and see", her voice was almost a whisper. "God bless, I really must dash now, darling." "Good-bye, . . . darling."

After he hung up the phone, the word lingered in his mouth, as though he had just discovered it.

CHAPTER NINE

MISSING IN ACTION

Satisfied that everything was shaping up properly for the next day's mission. Savage left the Ops room and walked over to the Officers' Club for a late dinner.

A few ground-pounder officers and a hand full of fliers, not scheduled for the mission, sat around the lounge drinking. Major Kaiser came over and offered to buy Savage a beer.

"Thanks, Doc", said Savage. "But I'm leading the mission tomorrow and beer makes me dopey." Kaiser looked concerned.

"Speaking as a Flight Surgeon, that reminds me of a question I've been wanting to ask the general. I hope you don't plan to lead all of the missions, sir."

Savage laughed.

"How many is too many, Doc?"

"It's a medical fact, general, that this high altitude bombing business is twice as hard on a man in his thirties, as on younger men in their twenties."

"Hell, Doc. I never felt better in my whole life as I do now. It agrees with me.

"I wouldn't guarantee that, sir. I don't want to sound alarming in any sense, but I've been keeping an eye on you since that last mission. And I know the first signs of overstrain when I see them."

Savage laughed, and patted the Flight Surgeon on the back.

"And I've been watching you too, Don. I've kinda noticed a course tremor in your drinking hand lately."

"But I'm serious, General."

Savage fetched Kaiser another pat on the back. He felt half drunk on the intoxication of Pamela's phone call.

"Cripes, Don, you quacks tickle the hell out of me. Why don't you psychoanalyze yourselves instead of worrying about non-excitable guys like me?" He held out his hand.

"Look at that. Like a rock."

Kaiser regarded the general with a protesting smile.

"I'm really serious, sir", he persisted. "Any man, no matter how strong, can succumb to a war neurosis, if the stress level reaches his threshold."

"It's all double talk to me", said Savage. "Neurosis. Thresholds. Hell, I can toss that lingo around too. But, any time I get to feeling flak-happy, Doc, I promise to take a rest.

Now, is there anything more important bothering you?" "No", said Kaiser, swallowing the rest of his beer'

His glance happened to fall on Gately, who was sitting in a corner, reading the Stars and Stripes.

"Oh, there is one other matter, sir", he continued. "Colonel Gately spoke to me awhile ago. About the mission. He seemed reluctant to see you personally."

"Yes?"

"He's complaining about his back, sir. It's been troubling him since that ditching . . ." "He wants you to ground him tomorrow?"

"Well, sir, he's not sure whether he's safe to go."

"So, now it's his back. It used to be head colds." Savage's expression seemed to harden.

"Hell, no. He'll go as scheduled."

Savage noticed a bare suggestion of a shrug in the Flight Surgeon's shoulders.

A week later, Savage stood atop the control tower, watching the bombers of the 918th approaching the field from a strike against Oschersleben, Germany. He had been on the tower for nearly an hour, trying not to let thoughts of his frustration about Pamela creep into the emptiness of the waiting period.

Due to a freak spell of clear weather, with missions coming thick and fast, it had been out of the question for him to go to Lowestoft, since the day the roof had fallen in on him at the Black Swan. But at the sight of the B-17s, all else was swept from his mind and, as always, he suffered a greater anxiety from being on the ground, instead of in the air.

Cobb had led the mission today, to give the general a breather after two missions in a row, in which, despite fierce air battles and heavy damage, Savage's record of not losing any crews was still intact. However, on one of the other missions, led by one of the Squadron Commanders, the Group had lost three crews.

For this reason, coupled with the increasing losses most of the other Groups had been sustaining, since the inception of strikes into Germany, had convinced Savage, anew, that the Eighth Air Force's most critical problem was still that of combat leadership. The 918th, he knew, would be needing him for a long time.

His tired face tensed up as he counted the planes in formation. Three were missing.

Then, off in the distance, he spotted two stragglers, down low, heading for the runway, one of them trailing smoke. He waited several minutes longer, scanning the horizon, in vain, for the third missing aircraft, then he hurried below to his car and drove directly to Cobb's hard-stand.

As soon as the props had stopped turning, he called up to Cobb, who thrust his head out the cockpit window.

"Did you hit it", Savage asked? "Clobbered it, I think, sir."
"Who's missing?"
"Bishop."

Savage's heart sunk like a stone. He felt wobbly in the knees, but he gave no sign of it. Instead of asking questions about what had happened, he waited until Cobb left the cockpit and swung down out of the nose hatch.

"Didn't look too good, General", he said, as he lit up a cigarette. "Jesse got a direct burst right over the target area. He went into a vertical dive towards the deck and disappeared into some low clouds. No chutes seen by my crew."

Savage listened to Cobb's description of what happened, attentively, but his eyes did not falter once. Cobb, on the other hand, looked like he was close to tears.

"The best damn little son-of-a-bitch in the whole Group", concluded Cobb.

"I hate to lose anybody, Joe", said Savage. "But it could have been a lot worse. It's just one crew. Don't let it get you down."

Back in his office, Savage relayed Cobb's firsthand mission report by phone to General Henderson, who expressed official satisfaction with the damage assessment indicated by the strike photos, but grumbled to Savage about the severe losses two other Groups had taken. The 918th had been the lead Group, and Cobb had admitted to having gotten slightly off course going into the target.

Savage immediately stood up for Cobb, reminding Henderson that it was always easy to lead a good mission from the ground. Henderson agreed and changed the subject.

"By the way, Frank", said Henderson, "General Barker is visiting from Washington, and he'd like to come down and make a mission with your Group. Shall I send him on?"

"How much does he weigh?"

Henderson was undecided as to whether or not Savage was joking. "Oh, about a hundred and eighty, I guess."

"I wish General Barker had brought along about a hundred and eighty pounds of the armor plate that I've been begging for, from Wright Field, to save our crews the trouble of pulling flak out of their butts. How about doing me a favor and send him somewhere else."

"He specified your Group."

"Hell, I thought the waiting list had dropped to zero, lately, since we started going to Germany." "It's slumped, all right. But Barker wants to go."

"To be honest with you, sir, it's a damn nuisance. These V.I.Ps. worry the crews they fly with. And what's worse, they hurt morale."

"That's news to me. How?"

"By coming back from one ride as a passenger, trussed up in two chutes, climbing out at the hard- stand and bumping right into a Silver Star, that's waiting for them."

Savage knew that Henderson's blood pressure was taking a jump, for Henderson had been awarded a Silver Star after his lone mission.

"I didn't ask for that ribbon they gave me", said Henderson, tartly.

"I'm referring to visiting firemen", said Savage. "And believe me, it's a real problem . . . one that the other Group Commanders have hesitated to bring up."

"What am I suppose to tell Barker?"

"Tell him that we have scarlet fever down here."

"All right, all right, we'll skip it. Now, number two. How soon do you think you can wind up your job there?"

Savage almost clenched his teeth clear through his cigar. He waited so long to reply that Henderson clicked his receiver to see if the had been cut off.

"I'm still here", said Savage. "But your question is a little baffling. I'll leave the day I have air leaders experienced enough to keep the Group out of trouble. It was my impression that we had reached an understanding about this."

"That's just fine. It settles everything, except for the fact that I don't have an understanding with the Pentagon, and I've got to fill that OTU assignment. Pritchard's saving it for you and he seems to think that it's about time you were available."

"He's been misinformed."

"Well, you think it over. And congratulations on staying on the ground today, for a change." Then Henderson rang off.

Savage stood on his feet, somewhat perturbed, and began to pace the floor. He was resisting the impulse to call Pritchard, whom he had not had a private conversation with since their meeting, at the duck pond, at PINETREE. But Savage knew that Pritchard had been snowed under by the mountainous problems confronting his fast growing air force.

He'd cross that particular bridge, he decided, when he had to. For now though, he quickly forget about Henderson, under the pressure of an emotion with a higher priority.

Jesse Bishop forced his way into the general's consciousness, filtering into his feelings through the anesthetic which had frozen him against the first shock of the news. But now, the anesthetic had worn off.

Savage was face to face with his pain, and he hated the pain. Not only because it was there, but because he dared not acknowledge it, even to himself. It had no place here at Archbury Field.

Terribly unforgiving of any weakness in others, demanding by his own example that his men be harder than the metal of their B-17s. Savage now combated with his own strength, against any indulgence of his own personal feelings.

Pamela. That was another threat. Pamela, Henderson, and Bishop. A three way tension tore at his mind and feelings, turn- ing his face blank.

Stovall came in, carrying some papers, but stopped halfway across the room when he saw Savage's face. His skin was the color of dough.

"Excuse me, sir", he said, quickly. "I've got the wrong papers here..."

He turned and left, after noting the instant reversion of the general's expression back to normal. Savage started to call out to Stovall, but was afraid of his voice, afraid that it would betray him.

Stovall came back and now it was his turn to cover his feelings. For, he had seen something he had never expected to see, the first chink. The first crack in a piece of human steel.

The lights were on late, in Stovall's office. With his tie undone and his shirt collar open, the Ground Exec was having an unusually difficult time with a Missing In Action report. A pile of ashes, and his pipe, laid in his ashtray and a half empty cup of cold, black coffee was at his elbow.

Over and over, he shuffled through a stack of Interrogation forms, with which the Intelligence Officer had supplied him - a summary of eyewitness reports from the crews who had seen Bishop's plane go down.

Savage wandered in.

"Working kind of late, aren't you, Harvey?" "Yes, sir."

He leaned back in his chair and stretched. "Maybe I'm just slowing down."

Savage glanced casually over the papers in front of the major. "Need any help?"

Savage's voice was still casual, but Stovall knew him well enough to detect that it was a little too casual.

"M.I.A. report", he said. "Kind of hard to make heads or tails of some of these gunner's accounts." He was careful not to mention Bishop's name. But, in the minds of all of the men at Archbury,

Stovall knew, that the name was present, like a flag fluttering at half-mast over the airfield.

Savage sat down and pulled out a cigar, clipped it and then discovered that his lighter was dry. Stovall knocked the ash from out of his pipe, sucked on it until it glowed red, then handed it to the general.

"Thanks, Harvey."

Stovall had barely returned his attention to his work when Savage interrupted him, again. "Tail gunners are your best bet", he said. "From a crew flying a wing position."

From his tone, he might just as well have been discussing a weather report.

"Yeah, I know", said Stovall, sliding a sheet of paper to one side. "This guy's got about the only specific information I can use."

After a pause, the general stood up and slowly walked past the desk toward the door. But Stovall noticed that Savage's eyes had flicked down, surreptitiously, at the tail gunner's name - Hillery - scrawled on the report.

"Better turn in, Harvey", he said. "I'll get over to the quarters soon. I think I'll drop by the Sergeant's Club and have a beer with the men. I haven't been by there for over a week."

As Savage's footsteps died away, down the hall, the Ground Exec's eyes dropped their guard, disclosing an expression of profound sympathy and understanding, of another man's suffering.

Savage warmed to the reception which greeted his arrival at the Sergeant's Club. There was no stiffness, or evidence that the men felt that their style was being cramped by the presence of a general officer. Those whom he came into contact with, were glad to see him, and showed it, while the rest simply went about their business.

Sergeants Nero and Coulter steered him to the bar for a beer, pulling rank on him when he tried to pay. After some shop talk about generator failures, Savage asked whether a gunner named Hillery was present.

"Over there, sir", said Nero. "Do you want me to get him?"

"No", said Savage. "I was just curious. I heard something about him the other day."

"He's a pretty sharp tail gunner ", chimed in Coulter. "He got credit for three FWs on the Vegesack mission."

"Of course", said Savage. "That's what it was."

Presently, Sergeant Hillery walked over to order another beer. Savage edged his way along the bar, until he was standing next to him.

"Nice going, Sergeant Hillery", he said. "How's that, sir?"

"That bag of FWs over Vegesack." "Oh . . . well. Gee, thanks, General."

The sergeant was delighted, and entirely without vanity, but with an honest pride in an achievement that constituted a high-water mark in his Army career. He never stopped to wonder how the general knew his name.

"I must have closed my eyes tight and squeezed the triggers", he added, modestly. Savage laughed.

"There's nothing wrong with your eyesight from what I hear, Sergeant", he said.

They chatted for several minutes until, suddenly, Hillery perceived that he had attracted closer attention from the general. The sergeant had just started talking about the day's mission and was describing enemy fighter tactics, in detail, continuing to hold the absorbed interest of the Group Commander.

Finally, he got around to his version of how Bishop's crew had gone down, noting that Savage's curiosity seemed to relax somewhat.

"There were no signs of any chutes, sir", he concluded. "They went straight down into the clouds. I'm afraid to say it, but it looked to me like they all bought it."

Savage bought Hillery a beer. He chatted a little longer, then said good night, leaving his beer half finished on the bar.

Savage was at his desk early the next morning, working at top speed, when he heard a knock and saw Major Kaiser standing at the door.

Come right in, Don." "Yes, sir."

The Fight Surgeon was carrying a large flat carton under his arm. But the general scarcely noticed it, because he was struck by the peculiar expression on Kaiser's face.

Savage could have sworn that the man had just been involved in some kind of serious accident. "May I sit down, sir?"

"Yes. Sure, here's a chair."

The general pushed the chair toward Kaiser, who sat down and looked at Savage with anxious eyes. The general conscious- ly exercised his self control, forcing his brain into readiness to absorb a new problem for which there was precious little room.

"I'm guilty of a terrible miscalculation, sir", said Kaiser. "What's wrong now, Doc?"

Savage frowned with concern.

"It's Ben Gately. He's over in the hospital and I've got him in a plaster cast. He couldn't even walk to the mess for breakfast this morning."

"Why wasn't I told that he was wounded yesterday", asked Savage, sharply? "That's the hell of it, sir. It wasn't yesterday. Here, take a look at this."

Kaiser opened his package, took out an X-ray plate and stood it up on the general's desk, against the glare of the desk lamp. Savage bent down, quickly, staring at the spinal column limned on the glass.

The Doc took a pencil and pointed to one of the vertebrae. "A crack of the anterior lip of the vertebral body". he said.

"Keerist,", said Savage, beginning to turn a bit pale. "You mean he broke his back in that ditching?"

"Not exactly. But that's what it amounts to."

"But . . . criminy, Doc, he's flown two missions since the ditching." "Yes, sir."

Kaiser cleared his throat.

"And without a complaint, since his original request to be grounded. If he'd reported back to me I might have become suspicious of a more serious condition. It's absolutely my fault, sir."

Savage walked over to the window and back again, crumpling up his cigar in his fist, until shreds of tobacco fell to the floor.

"I only wish it were your fault, Don. Or somebody else's. But it's all mine!" He walked back to the window, again, and turned around.

"Why the hell am I standing around here for, Don? Come on, we're going over to your place."

Kaiser and the general arrived at the hospital in double-quick time. They walked down a center aisle, connecting several of the Nissen huts and, at length, turned off into a round ceilinged ward filled with Purple Heart cases.

Gately, lying in a cast and with weights attached to his feet, looked up from one of the beds at the far end. Savage approached the bed slowly, painfully aware of a more intense hostility in Gately's eyes than he had anticipated.

Meeting those eyes, rejected by them, Savage had to force himself to cover the last few feet, until he was standing beside the bed. Now that he was confronted by its occupant, he felt completely at a loss on how to begin.

He swallowed hard.

"How, . . . how do you feel, Ben", he finally asked?

Gately gave him a long, cold stare and Savage began to wonder whether Gately would answer at all. Then the former Air Exec raised himself, slightly, up on his elbows.

"Come to think of it, General", he said, with bitterness, but without self-pity, making every word count, "I can remember times when I've felt worse."

Gately's reply was so cogent, so aptly to the point, that the general lost track of the words that he had come to say. He remained silent for a moment, then looked at Kaiser.

"How long, Major", he asked, grasping for any conversational straw, "before he'll be okay?" "A couple of months, probably, sir. Although one month is possible."

"One month", said Gately, looking at Kaiser, not at Savage, "is more like it, Doc. The sooner you get me out of this iron maiden the better."

"We'll do our best, Ben", replied Kaiser. Savage regarded Kaiser anxiously.

"Are you equipped to give him the proper treatment here", he asked?

"I believe so, sir. But we can move him to a rear hospital, if you think it advisable."

"Just leave me here, Doc", said Gately, vehemently. "I'm not going anywhere . . . except back to flying duty. As soon as you get rid of this backache for me."

"There's nothing to get upset about", Kaiser told him. "We'll have you up and around soon enough."

"Okay", said Gately, making the word sound more like: See that you do! By now, Savage had collected his thoughts.

"Ben", he said. "I'm not much of a letter writer, but I want to write a letter to your father. I'd like to get his address."

Gately stared at him, dubiously.

"Why worry him, General", he asked? "By the time he gets a letter, I'll be out of here." "What I want to write", said Savage, "won't worry him a bit."

Across Gately's mind there flashed a vivid picture of another occasion, and the sarcasm of Savage's voice saying: "Why don't you cable your father? He'd be goddamn proud of you!" Mixed emotions stirred within him.

"Care of the Joint Chiefs of Staff", he said, coldly. "Washington, D.C." "Thanks, Ben. I'm going to write to him tonight."

Savage studied Gately's unrelenting expression. Then the general moved a little closer to him, while clearing his throat.

"You don't hate me", he said.. "You just think you do." He waited, but there was no answer.

"You never did hate me. You hated the things inside yourself that didn't belong there. You thought you hated me when I dragged them out of you into the open . . . and showed them to you."

Still, no answer. Then Savage perceived that Gately had begun to look terribly tired. "I'm shoving off now."

He reached out his hand, halfway towards Gately, but the latter made no move and merely stared up at him, blankly. Savage lingered a moment longer, his eyes looking at the floor.

He looked up.

"Get some shut-eye", he added, gently.

After Savage and Kaiser had gone, Gately lit a cigarette, blew the smoke upward and gazed at the ceiling. He heard footsteps on the concrete walk outside the window and recognized the general's voice.

"Pretty painful", asked Savage?

"Agonizingly so, sir. There's bone impinging on the nerve, you know. Long hours at high altitude. I know better men than Gately that couldn't have stood that kind of pain for one mission - let alone two."

There was a pause.

"You're dead wrong, Don."

Gately could hear Savage's voice distinctly. "There are no better men than Ben Gately."

For a long time the former Air Exec stared at the ceiling, as though he were paralyzed. Everything that had been pent up inside of him - the humiliation - the hate - the bitterness - the frustration - all at once let go.

He turned his head and buried his face in his pillow.

CHAPTER TEN

WIDEWING

The following morning Savage entered the hospital carrying a small paper bag, containing six eggs. And although it was early enough that most of the men in the ward were still asleep, he found Gately lying awake and listening to a news broadcast, turned down low, from a small radio beside the head of his bed. Upon seeing the general, Gately smiled. While wondering what had come over him since the previous evening, Savage held out his hand, Gately took it, and the two men exchanged a long handshake. But there was an even warmer greeting in the meet- ing of their eyes - Gately's being clear, Savage's being a little misty.

"Morning, sir", said Gately, belatedly. "Good morning, Ben . . . how's the back?" "I'm a cinch, sir. Just give me about a week." "I'll give you anything you say, Ben."

Gately glanced over at his radio, turning it off.

"You shouldn't have given me your own radio", he said. "I wish you'd take it back, sir . . . there's a big one over there in the corner."

"Keep it", said Savage. "I never use it anyway." "Thanks, General."

"I've got something else you may be able to use", he said, rolling his six eggs out on the blanket. Gately's eyes opened wide with pleasure.

"That sleeping pill must still be working, sir", he said. "For a second I dreamed I was looking at six eggs . . . in the shell."

Savage just grinned.

"Sergeant McIllhenny's a pretty fair scrounger, since he got married. He sent these to you with the compliments of him and Misses McIllhenny."

"Cackle berries", said Gately, picking up one of the eggs and examining it, as though it were a precious jewel. "A genuine cackle berry." His face then assumed an expression of frowning calculation.

"Well, now I've got a problem, sir", he continued. "Whether to stretch these out for six days . . . or eat them in pairs for three days."

"Eat 'em all for breakfast this morning", said Savage. "Not me, sir. I think I'll kind of stretch them out."

"There's more where those came from, Ben. McIllhenny told his wife that if any hen fails to make a maximum effort, the bird goes in the pot."

"Seriously, general. I'd be embarrassed if you brought any more. These are plenty. Hell, I'm rich."

After chatting with Gately a few minutes more, Savage said good-bye, promising he'd be dropping by again soon. On his way out of the ward, he stopped to talk with a couple of wounded gunners, who were awake, waved again at Gately from the door, and left.

Later, after Savage had made a thorough analysis of the noon-weather sequence, he gave Stovall a telephone number where he could be reached at Lowestoft in an emergency. Then he went to his quarters, changed into his best uniform, drove to the hanger line and took off from Archbury Field in a small staff aircraft.

It was typical English flying weather - a bagful of visibility and a couple of yards of altitude. This kind of flying demanded Savage's close attention to his navigation, as identical looking villages and fields appeared in the mist beneath the low clouds, and sped by under the nose of the plane.

In the States, he told himself, you wouldn't dream of taking off in such weather. But, in England, you had to go fly or let your airplanes rot in storage.

Twice, when he was forced down to chimney height and squinting through his rain smeared windshield at shiny wet roofs, he almost decided to turn back. But each time, the ceiling lifted just enough.

Deep down, he was enjoying his contest with the weather, a purely physical obstacle separating him from Pamela, and one that could be surmounted. Actually, the dirty weather was his friend, for it had enabled him to leave Archbury with a clear con-science.

He found himself wishing that some obstacles of the mind and emotions were as readily susceptible to a solution. For days he had alternated between giddy confidence and qualms of doubt, about Pamela's ultimate reaction to his proposal.

Before long he landed on a small sod field near Lowestoft, just behind another small plane. He met the planes pilot, an R.A.F. officer, in the Operations Office, who introduced himself as Group Captain Heeley, and he told the general that he was now the Liaison Officer from PINETREE, for RT- Intercepts.

During the short drive over to Pamela's station, Savage was gratified to learn that Heeley's original one-man section had grown to two officers and eleven enlisted men - a reflection of the increasing importance General Henderson had been attaching to the work of plotting enemy fighter reaction. Armed with a graphic record of enemy tactics on each mission, Bomber Com- mand was already doing a much better job at guessing what the Germans would try the next time.

Passing through a dense wooded area, which concealed some radio antennae, their car pulled up in front of a squat, unimport-ant looking concrete building. The sentry on duty recognized Group Captain Heeley and motioned him inside, but he stopped Savage to check his identification.

"Right you are, General", he said, promptly. "I have your pass already made out."

Savage walked down a long hall, past a large, low lit, room in which a dozen W.A.A.Fs. with earphones sat in front of radio receivers, and stopped at the open door of a small office. He looked in and saw that Pamela was sitting at her desk, entering pencil notations on a report.

He felt as though an invisible hand had suddenly reached up and put its fingers around his throat, choking his windpipe and preventing him from speaking. He just stared at her for several moments before she looked up.

"Frank!"

She jumped up, hurried around the desk and toward him, as he moved forward to meet her. He hugged her against himself, his mouth against hers, and then she moved her head back a little, looking into his eyes.

"It's about time, don't you think", she said?

He kissed her again - a much longer kiss. And neither of them heard the heavy footsteps coming up behind them, until a elderly R.A.F. officer, with a handlebar mustache, burst into the room.

He stopped dead in his tracks, his eyes wide open. Pamela, blushing a radiant pink, immediately released Savage, who swung around in confusion.

"I beg your . . . . ", began the R.A.F. officer.

Simultaneous exclamations from Frank and Pamela canceled him out. The intruder, extremely embarrassed, started to back out towards the door, nodding his head awkwardly, but Pamela stepped forward for a fresh start.

"Air Commodore", she said, "I'd like to present Brigadier General Savage . . . Air Commodore Satterlee."

"I'm quite delighted to meet you, sir", responded the air commodore, as he continued backing out.

Savage, trying to look calm, merely bowed his head.

"General Savage, is . . . my fiancé", said Pamela, as she straightened her blouse with one hand and smoothed back her hair with the other.

Savage's heart leaped at the word.

"Quite", said the air commodore, again, acting as though he were frozen, like the victim of a nightmare who couldn't move.

"You're a lucky chap, sir. Splendid . . . well . . . God bless."

Bowing, harrumphing and smiling, he backed out into the hall just in time to collide with the hurrying form of a rather large W.A.A.F., to whom he apologized hastily and then disappeared.

"Fiancé, eh", said Savage, as he grinned at Pamela. "Don't forget, I've got a high ranking witness."

W.A.A.Fs. constantly hurried in and out of Pamela's office, and her phone rang incessantly, rendering any conversation with Frank, who sat on a chair beside her desk, nearly impossible.

"Hello, Eleven Group", she said. while Savage listened more to the lilting, clipped enunciation of her speech, than to the sense of what she was saying. "DDI-Four-B here. Can you scramble? Have you one missing on your last sweep? . . . . Here's a Jerry intercept for you; I believe you'll find your man drifting about in his dingy, in the middle of a bloody mine field . . . Will you take the co- ordinates?"

He was happy just to sit there, watching her face and hands, listening to her voice and the occasional trill of her laugh. He felt a little bit like the way he once did when, just out of college, he had sat across the aisle, in a train car, from a famous movie act- ress, whose simplest words and gestures assumed the quality of high drama.

Taking advantage of a lull, Pamela explained that her deputy was in the hospital with the flu.

"It's double the work for me", she told Savage. "But there's one consolation. I shall be off at sixteen hundred, and we'll have a place where we can go and talk, alone."

"I'm not wishing your roommate any hard luck, but . . . ." Pamela laughed.

"Not my roommate", she said. "My house mate. We were lucky enough to get a small cottage down the road. I'll make you a spot of tea and you can stretch out in front of the fire, in your slippers."

"Great", said Savage, beaming. "I didn't bring any slippers, though. And I ought to get back to Archbury some time tonight."

"But you mustn't", she replied. "Not in this weather. There's a bed for you in the visitors' quarters."

"Well, we don't have to worry about that right now", he said.

Another W.A.A.F. entered with a message for Pamela, which occupied her attention for several minutes. When she was free again, Savage told her about Gately's hospitalization and about the tremendous respect he now had for the man.

He also told her of his remorse over ordering him to fly with his injury, and of their reconciliation as of that morning. She let him know, without any hint of I-told-you-so, how wonderfully happy she was about it.

Then her face seem to cloud over with sadness and concern, when she was told about Bishop's aircraft being shot down.

"But you didn't mention it in your letter", she protested.

"I couldn't think of anything else, except you ", he lied, "while I was writing." She reached over and squeezed his hand, then frowned as something else occurred to her.

"What day did Jesse get shot down, Frank", she asked?

"On the eighth", he said, promptly. "Pam, I'm just beginning to notice that your hair . . . ."

"Do you remember the time", she interrupted, in spite of his obvious desire not to discuss Bishop any further.

"1423 hours, GMT", he said. "You know, from a certain angle, it's got red highlights in it. What do you do to it?"

"Were there any parachutes", she persisted? "No-one saw any, so apparently not."

"Do you know the co-ordinates where Jesse went down?"

"Not in my head. Somewhere near Oschersleben. I wasn't there. Joe Cobb was." Pamela called in a W.A.A.F. sergeant.

"Bring me the log for the eighth", she told the sergeant, referring to her note pad. "Oschersleben. I want all the RT-Intercepts within a half-hour before and after 1423, GMT."

Savage sat bolt upright. The sergeant was gone for several minutes, during which Savage sat in his chair with ill-concealed impatience, thankful that Pamela was busy on the phone.

Finally the sergeant returned, carrying a type written file, which she placed on the desk in front of Pamela. Savage stood up and leaned over her shoulder, staring at the cryptic entries in the file, until she had hung up.

"Now, let's see", she said, running her pencil down along the margin and reading rapidly. "There were several shoot-downs before 1423 . . . the last one was at 1418 . . . which would have been too early. And there's nothing listed at 1423 or 1424."

She read further, silently, then suddenly paused.

"Hold on", she exclaimed! "At 1425. Maybe we've got something." Savage leaned over still closer.

"A shoot-down by flak. Dickeauto Amerikanische." "That's right", breathed Savage!

"Reported by a Me-109 pilot, named Heinz. Call sign - Schwarzkopf Acht." "Go on", said Savage, getting a bit closer!

"Please, dear, your in my light . . . Nothing at 1426 or 27. And look, Frank! 1428, same pilot, same call sign . . he contact- ed a Luftwaffe airdrome north of Oschersleben . . . Send troops. Farm. One mile east of your airdrome. Crash landing. American heavy bomber. Ten survivors scattering south towards woods. Will circle area. Over."

Savage straightened up, slowly, and then sank back onto his chair, while Pamela, in great excitement, continued to check through a few subsequent entries.

"The next B-17 shoot-down", she told him, after finally looking up, "was eleven minutes later, and about forty miles west of Oschersleben. Frank! This 1428 could only have been Jesse!"

Savage, smiling, in almost tearful relief, stood up and began taking short paces, back and forth, in front of her desk.

"All of them are okay", he said, quietly, but jubilantly. "All ten of them, okay!" His eyes shone. He pulled Pamela from behind her desk and hugged her.

"I get magic from you", he said. You're wonderful."

"I just hope this won't spoil it for you, darling", she said, "but you didn't let me finish. Jesse will be eating out of a Red Cross parcel for a long time. That pilot that circled. He reported the whole crew was taken prisoner. All of them."

Savage was still grinning

"So what", he asked? "I can think of worse places than a P.o.W. camp." Another thought occurred to him.

"How about our headquarters? Did they get a report on this?" "Of course. Air Ministry passes it all on to you."

She smiled at him, mischievously.

"What your chaps do with it after that, I can't say." Savage wagged an admonitory finger at her.

"You need to watch your Anglo-American relations", he said. "Remember?" "I'll do my bit right now", she said.

Glancing first at the door, she gave him a quick kiss.

A slanting rain beat down, in gusts, against the windowpanes, but inside Pamela's cottage all was snug and warm. She and Frank sat in stuffed chairs, drawn up close together before the hearth.

On a nearby table, next to Savage's empty musette bag, lay a heap of the general's burnt offerings. They included, four cartons of American cigarettes, two bottles of Scotch, three cans of salted peanuts, two cans of anchovies, a jar of strawberry jam, a box of Kleenex, some lipstick, and a pair of nylon stockings.

They were quite comfortable, sipping Savage's brand of tea - in this case, Scotch and soda. And for some time they simply sat, enjoying each other's company with small talk, each of them waiting for the other to turn the conversation to the momentous thoughts uppermost in their minds.

Pamela was the first to become serious.

"Frank", she asked, "if you'll forgive me for talking shop, isn't it about time for them to give you . .

. a different posting?"

"I've got a pretty good job", he said.

"Yes, but it means combat", she replied. Your second tour of combat." "I know", he said, quietly. "But it won't last forever."

She took a deep swallow of her drink.

"I should hope not", she remarked. "Frank, this is the first thing I've ever asked you to do. And it may be the most import-ant."

He set down his glass and turned his eyes from the fire to her face.

"Don't think that I'm cowardly", she continued, "but I'm asking you, for my sake, to stop flying combat, just as soon as you possibly can."

"I will", he said, guardedly.

"You've got to give me something more definite to go on", she told him. "How soon, Frank?"

"The minute, the second I know my job is done."

She ran her fingertip around the top of her glass, turning away from him to stare at the fire. When she spoke again, her voice was unsteady.

"I am a coward, an awful coward", she stated. "But an truthful one, anyway. I've been a coward ever since we met."

Savage took a long drink, then reached for her hand and looked into her eyes. "I met a war first", he simply said Both of them were silent, for what seemed to each other like a long time. After a while, Frank got up and poked at the fire.

"Reminds me", he said. "I'd better check the weather. Okay if I use your phone?" She stifled the urge to say no.

"Over there", she said, gesturing towards a small table.

Savage put in a call to the airfield, got hold of the weather forecaster, and listened thoughtfully. He returned the receiver to it's cradle and then found her staring at him.

"The stuff's lifting. I can get through."

As he walked slowly back to the fireplace, she stood up and went over to him, laying her hands on his shoulders.

"Darling", she said, shyly.

She reached up with her right hand and ran her long fingers over his forehead and back through his hair. Through her other hand she felt his shoulders tremble.

She led him over to the couch, stretched out with her head on a pillow, and pulled him down alongside of her. Taking her in his arms, feeling the softness of her against the whole length of his body, Frank was overcome by the turbulence of the deepest bliss he had ever felt.

A full minute passed, during which he believed that he could never let go, with their lips pressed firmly together. Finally, he forced himself to sit up and made a visible effort to get to his feet. But, instead, he turned and laid his head on her lap, as she also reached a sitting position.

"Frank, . . . dear", she asked, out of breath?

She stroked his hair and gazed at his face, with eyes that were liquid with tenderness. "No, Pam, don't talk."

"I must, darling . . . I don't want you to go back tonight . . . even if there isn't a cloud in the sky. I want you to stay here, in the cottage. With me."

He stared at her, and then toward the rain swept window, his eyes gradually losing their charge of emotion and longing. His expression altered, radically, into one of meditation.

"Are you thinking", she asked? He cleared his throat.

"Yes", he murmured. "Thinking." "Don't", she whispered.

But he continued to stare at the window, as though it were a windshield of an airplane. And looking as he must look, she imagined, when he was sitting in the cockpit, leading hundreds of bombers, weighing the factors of enemy fighters, flak, weather, and all the other variables confronting him.

Actually, the old Frank Savage was fighting at close quarters with the new Frank Savage. Where his old self told him, as it had once told Pamela: "I don't think a roll in the hay is too important"- his changed outlook told him that any relationship of intimacy with Pamela would be devastatingly important to him.

He knew that he couldn't take her in his stride and then forget about her, because he would end up spending half of his time at Archbury wondering how soon he could get back to Lowestoft again. He also knew that he would be rationalizing himself into excuses for going back, at the expense of the single-minded concentration demanded of him in his command of the 918th.

Did he have the right to let himself become more interested in living, than reaching the target? Did he not once say to a bunch of young airmen:

"Consider yourselves already dead." Didn't that go for him too?

He lit a cigarette and inhaled deeply. Finally he stirred, sat up, paused for a moment, then got to his feet, facing her.

He flicked the cigarette into the fireplace behind him and then gave her his answer, which was the shortest, and yet the longest, she had ever heard.

"It's no good", he told her.

She wanted to be angry with him, plead with him if necessary, but his eyes told her that it would be futile. He had thought it through to a decision and that he would not alter it . . nor explain it.

She stood up, too. He took her in his arms and held her in a prolonged, breathless, embrace. Then, without looking back, he walked to the door, picked up his hat and musette bag, stepped outside into the drizzle, and was gone.

Pamela quickly moved to a front window and watched his figure retreating through the gloom.

Two days later, Savage was instructed to attend a meeting for all Group and Wing Commanders at WIDEWING. He felt a novel sense of appreciation as his fellow commanders began fill- ing the conference room.

All of their faces were tired. Probably, reflected Savage, at no place in the world and at no time in history, could one room have been occupied by so highly a select group of men.

These were the main bearings about which the wheel of the air war revolved. Any burned-out bearing here could mean a breakdown of the complex machinery which began with the enlisted technicians at the air bases and spread up to the highest levels of command in Washington.

The blank checks written by Roosevelt and Churchill, to fight this war, were being honored, or repudiated, at the bank window of combat by these leaders. For they functioned just below the precise dividing line between personal leadership and the upper echelons, where responsibility became increasingly impersonal and remote from the flesh and blood of human pawns.

When General Pritchard and General Henderson walked into the room, their faces were unusually solemn.

"Gentlemen", began Pritchard, "I must begin by cautioning all of you, as emphatically as I know how, that the plans we will be discussing at this meeting are for your eyes and ears alone, with the exception of the minimum number of your subordinates who will be directly concerned. I repeat that any breach of security will completely nullify the chances for success of the most vitally important assignment yet given the Eighth Air Force."

Henderson nodded gravely in agreement.

"It's going to be a tough one", continued Pritchard. "It must be exactly planned down to the last pint of fuel, the last round of ammunition, and the last second of time. Losses in men and aircraft are estimated to be heavy, but if the mission is successful, the military cost will be cheap.

My directive for this mission was worked out in Washington by the Combined and Joint Chiefs of Staff. That directive makes it clear that, aside from purely military considerations, grave political considerations are involved, that will affect the morale of our Allies, and operations in other theaters.

And one last thing. Because of the continuing expansion of the Eighth Air Force and the creation of the Ninth Air Force, I'll be moving my operational headquarters to PINETREE after this meeting."

He paused.

"General Henderson will take it from here." Henderson stepped forward.

"First", he said, "if any officer present is certain that he will be required to fly over enemy territory in the next six days, I must ask him to leave the room now."

Three colonels excused themselves and left.

"I will briefly outline the operation, and then we'll go into the details."

He motioned to a sergeant, who rolled up a screen in front of a huge wall map. Henderson then picked up a pointer, but stood to one side for several seconds, to allow his audience to absorb the story told by the red strings stretched across part of the map.

Savage, along with the others, caught his breath.

A red string was stretched from England, to a point deep into Germany, then split into a fork. Part of the fork led northeast to Hambrucken, the other ran southeast to Bonhofen. From Bonhofen, the string continued east, to a base in the Soviet Union, at the extreme range of a B-17 equipped with "Tokio" wingtip fuel tanks.

Savage's heart pounded, as the skeleton of the plan quickly crystallized in his mind. It was a bold plan, a dangerous plan, he told himself, but it might work. It had the virtues of simplicity and, if properly executed, of surprise.

Henderson waited for the rustle of tense comment among the commanders to subside. Then, he reached into his pocket and brought out a shiny round object, which he held in his hand so that all could see it.

"Approximately half of these German ball bearings are manufactured at Hambrucken", he stated. "Last night, Air Chief Marshall, Lord Charles Portal, handed me this one. I'll repeat what he said to me: 'If you can stop the Jerries from making these things, it's going to be a much shorter war.'" He paused for a moment.

"General Pritchard and I agree with him. These bearing are essential not only to the production of German aircraft, but to much of the equipment critically needed by the Nazi ground and naval forces." He paused again.

"At Bonhofen", he continued, pointing to a spot on the map, "the Nazis have their second largest factory for the production of the Messerschmitt Me-109. Knock it out and we estimate that thirty percent of the German single-engine fighter production will be knocked out.

As to the overall importance of these two targets, I'm sure that I don't need to labor the point. Now, for the plan.

Its essential features are tactical surprise and saturation of the defenses. We expect you to put every bomber in the air that will get off the ground. Half of the bombers will go to Hambrucken, the other half to Bonhofen.

The Bonhofen task force will penetrate first, and will have fighter escort through the German fighter belt - all the fighter support that we and the R.A.F., combined, can furnish. This, plus whatever degree of surprise we can achieve by diversionary attacks, should hold down your losses. Every airplane in England that isn't participating in the mission - including British Bomber Command, medium bombers, fighters - will make large scale feints at other points, timed towards maximum deception.

All right! The Bonhofen force, instead of retracing its course back to England, against the concentrations of fighters that will be waiting for them along the normal route of withdrawal, will, instead, continue on past Poland to prepared airfields in the Soviet Union. To complete their shuttle- bombing operation, they will rest up for a few days, and then bomb targets in Germany on their way home to England.

The Hambrucken task force will follow the same route into Germany as the Bonhofen force. The plan is to time this second penetration fifteen minutes behind the first penetration, in order to catch the enemy fighters on the ground, refueling and rearming - in other words, flatfooted.

After bombing Hambrucken, our bombers will have to fight their way back out from the target area, until they are met by a maximum force of our fighters, who will give them withdrawal support from the limit of their range."

He laid down his pointer and turned to face his listeners.

"In all probability", he concluded, "as soon as the Luftwaffe wakes up to where we are headed, it will throw everything in the book at us . . . everything they've got. But that cuts both ways.

It's a chance for us to break the back of the enemy fighter re- sistance in the air, as well as on the ground. If the whole operation is flown as planned, our own losses may not be excessive.

Fundamentally, the whole plan hinges on weather. England, the entire continent, and Western Soviet Union, must be clear for twelve hours of daylight. That's a tall order, I know.

So, we must be prepared to take advantage of the first break in the weather. In the meantime, all other operations will be curtailed, so that you can start getting ready. You will have a minimum of six days.

Then the plan will go into effect until the mission is accomplished. Tonight, all of your lead navigators and bombardiers will attend a special briefing at my headquarters.

And now, one more thing before I turn the floor over to General Phillips, A-3, who will brief you in further detail. I have been advised that many reasons exist pointing to the desirability of our following up the Hambrucken-Bonhofen strikes, at the earliest opportunity, with our first daylight strike on Berlin."

A glint of fire flashed in Savage's eyes at the mention of the word, Berlin.

"We won't get into that this morning. Just keep it in mind, and start getting ready." Henderson then motioned to an officer in the front row.

"General Phillips", he said, then returning to his seat next to Pritchard.

"You and I", said Pritchard, offering Savage a cigar from a box on his desk, "are overdue for a private bull session, Frank."

His smile was warm and sincere. "How's business?"

"We're choppin' and the chips are flyin', sir", replied Savage, sniffing the cigar, appreciatively. "How about yourself?"

"Rugged, Frank. Every time I turn around, they're trying to take my airplanes away from me. The build up is way behind schedule, but we're growing anyway. Little by little."

He lit up a cigar for himself.

"But, as for you, I'd say, offhand, that you're doing better than just getting by." "I'm not complaining, sir."

"You took the worse Group we had and made it into the best. And that didn't surprise me a bit." He blew out a puff of smoke, then crinkled his eyes at Savage.

"I know that you hate a desk, Frank", he observed. "You're a fightin' man. But Ed Henderson shares my opinion that there's no sense in your fighting until you get shot down. You know that I'm referring to that job in the States."

"Yes, sir, I know."

"I'm wondering if it isn't about time that you took it? Ed says that you're reluctant."

"I am, sir. Pretty soon I'll have a couple of my men that can handle the Group . . . Ben Gately, or maybe Joe Cobb. But they aren't quite ready . . . not yet. With the Hambrucken and Berlin missions coming up, I want to make those two, sir. Then the crews will have seen everything, and I won't care where you ship me."

"I think the time is now, Frank. Before it's too late. I can send Charley Fisher down to take over. He just got here from the States . . . and he's looking for a job."

"Fisher's a good man, General, but he hasn't any combat in this Theater. He's too green. I wouldn't sleep nights."

Pritchard began to scowl and his jaw assumed a stubborn line, which Savage had seen, on occasion, when the Old Man was in no mood to argue about something.

"I've tried to tell you the easy way, Frank", he said. "The fact is, you're not going on any more missions. I won't approve it."

"I'm just asking for those two, General."

"Nothing doing. I'll be the first to admit that you're the best damn leader we've got. But, do you deny that we have others who can do the job?"

"Of course we have, sir. We've got some good Group Commanders. But I've got the experience, and that may make the difference on a strike to Hambrucken, or Berlin." "Others have experience now, too."

"Yes, sir. But I've got more. More than anyone!" Pritchard's scowl deepened.

"I'm not arguing about it, Frank. I'm telling you." Savage turned a shade paler, and stood up.

"Sir", he said. "In all the years I've known you, and served under you, and they've been the best years I've spent in my life, I've never questioned an order from you, and I never thought that I would. But, on this issue, I'm going to have to insist that you allow me to fly on these last two missions."

Pritchard stood up also, and his face had hardened.

"General Savage, you are not in a position to insist on anything", he stated, evenly. "I believe I am, sir."

"What?"

"Let me put it this way, sir. All you can do to me if I disobey your orders is to court-martial me. Am I not right?"

"Correct. And I wouldn't hesitate to do it."

"All right. So, I tell the public why I was court-martialed . . . . for insisting on the right to fly a combat mission I believed that was my duty to fly. A general insisting on getting shot at!"

He took a step toward Pritchard, until his face was close to the other man's.

"And you know, General", he shot out the words, "who would win that argument, don't you?" Savage perceived that he had scored a direct hit. Pritchard squinted at him for a brief moment from frustration, jabbed his cigar in his mouth, swung around his desk, sat down and began visibly to cool off.

"You win, Frank", he said, quietly. "But you had an even better argument. And I was afraid that you were going to use it."

He waited until Savage's curiosity gained the upper hand. "What argument, sir?"

"On second thought, you actually had two. Number one: you delivered the goods for me at Archbury, and you could have asked anything, in my power to grant, in return. But I knew that you'd never use that one."

Again he stopped, but this time Savage also waited.

"But, I was afraid you were going to read my thoughts and play the ace. I was afraid that you were going to tell me that you knew that I wanted you to lead those two strikes."

He stood up, again, and walked over to Savage, shaking his hand.

"I couldn't have lied to you, Frank", he told him. "I've done everything I can to talk you out of it. Now, my conscience is clear."

Five times, within the next four weeks, the Hambrucken-Bonhofen missions was laid on by a warning order. And five times the lead navigators and bombardiers were summoned to secret briefings the night before, only to discover, upon returning to their stations, that the Big Show was being scrubbed on account of the weather.

A few missions were flown to avoid arousing any enemy suspicions, but all of them were planned so as to conserve the units strength and rest the aircrews, while keeping them from getting stale. Savage, preferring to let the younger men gain more experience on easy missions, remained on the ground.

He worried constantly about security, for it was obvious that too many people now knew that something was in the wind. And he missed Pamela, terribly.

She had not been able to leave her post at Lowestoft, but her letters were frequent, and filled with words which he treasured in his heart for days after reading them. And he never ceased to be amazed at the extent to which, having found her man, she went flat out in making it clear that this was so. Twice he called her, long distance - an almost impossible feat in the face of the pyramid of official priorities standing in the way of the personal use of England's war-burdened, over-worked telephone system.

Ben Gately dumbfounded everybody, especially the Flight Surgeon, by recovering sufficiently to leave his hospital bed after only three weeks. And, within a couple of weeks of being up and around, he persuaded Savage and Kaiser, after a final X-Ray, to let him make a mission, from which there appeared to have been no ill effects.

The general was sitting in his office, perusing through a series of weather sequences, which led him to anticipate the possibility of the Big Show's being laid on again for the next day, when Joe Cobb walked in. Looking slightly hung-over, the Air Exec had avoided the Officer's Club bar faithfully, since his first encounter with Savage, that is, until the previous evening, when the general had given him the nod, and with good reason.

Cobb was now wearing the silver oak leaves of a lieutenant colonel, and so was Harvey Stovall. Because a batch of promotions had finally been approved.

"Pull up a chair, Joe", said Savage, with a slight grin. "Or, should I say, Colonel Cobb?"

"I just can't get use to these things, sir", responded Cobb, grinning and looking down at his shoulders.

He took a seat.

"General", he began, cautiously, "I've been thinking. We've got a Squadron Commander vacancy. And well, I was wondering if you'd let me take the squadron for awhile?"

"You tired of being the Air Exec?"

"Oh, no, sir. It's been great, but . . . well, you know how it is, more or less of a staff job. With a squadron . . . well, you've got a command."

"I'd like a squadron myself", said Savage. "It always has been, and always will be, the best job in the Air Force."

"That's right, sir. That's what I mean. Is there any chance?" Savage looked at Cobb, shrewdly, for awhile.

"I can't say that I have any particular objection, Joe. If that's what you really want. Your new rank's no obstacle . . . a new T.O. authorizes lieutenant colonelcies for heavy bombardment squadrons."

"Thanks", said Cobb, genuinely pleased. "Thanks a hell of a lot, General." "Only one thing, though, Joe. What am I going to do about a new Air Exec?" Cobb was prompt with his reply.

"What's wrong with the old one? How about Ben?" Savage reached for a cigar and bit off the end.

"Now, hold on there, Joe", he said. "Gately would be fine. But, if you're making me a proposition just so that I can put him in your place, you're all wet. You're doing a good job."

"No, no, sir. It's nothing like that, honest. I'm not trying to be noble, or anything. I've really missed my squadron, General. That's the honest truth."

He studied Cobb closely, with the look of a man who doesn't miss much. "Okay, Joe", he said. "Colonel Stovall!"

The Ground Exec appeared.

"Harvey, . . assign Colonel Cobb to his old squadron, and reassign Colonel Gately as Air Exec. Effective as of now."

"Yes, sir. Right away, sir", said Stovall.

Savage noticed that Stovall had left with a pleased expression on his face, almost as though it had been his own idea.

Cobb stood up.

"I'll go move my stuff out, sir, so that Ben can move in."

"No", said Savage. "Don't bother with that, Joe. I've got a better idea. You stay where you are; but get hold of Gately and tell him to move his gear into my quarters. He can have the spare bed.

Tell him that it'll save cluttering up the place whenever visitors come around." "Yes, sir", said Cobb, who then saluted and left.

Later that same day, Colonel Stovall came into the general's office and laid a pile of papers, including a postcard, in front of Savage. He picked up some papers from the OUT basket on the desk, and pretended to examine them, while he watched until Savage got around to looking at the postcard.

Stovall saw no change in the general's expression as he read it, although when he had scanned the brief lines, he had barely been able to stop himself from shouting aloud. It was a card from Jesse Bishop, stating that he and the rest of his crew, none of them seriously injured, were in P.o.W. camps, he being in StalagLuft Nine.

Savage initialed a corner of the card, then tossed it in the OUT basket.

"Anything else from behind the barbed wire", he asked, casually? "No, sir. That's all for today."

Savage reached over, unconcernedly, to his IN basket and lifted out a report.

"The more of them that we hear from, the better", he said. "You know, Harvey, I figure that we'll find out after the war, that at least half of the guys that get shot down will turn up okay."

"I certainly hope so, sir. And I wouldn't be surprise that it might be even more then half."

The general concentrated his attention on his report, as Stovall left to return to his office, carefully closing the door behind him. With Stovall gone, Savage tossed the report aside and, his mouth relaxing into a smile, fixed his eyes on an object beyond the windows of his office.

His reverie continued until he heard a hesitant knock on the door. "Come in, McIllhenny", he said.

The sergeant stepped briskly forward and rendered his best Sunday parade salute. Savage divined something unusual in McIllhenny's manner.

"What have you done this time, Sergeant?"

"Since the General has put it that way", said McIllhenny, "I'll come right to the point, sir." "That's always a good idea with me", commented Savage.

"Yes, sir."

McIllhenny reached into his breast pocket, pulled out a black cigar, and handed it to the general. "With my compliments, sir."

"It's your birthday", asked Savage?

"No, sir. At 0930 hours, I became a father, sir."

Savage immediately stood up and shook the sergeant's hand.

"My congratulations, McIllhenny. That's great. Is it a boy or girl?" McIllhenny beamed. "A ten pound boy, sir."

"Sergeant, that's wonderful! That's . . ." He stopped, at a momentary loss for words.

"You're a credit to the 918th, McIllhenny, that's what you are. A boy! Do you realize what a lucky guy you are?"

"I hope I do, sir."

"Well, Sergeant, this calls for a celebration. Wouldn't you say?"

"Yes, sir. Thank you, sir."

Savage caught an expectant look in the other man's eyes.

"Do you think that boy of yours is worth a stripe, by any chance?" "At least one stripe, sir."

"I see your point. All right, Sergeant McIllhenny, you can warm up that typewriter of yours right now, with an order presenting you with three additional stripes."

"Comes out just even, sir. A master sergeant. Three on top and three below. The general has my deepest thanks."

"You're extremely welcome. I consider that you earned those stripes the hard way", he added. "You're a family man, now, Sergeant. No more combat missions for you."

McIllhenny's face fell.

"But, General", he protested. "Two more missions and I'm eligible for that Air Medal I've been sweating out."

"Sorry", said Savage. "You're positively through." McIllhenny stared at his shoes for a moment.

"You're not doing me any favor, sir", he said, with a strange, emotional overtone in his voice. "You're actually punishing me, you know, sir. I've gotten right handy with a fifty cal. I can pay my way up there with you."

"I know that you're a good gunner", interrupted Savage. "But that's not the point."

"The point is, sir, I'd rather take a beating, than have to wait up on the control tower . . . sweating it out. It's a lot easier to go along."

It gradually dawned on Savage that McIllhenny's words concealed a deeper feeling.

"Nobody likes sweating them out from the ground, Sergeant", he said. "And nobody knows that better than I do. Still . . . I don't know . . ."

"General Savage", interposed McIllhenny? "Why couldn't we . . . I was thinking, sir, maybe the general and I could kind of finish up combat together . . . at the same time."

He watched Savage closely.

"Two more", said Savage, finally. "Two more will give you your Air Medal. Okay, just two more, Sergeant. And that's final."

"Yes, sir. Very well, sir", said McIllhenny, exhibiting enormous relief.

CHAPTER ELEVEN

TWELVE O'CLOCK HIGH

Savage became wide awake during the two seconds it took him to reach out, in the dark, and turn off the clangor of his alarm clock. The luminous hands pointed to two-fifteen.

In the next bed, Ben Gately sat up and rubbed his eyes. "Here we go again", he said, drowsily.

"I sure hope so", said Savage.

He walked over to an open window and stared through the blackout, but it was too early for any omens of weather. He then closed the blackout curtains and switched on the lights.

"I thought I saw a couple of stars through the mist", he said. "But I'm not sure." "Maybe the stuff is thin", said Gately. "It'll probably burn off later."

The two men began to get dressed in silence, each permeated with that inner flood of excitement peculiar to the morning of any scheduled mission. However, this was extra special.

The Big Show had been laid on at last. Today, if only the weather forecast held true, they would go.

"You know, General", said Gately, reaching for his pants, "I've been awake for awhile - and been lying here thinking."

"I can't think until I've had my coffee", remarked Savage, yawning.

"Maybe I do too much thinking", said Gately, hesitantly. "Ever since this show started, I've been trying to sell myself on it. It seems as though, for a hundred years, I've been getting up in the blackout, like this, and taking off for somewhere with a load of bombs."

He paused.

"Do you have to sell yourself on it?" "No", replied Savage.

Gately waited a moment, but the general didn't amplify his statement.

"Well", continued Gately. "There's one thing I am sold on, General, and that's when this is all over, after the brains and skill and lives that have gone into it, somebody at the top has got to figure out a better way to run the world - without dictators, and armies, and secret weapons."

He lit a cigarette.

"I know one thing, for sure. If there's still any need for an army after this war, old man Gately isn't going to be in it. You'll find me in a pinstripe suit, running for Congress, and I'm going to have my say."

"Me", said Savage. "I'm thinking about getting the war won first, before I start sweating about the state of the world."

Savage had started his ritual of mission preparation by taking out a fresh, clean pair of G.I. long- handled, winter underwear. As he donned the underwear, the clean wool came into contact with his clean skin, because he had scrubbed himself thoroughly, in a hot bath, before going to bed. A little thing, but important. And he had seen to it, through the Flight Surgeon, that all combat crews understood the necessity, in the interest of safety, of good personal hygiene.

You needed fresh underwear to absorb pre-take-off moisture, before the climb to North Pole temperatures. And, even more important, to reduce the danger of infecting wounds opened from flak and cannon shells.

Next, he powered his feet, copiously, and slid on a pair of silk socks, following them with an outside pair of heavy cotton socks. Then he put his feet into a pair of muddied, heavy-duty, G.I. en- listedman's, broad-toed shoes. If a man got shot down, he might have to walk hundreds of miles to escape. Without heavy-duty shoes, he might pull up lame in fifty miles, or, if the shoes were shined, or noticeably different from those worn by common European folks, he would invite suspicion and possibly capture.

Then, he climbed into a pair of light weight flying coveralls, preferring them to the bulky winter flying clothes. Temperatures in the cockpit were not so dangerously low, even if the heaters failed. And if, for any reason, he had to leave the cockpit temp- orarily, to assist in some more frigid part of the airplane, Savage preferred to be unencumbered.

But, at best, it was a compromised that irritated him whenever he thought of the delays that had deprived the crews, thus far, of light weight, electrically heated flying suits, shoes, and gloves,

that could be depended on to work properly.

After rolling his sleeves up, above his elbows, he zipped the coveralls up the front, so as to leave the neck open for coolness while on the ground. Then, he went to his washbasin and gave his face a final once-over with a new razor blade, out of defer- ence to the torment that would surely result from wearing a tight oxygen mask, chafing against unshaven whiskers.

Next, he lifted his kit bag onto the bed and emptied out its contents, and, as he did so, he crossed each item off a mental checklist. A "Mae West" life preserver, a parachute harness and chest pack parachute, an oxygen mask, a throat microphone, a pair of fur-lined gloves, a silk scarf, and a small chart board with large clips, on which to mount his maps and mission data.

Then, he checked the inflation cartridges of the "Mae West", and insured that the handles were properly safetied. And finally, he opened the cover flap of the chest pack, to see that the seal had not been broken, or the copper safety wire, leading to the ripcord handle.

Savage and Gately, who had basically followed the same pro- cedure, were now ready, even though barely twenty minutes had passed since the alarm clock went off. To both men, as with most of the combat crews, this pre-mission routine of meticulous attention to detail, had long ago become second nature.

While Savage had been equipping himself, outwardly, for the job ahead, inwardly, his mind was undergoing a familiar process of preparation. He counted over a score of important details on his mental fingertips - like Joe Cobb.

He must remember to tell Cobb to fly the low squadron a bit farther forward than usual, today. In addition to miscellaneous items such as this, all of which could be forgotten tomorrow, but any one of which might be a matter of life and death today, his mind held a photographic copy of a mass of details bearing on the mission.

Details of the route, headings, positions of other Groups, call signs, control times, navigation check points, flak areas, fighter escort plans, and weather data. There might, or might not, be time, in an emergency, to dig these things out from his written data. Like other experienced Group Commanders, once a Field Order began clicking out of the teletype machine, Savage had learned the trick of converting his brain tissue into a sheet of car- bon-copy paper.

But, beneath all of these things, he was experiencing the most vital part of his personal preparation. He was enclosing himself in his psychological armor. To some extent it was always there, had always been there, while he was in command of a combat unit. But before every mission, it required an extra thickness and hardness, shielding him with a profound sense of confidence.

Each time, this conditioning left him devoid of fear or weakness, when he faced his crews at Briefing. And this morning, he knew, he would need every last particle of strength of mind, and heart, he could muster. Because, this time, he was leading eleven Groups - the second strike force of the Eighth Air Force - to Hambrucken.

Two hundred and forty combat crew members strained forward in their seats, soaking up every scrap of information during the crackling tension of the long Briefing. When Savage stood to speak, at the end, he could have heard a rubber oxygen mask hit the floor.

"Gentlemen", he began, "if you destroy this target today, you destroy nearly half of the ball bearings that go into FWs and Me-109s. You fellows know what that means to you personally."

There were a few hollow laughs.

"Furthermore", he continued, "this is the most vital target we have ever gone after. And it is appropriate that we attack it to- day, on the anniversary of the first mission flown by the Eighth Air Force.

As most of you know, that mission had a maximum effort of twelve B-17s. Today, we're going to put thirty times that number of heavies into the air, half to Hambrucken and half to Bonhofen, both of them deep in the guts of the Third Reich."

Savage was interrupted by a scattering of hand claps, initiated by Gately and Cobb, which snowballed into cheers, and finally an ovation. For not a man in the room was ignorant of the fact that Savage had led that first mission.

"Thanks", he said, trying to hold his voice steady. "Thanks to all of you. But you had better save the cheering for tonight."

His face brightened into the kind of smile he might have worn if all of them had been going to a ball game.

"Good luck to all of you", he simply said, and then he jumped down from the platform. After the crews had begun to file out, Savage walked over to complimented the Intelligence Officer on his excellent briefing.

Then he led him over to the wall map.

"I've always been curious about these P.o.W. camps", he said. "Do you happen to know where Luftstalag Nine is?"

"Yes, sir. Right about here", said the officer, pointing to a spot on the map. "Almost twelve miles north of your course today."

The general studied the location carefully. "Thank you, Captain", he said.

"Yes, sir."

At 5:30 A.M., fifteen minutes before taxi time, a jeep drove around the five mile perimeter track, in the semi-darkness. It paused at each dispersal point long enough to notify the waiting crews that poor local visibility would postpone the take-off for an hour.

Savage, sitting in the grass with his co-pilot, Rexall, received the news with a scowl. Timing, he knew, was everything Suppose the weather permitted the other strike force, whose bases were in East Anglia, to get off on schedule? An hour's delay for his own force would give the enemy fighters plenty of time to reform between thrusts.

"Notify me immediately", he said to the officer in the jeep, "when the Bonhofen air division takes off."

The minutes crept by painfully slow. Rexall got up and gave the Piccadilly Lily another once-over, with special attention to the oxygen system - human fuel, as important for this mission, he knew, as aviation fuel was for the aircraft.

The gunners field-stripped their fifty calipers again, and oiled the bolts. Master Sergeant McIllhenny lay in the grass with his head on his parachute, feigning sleep, sweating out his fourth start.

Forty-five minutes later, the jeep drove up at a high speed and advised Savage that the Bonhofen force had just taken off. But, what was worse, was when the 918th received an order for a further postponement of an hour, Savage lost his temper.

Calling for McIllhenny, he got into his car, drove to his office and waited impatiently while Colonel Stovall tried to place a call through to General Henderson. Gately came in.

"Hell, General", he exclaimed, "they've got to scrub us. In another half-hour all of southern England will be fogged in . . . and none of our fighter escorts will be able to take off."

"I know, Ben, I know . . . I'm trying to get Henderson now."

With growing impatience, Savage waited for over ten minutes before Stovall succeeded it getting through to PINETREE. Grabbing his phone, Savage asked.

"Well, how about it, Ed . . . are we scrubbing it . . .? What's that . . .? But damnit, Ed, the timing's all shot to hell. Surprise is out the window. The plan has failed!"

He paused to listen longer.

"Do you really mean that . . .? Okay . . . Roger that."

Wearily he hung up the phone. Then, turning to Gately and Stovall, he said.

"It's still on. Henderson said that there's still a chance our fighter escort will be able to get off. And maybe the Germans will get too badly scattered in the first show, to meet us in any strength."

He throttled his urge to express his own opinions.

"So, come on, Ben", he added. "We'd better get back to our ships."

At the hard-stand, Savage began looking at his watch two or three times a minute, burning up valuable energy in his frantic anxiety to get started, before it was too late. Every fifteen minutes of postponement meant just that many more cannon shells waiting for his crews.

A few minutes before the revised start-engines time, his eyes lighted up when he saw the jeep approaching, once more. But his hopes plummeted as soon as he saw the Operations Officer's expression.

"Set back another hour, sir", said the captain.

Savage threw down his cigar and stomped on it with his heel. Once more he drove back to his headquarters and, again, Stovall struggled to get a free circuit to PINETREE, without any success.

"I'm afraid, sir, that every Group and Wing Commander in the Air Division is trying to get hold of General Henderson at the same time", said Stovall.

"I know damn well they are, Harvey", responded Savage, as he stood up, looking at his watch. Just then, a clerk hurried out of the Adjutant's office.

"A long distance call for you, General. From Lowestoft." "I'll take it", said Savage, hurrying back to his desk.

Pamela was on the other end, and her voice sounded urgent. "Frank", she said, "I've got to talk in the clear. Can you hear me?" "Shoot", he said.

"Frank . . . Captain Heeley is on his way to PINETREE with the intercepts. But he may be too late. You've got to scrub!"

"Give it to me as fast as you can, Pam!"

"The Germans are putting up everything in Germany against your first strike. Most of their fighters have already landed, refueled and rearmed. They're sitting on their airfields all along your whole route . . . waiting. Waiting for your other people to come back out. You're going to run right into an ambush, Frank. It's suicidal. You've got to scrub!"

"Bless you, Pam. Good-bye!"

He slammed down the receiver and sprinted out to his car. And McIllhenny set a new record from Archbury to PINETREE.

Anticipating, correctly, that Henderson would be in the brand new underground Ops Block up on Daws Hill, Savage left his car at the entrance to the tunnel and rushed along the subterranean corridors, until he came to Henderson in the Ops room.

"Is it still on", he asked, without any preliminaries, and breathing hard? Henderson just glared at him, while passing a hand through his rumpled hair. "Yes it is", he said. "And what are you doing here, Frank?"

"I got a call from the R.A.F., about the latest RT-Intercepts. Do you have them?" "No! But I'll have them soon."

Savage quickly repeated what Pamela had told him. And, while Henderson showed his alarm at the intelligence, he showed his annoyance even more.

"There will be no more postponements", he said, firmly. "In forty minutes we go. So you'd better start back, now."

"But, Ed! You can't mean that! They're laying in wait for us, right now! We'll catch hell, going in and coming out!"

"Look, Frank. I'm sick and tired of having everybody trying to talk me out of this strike. They'll go!"

"Why? Just to celebrate an anniversary? To buy a lousy headline with blood?"

"YES", roared Henderson, with more conviction than Savage had ever seen in the man. "Exactly! To buy a headline we need! To buy the politicians! To buy the skeptics who don't believe that we've got the stuff to hit a tough target in spite of hell! To buy the airplanes that the pressure groups want to send some- where else, if we let a thin fog stop us from hitting the most im- portant target they ever gave us! Now do you understand?"

Ignoring the question and calling on every bit of persuasiveness at his command, Savage stepped closer to Henderson.

"Thin fog", he said! "That's a load of crap! It's thick enough so that we'll need jeeps with spotlights just to find the end of the runway for us! It's thick enough to cost us a bunch of aircraft colliding in the soup, before we even get assembled!"

"You're exaggerating", claimed Henderson.

"Am I? You've already scrubbed this show twice when the weather was better than today's!

Hambrucken will keep . . . until another day, and better weather! Ed, it's a foolhardy waste of men and planes! And for what? Is an anniversary, or another star, worth that to you?"

"General Savage, there are a lot of things that you don't know about! And I still make the decisions around here! And I don't give a goddamn what you think! They'll GO this morning . . . . even if we don't get one airplane back."

Savage held Henderson's gaze for a long moment. His reply consisted of only two words. But they were the two words which win wars.

"Yes, Sir", he said, in a voice like ice.

It's brakes squealing, as the B-17 crept along the perimeter track, in fits and starts. Savage glued his eyes to the red halo of light, on the back of the jeep, a few feet in front of the aircraft's nose.

The red light was all that he could see, through the dense fog, which had rolled in over Archbury Field. Cursing the delay, in- wardly, he sweated out the slow journey to the head of the run- way, and hoped that a wheel wouldn't roll off the edge of the narrow strip, and mire his ship in the mud.

When the driver of the jeep had lined him up on the correct heading of the runway, only twenty yards of which Savage could see in front of him, he run up his engines and then focused his gaze on the Directional Gyro. Gradually, he advanced the four throttles, until their manifold pressures were exactly equal, and then released the brakes.

Rolling forward and gathering speed, he held the needle in the Gyro on dead center using the rudder pedals, and completed his instrument take-off without seeing the ground. Climbing slowly on instruments, he wondered, in the back of his mind, how many B-17s from other nearby bases were milling around, fighting with him for the same piece of sky.

The LaGuardia Airport control tower would have its hands full, if a score of transports were stacked up over the field, at one thousand foot intervals. Savage wondered, how would they like having a couple of hundred aircraft at unknown altitudes, overloaded with bombs and fuel, crowding the sky in their immediate vicinity?

He recollected the helpless moments he had spent in the Archbury control tower, listening to the desperate calls of a young pilot, caught just after a take-off, on instruments, with the most dreaded of emergencies - the failure of an engine from a runaway prop or turbo. Fifty feet off the ground, too heavy to climb, and unable to land, the pilot's dilemma was classic - and often fatal.

At 0900 hours, heaving a sigh of relief, Savage's plane broke out of the cloud tops, and into the glare of the sun. Beneath the Piccadilly Lily, the fields of England lay blanketed in the, now, undercast, from which many other B-17s were surfacing and from which a few, colliding in mid-air, never emerged.

The Lily continued to climb slowly, her broad wings shouldering a heavy load of incendiary bombs in the bomb bay, and a burden of fuel in the main and wingtip tanks that would keep her in the thin air, of the upper altitudes, for many hours. From his window on the left hand side of the cockpit, Savage anxiously watched the white surface of the undercast where his pilots were puncturing the cloud deck, rising clear of the mist with their Plexiglas tipped noses slanted upward, for the long climb to the base altitude.

The general had a green-red flare fired that identified him to Cobb, of the low squadron, and to Gately, of the high squadron. Five Fortresses had already tacked onto Savage, to form the lead squadron, and soon Cobb pulled into position with his cluster of six, with Gately joining up with his clutch of nine. The Group was now assembled, and intact.

The skies over England grew heavy with the weight of thousands of tons of bombs, fuel, men, and machines being lifted four miles up on a giant aerial hoist, to the western terminus of a twenty thousand foot elevated highway that led east, to Hambrucken. At intervals, arcs of sputtering red, green or yellow flares shot across the deep blue backdrop, as Group Leaders identified themselves to Wing Leaders.

For nearly an hour, while still above the English landscape, the bombers climbed, nursing their straining Cyclone engines in a three hundred foot-per-minute ascent. Gradually, they formed the three squadrons into a compact group of staggered formations - the low squadron down and to the left, and the high squadron up and to the right of the lead squadron.

Groups assembled into looser Combat Wings of three Groups each, along the Combat-Wing assembly line, homing in over pre-assigned splasher beacons by radio compass. Then finally, they cruised along the Air-Division assembly line, to allow the Combat Wings to fall into place, in trail, behind Savage's lead Group.

Formed up at last, with each flanking Group in place, one thousand feet above or below its lead Group, Savage's fifteen mile long parade moved eastward, toward Lowestoft, the point of departure from the friendly coast. He looked down for one last glimpse of Lowestoft, a speck on the curving coast line of another world, and gave a little wave of his gloved hand.

Unwieldy, but too dangerous for fighters to fool with, the bomber stream moved with stately purpose, out across the North Sea. In the co-pilot's seat of one of the last B-17s in the long procession, General Ed Henderson watched the spectacle with the breathless suspense of a man on only his second combat mission, coupled with the knowledge of backing a terrible gamble with his own life.

From Henderson's perch, the task force resembled huge, anvil-shaped, swarms of locusts. Not on dress parade, like the bomb- ers of the Luftwaffe that died in droves over Britain in 1940, but deployed to uncover every gun, and to permit maneuverability.

The English Channel and the North Sea glistened brightly, in the clear visibility, as the 918th left the bulge of East Anglia behind. Savage knew that his force was already registering on the German's radar, and that the fighter controllers of the Luft- waffe were busy alerting their Staffeln of Messerschmitts and Focke Wulfs.

He stole a quick glance back at the cloud covered English countryside, hoping to see some sign of friendly fighters on their way to the rendezvous. But all he could pick out were a dozen or so B-17s, which had followed the strike force to fill in for any aborts from mechanical failures in the hard climb, heading for home.

Savage fastened his oxygen mask a little tighter and looked at the gauge, on the instrument panel, that indicated a proper oxy- gen flow. It was opening and closing, like a visual heartbeat, registering normal as he breathed.

Back in the rear of the aircraft, the gunners were already sear- ching for enemy fighters and, occasionally, the ship shivered as their guns were tested with short bursts. Savage could also see puffs of blue smoke from Cobb's squadron, close below him, as each gunner satisfied himself that he had lead poisoning at his trigger finger tips.

As the coast of Holland appeared, in sharp black outline, he drew in a deep breath of oxygen, consulted his map, and saw that his navigator was going to hit the enemy coast, right on the nose. At 1108 hours, Savage's aircraft crossed into Holland, south of The Hague. Near Woensdrecht, at 1117, he saw the first flak, in his vicinity, blossom out. It was light and inaccurate.

A few minutes later, McIllhenny called out, from his waistgun position. "Bandits at ten o'clock, and low."

Savage saw them, climbing above the horizon, ahead of him and to the left - a pair of them. For a moment he hoped that they were P-47 "Thunderbolts", from the missing escort, but he didn't hope long.

The two were FW-190s, and as they turned for and whizzed through the formation, in frontal attacks, they nicked two of the low squadron's B-17s in the wings, then broke away in half rolls. Savage got a good look at one of them, when it flashed past at a six hundred mile-an-hour rate of closure, its yellow nose smoking and small pieces flying off near the wing root.

The gunners of the 918th were in action, and the strong pungent smell of burnt cordite filled the cockpit, as the Lily trembled to the recoil of the nose guns, and upper and belly turret guns. Smoke immediately began trailing from the hit B-17s, but they were able to hold their positions.

Here was an early fighter reaction, much earlier than even Savage expected. And there had been something desperate about the way the two FWs had come in, fast, right out of their climb, without any preliminaries.

The innercomm was active for a few seconds with brief admonitions: "Lead 'em more". . . "Use short bursts". . . "Don't throw rounds away, we've got a long way to go". . . "Pilot to left waist, don't yell. Talk slow." Three minutes later, the gunners were reporting fighters climbing up from all around the clock, singly and in pairs, both FW-190s and Me-109s.

The approaching fighters that Savage could see on his side looked like far too many for sound health, and there were no friendly Thunderbolts visible, anywhere. From now on, Savage knew, the Group was in mortal danger, but he was use to it. His brain, clear as a bell, was able to ignore it.

A co-ordinated attack began, with most of the fighters diving out of the sun, head-on, from TWELVE O'CLOCK HIGH. The nine and three o'clock attackers were approaching from about level, and the rear attackers were coming in from slightly below. The guns from every plane in every Group in the Combat Wing were firing simultaneously.

Lashing the sky with streams of orange tracers, to match the chain-puff bursts coming from the 20 mm cannons, blinking red, from the wings and noses of the German single seaters.

Both sides were getting hurt in this clash, with the entire second element of three B-17s, from Cobb's squadron, falling out of formation on fire, and the crews bailing out. One Fortress from

Gately's squadron disappeared in a brilliant, explosive flash, and several fighters headed for the deck in flames, or with their pilots lingering behind under the dirty yellow canopies that distinguished some of their parachutes from those of the Americans.

Savage swallowed hard, against his dry throat. Already, in this first fight, he had lost four aircraft, as against none in twenty-three previous combat missions he had flown. He ordered Gately and Cobb to move their squadrons in closer, for mutual support.

One thought that was uppermost in his mind was, that son-of-a-bitch Galland had finally gotten smart. He's going to concentrate on shooting the entire lead Group out of the sky! If he gets me, he told himself, he knows it's worth two Groups farther back.

Savage glanced over at Rexall. It was freezing in the cockpit, but sweat was running down from the co-pilot's forehead and over his oxygen mask, even though the aircraft was on automatic pilot and neither man was exerting himself, physically.

The general pulled his mask down, leaned over to the man's ear and yelled. "I don't think they like us."

Rexall returned a halfhearted grin, from under his mask.

Savage then checked with the navigator and found that they were still on course, and on time. He felt a considerable relief, during this brief distraction, from just sitting there and watching the fighters take aim between his eyes.

Every alarm in his brain and heart was ringing a high pitched warning, but his nerves were steady and his brain calm. He knew that the largest, and most ferocious, fighter resistance of the war was rising to stop his formations, at any cost.

A few minutes later, the strike force absorbed the first wave, of a hailstorm, of individual fighter attacks, that were to engulf it all the way to the target, in such a blizzard of bullets and cannon shells, that many a co-pilot closed his eyes. At 1141 hours, over Eupen, Savage looked out the window, after a minute's lull, and saw that two whole Staffeln, twelve 109s and eleven 190s, were climbing parallel to him, like they were on a steep escalator.

The first group of fighters had soon reached Savage's altitude and were pulling ahead to turn into him, with the second group not far behind. And several thousand feet below were many more fighters, their noses cocked up in a maximum climb.

Over the innercom came more reports of an equal number of enemy aircraft, deploying on the other side of the formation. Pamela, thought Savage, you were right.

Suddenly he noticed, for the first time, a twin-engine Me-110 long range fighter, painted a crimson red, sitting just out of range and exactly level, out to his right. It would stay with the 918th all the way to the target, apparently radioing its position, and bomber stream weak spots, to fresh Staffeln, waiting farther down the line. But, what Savage didn't know, and Pamela did, by reading intercepts back at Lowestoft, was that Adolph Galland was sitting in that Me-110, biding his time.

Swinging their blue noses around in a wide turn, the twelve plane formation of 109s came in from twelve o'clock, dead ahead, in pairs. The main event was on, and Savage had to fight the impulse to shut his eyes.

He kept his eyes open and then, to his amazement and relief, he saw the fighters going after the high and low Groups of his Combat Wing. Other fighters, he was now seeing, were turning into their attacks before they caught up with the 918th, and were taking their revenge out on Groups farther back.

To Savage, it meant that they were beginning to encounter German pilots with less experience than the earlier yellow nose, Abbeville boys. Far back in the bomber stream, Henderson sat frozen in his seat at the sight of so many enemy fighters.

Struggling against the anxiety that convulsed him, he became convinced that he was going to die. And he watched as a shining silver rectangular piece of metal went sailing past, over his aircraft's right wing.

He recognized it as a main entrance door and, seconds later, a black lump came hurtling through the formation, barely missing several propellers. It was a man, clasping his knees to his head, revolving like a diver in a triple somersault, shooting by so close that Henderson saw a piece of paper blow out of his leather flight jacket.

A B-17 ahead of him began to gradually turn to the right, out of the formation, but maintaining its altitude. Then, in a split second, it completely vanished in a yellow explosion, from which the only remains were four balls of fire, the fuel tanks, which were quickly consumed as Henderson watched them fall earth- ward.

Up front, Savage made mental notes of the different fighters. Some of them shot at the formation with rockets, and he saw one attempt an air-to-air bombing with little black time-fused sticks, dropped from above, which exploded in small gray puffs, off to one side of the low squadron.

As the minutes passed, the 918th sustained no further losses, although some of the fighters were pressing home their attacks to 250 yards, and less. While others were bolting, flat out, through the formation, firing long twenty second bursts, and often presenting themselves as pointblank targets on their breakaway.

Some committed the fatal error of pulling up, instead of going down and out. And upon hearing McIllhenny claim one of these, Savage felt a strange reassurance at the sound of the sergeant's businesslike voice.

But no enemy tactics could halt the close-knit juggernauts of the Flying Fortress Groups, nor save the single-seat fighters from paying a terrible price. Henderson, watching in horrified fascination, began to perceive that his aircraft, flying in the cluttered wake of a desperate air battle, was endangered by various kinds of debris, as well as by enemy fighters.

Nose hatches, entrance doors, tail gunner's hatches, premature opening parachutes, bodies, and assorted fragments of B-17s and German fighters breezed past him in the slipstream. He watched as two fighters explode, not far below, and disappear in sheets of orange flame.

B-17s were dropping out of formation in every stage of distress, from engines on fire to controls shot away. Friendly and enemy chutes floated down and, on the green landscape below, funeral pyres of smoke from fallen aircraft marked the route.

Disintegrating aircraft became commonplace, and the white dots of sixty chutes in the air at one time, were hardly worth a second look. The spectacle registering on Henderson's eyes grew to be so weird, that his brain turned numb to the actuality of the death and destruction that was all around him.

Had it not been for the squeezing of his stomach, which was trying hard to purge itself, he might easily have been watching an animated cartoon in a movie theater. Vaguely, he wondered how Savage, sitting up ahead in the lead aircraft, with nothing in front of him but Germans, had the stomach to keep on going.

The minutes dragged on into an hour, and still the fighters kept coming. Savage's gunners, coolly and briefly, called out to one another, dividing up their targets, fighting for their lives, and the life of the formation, with every round of ammunition.

McIllhenny called out that he was out of ammo, so the radio operator took another belt back to him. Now, here was a new hazard, and Savage began to worry whether or not they would run out of fifty caliber bullets, even before reaching the target.

Henderson looked out his window and watched, while a Fortress turned slowly out to the right, its cockpit a mass of flames. He saw the co-pilot crawl out through the window, hold on with one hand as he reached back for his chute, buckled it on, then let go, and was whisked back into the horizontal stabilizer of the tail. Henderson figured that the impact must have killed him, as his chute never opened.

Henderson then looked straight ahead, and instinctively ducked his head, as he watched the tail gunner of a B-17 in front of him take a bead on his windshield. The gunner then cut loose with a stream of bullets and tracers that passed a few feet overhead, on their way toward an enemy fighter that was attacking from behind.

Still, there was no letup. The Germans queued up like a bread line and let the Fortresses have it, and each second of time had a cannon shell in it.

The strain of being a clay pigeon, at the wrong end of this aerial shooting gallery, became almost intolerable for Savage. And, as on previous missions, he felt an impulse to grab a flare pistol - or anything - and fight back.

The Lily shook steadily with the constant firing of the fifties, and the air inside her was wispy with smoke. Savage checked the engine instruments, for the hundredth time, and every one of them read normal.

None of the crew had been injured yet, which seemed like a miracle. So, maybe, he thought, just maybe, he'd would get to the target, in spite of the 918th's reduced fire power from the four aircraft that had been lost.

Now, a new problem arose, calling for a decision - one of those decisions that could mean the success or failure of an entire mission. A decision that was easy to make on the ground, but, as bitter experience in the Eighth Air Force had repeatedly proven, was weirdly difficult for a man to make, when thousands of lives were at stake. Where he was alone in the milky never-never world of the frigid sub-stratosphere, while sucking at an oxygen mask. When his eardrums were aching from the maddening splinters of static and enemy radio interference. When he was feeling cramped and acutely uncomfortable, physically, and taut with the stress of the mortal anxiety that subjects a man, under enemy fire, to a sensation akin to having a pair of ice tongs hook- ed into his guts.

The navigator had just informed Savage that the winds aloft, blowing at 120 miles-per-hour, had suddenly shifted and were now blowing in the opposite direction. Should this condition still exist when the target was reached, it would mean that the bomber force would have to approach Hambrucken upwind, from the assigned I.P. (Initial Point), adding minutes of vulnerability to the bomb run and presenting the German flak defenses with a beauti- ful, slow moving target. Thus, Savage began formulating his de- cision with the painful concentration of a patient trying to solve a crossword puzzle, while the dentist is drilling a tooth.

Fifteen minutes from target time, after a breather of several minutes, a new wave of fighters bore in on the 918th. Battle damage soon overtook the Piccadilly Lily with a rush, as several twenty millimeter cannon shells raked her.

The first shell penetrated the right side of the cockpit and ex- ploded below and behind Savage's armor plate, peppering him slightly about the calves, but damaging the electrical system, and wounding the top-turret gunner in the legs.

A second shell entered the radio compartment and a third shell entered the left side of the nose, tearing out a section about two feet square, damaging the right-hand nose gun installation and injuring the navigator in the head and shoulders. The navigator reported to Savage that he was okay just as another shell penetrated the right wing root, going into the fuselage and shattering the hydraulic system, releasing the blood-colored fluid all over the cockpit floor and creating a fire hazard.

A fifth shell punctured the cabin roof and severed the rudder cables connecting one side of the rudder. While a sixth shell exploded in the number 3 engine, which then caught fire.

Instantly, as the co-pilot activated the number 3 engine fire extinguishing system, Savage reached over and hit a red knob, marked "3", and then trimmed the aircraft for three-engine operation. The number 3 propeller slowed down, then stopped, as the blades rotated to a full-feathered position - leading edge to the slipstream.

As the engine fire reduced itself to a thin stream of smoke, the general unfastened his seat belt and shoulder harness, ordered Rexall to take over, then grabbed a small walk-around oxygen bottle and made his way aft, through the bomb bay, to the radio compartment. Feeling his strength starting to ebb, from even this small exertion at the high altitude, he entered the radio room and saw that the radio operator was dead.

He turned his attention to a small fire on the bulkhead, smothering it with a hand held fire extinguisher. Then, after the gunners in the waist waved to him that they were okay, he returned to the cockpit and made a check of the rest of the crew over the innercomm.

By advancing the throttles for some additional power, Savage managed to maintain his airspeed and pressed on towards the target. But, because of the fire in the number 3 engine nacelle, a partial loss of the controls, the structural damage and injured personnel, he didn't know if they could make it, or not.

There was every justification for abandoning the aircraft, a thought which had begun to obsess some of the crew. And with Rexall pleading with him, repeatedly, on the innercomm.

"General Savage! We've had it", he called out, hysterically. "Let's bail out while we still can!"

The others, listening to the co-pilot's voice, caught the panic and several began making preparations to leave - order or no order. Savage looked across and saw that Rexall had gone completely to pieces.

He pressed down on his mike button.

"You son-of-a-bitch", he enunciated, distinctly, "you sit there and take it like the rest of us!"

The psychological effect of those cold-blooded words, coming in the nick of time, had an immediate, and magical, effect on the whole crew, and averted a crisis.

The Lily pressed on.

At last, the fighters, their fuel exhausted from the long chase, diminished their attacks on the 918th, to almost nothing. Even the Me-110 executed a 180-degree turn, and disappeared from Savage's view.

The strike force was approaching the I.P., directly south of the target. Savage called the navigator, who told him that the winds were still blowing hard from the north.

Quickly, Savage discounted the possibility of their bombing upwind, from the designated I.P., and weighed the alternatives. If he selected a new I.P. north of the target, the bombers would benefit by a faster bomb run, with minimum time of exposure to enemy flak. However, the new flight path would take the force over the densest concentrations of the flak positions, which the briefed route had been carefully planned to avoid.

Secondly, the faster bomb run might be too short, with such a tailwind, for accurate bombing. Third, the delay in flying upwind to the new I.P., would upset the timing of the rendezvous of the bombers, with their fighter escorts, on the withdrawal. Hours later, the friendly fighters, at the limit of their fuel range, would be waiting to meet the bombers, but they wouldn't be able to wait very long: minutes, even seconds, could be decisive.

Savage elected to discard the alternative in favor of bombing cross wind, from an I.P. about ten miles west of Hambrucken, since an I.P. east of the target would take them farther into enemy territory, and prolong the mission.

"Pilot to navigator", he called. "How's the visibility west of the target area?"

To the navigator, the general's calm voice gave the casual impression of a man asking what was playing at the movies.

"Navigator to pilot", he called back. "Hazy west of target. No undercast." "Roger", replied Savage.

The general consulted his map.

"Pilot to tail gunner. How close is the next Combat Wing?"

"Tail gunner to pilot. They're right behind us, sir."

Savage breathed a little easier. He wouldn't have to break radio silence to divulge the change of plans to the commanders following him.

"Ah, pilot to navigator. Set course for Halstuben. That is the new I.P."

Firing an orange flare to alert the bomber stream in his wake, to a change of plan, Savage swung his aircraft around to its new heading. He then fired another flare over Halstuben, as the Lily turned again, into its bombing run.

"Okay, Roby", he called to the bombardier. "You take it on in from the I.P. Is everything okay?" "Bombardier to pilot. There's a hell of a crosswind, General. But I think I can hold the target." To himself, Savage hoped, almost tearfully, that his decision had been the right one. That, as he phrased it in his mind, "So some poor bastards wouldn't have to go back another day and do this all over, again."

The 918th proceeded on its bomb run, and as the bomb bay doors opened, a red light lit up on the instrument panel. Savage looked up ahead, and watched as ugly, black puffs of smoke began appearing level with the aircraft's nose. Flak, and plenty of it.

Enough to get out and walk on. But a lot less, he knew, than there would have been north of Hambrucken.

A black burst mushroomed so close in front of the Lily, that Savage could see the red flame in the heart of the smoke. Simultaneously, there was a metallic crunch and a jerk, as a heavy fragment of steel punctured the nose compartment up front.

Over the innercomm, he heard the single word from Roby - "Bombs . . ." But the word "away" did not come. The red light blinked out, and the B-17, relieved of its bomb load, surged upward.

The navigator called out, frantically . . .

"Roby's hit bad! Let's get the hell out of here!"

Savage gripped the control wheel and turned it to the left, away from the target, while looking down to see that Cobb, on the inside of the turn, didn't overrun the formation. In the next instant, Savage was appalled to see a burst of flak catch Cobb's B-17 directly in the tail, severing it.

The aircraft started straight down, but almost immediately, it exploded into a thousand fragments, no bigger that a man's fist. And there was no sign of any chutes.

Cobb's instant death registered on Savage's eyes, but not in his brain. He pressed his mike button. "Able leader to Charlie two and Charlie three, tack on behind Able Squadron", he called, sharply! The two surviving Fortresses of Cobb's six-ship, low squad- ron, dropped back behind Savage.

Calling on the bottom most depths of his self control, Savage set course for home. He sent Rexall below to check up on Roby, then he looked back towards the target.

Pillars of smoke rose from the vicinity of the Aiming Point, at the ball bearing plant, and above it, boring in through dense barr- ages of smoky flak, the other Groups were raining down their bombs.

The mission had succeeded.

Breaking radio silence, Savage called to Gately on the V.H.F. radio. "Able leader to Baker leader, over."

"Baker leader to Abler leader, go ahead."

"My radio operator is dead, Baker. Can you send the strike report to headquarters for me?" "Roger that. Baker leader out."

Hundreds of miles to the west, at Lowestoft, this conversation was being monitored by a W.A.A.F., who immediately carried it to Flight Leftenant Mallory. Pamela's brain reeled with relief, as she said to herself; "Frank is still alive".

The sending of the commander's strike report indicated that, yes, Savage was still alive. And it was the first RT-intercept from the Americans, as all the rest had been German. And all of them portents of disaster, spearheaded by an intercept from Adolph Galland, indicating that he had landed to refuel, before resuming the chase.

Pamela hid her face in her hands.

When Rexall returned from the nose compartment, he gave Savage an incredible report. An instant before bombs away, Roby, crouching over his bombsight, had been hit in the chest by a piece of flak, which hurled him back six feet, to the rear of the compartment. He had force himself forward, released the bombs and dropped dead over the bombsight, in the middle of saying,

"Bombs away".

Savage gradually hypnotized himself into sort of a coma, in which his mind, grasping like a drowning man at a straw, clung to just one thought - stay on course and get home. The death of Cobb, of Roby, of the radio operator, and even the overwhelm- ing fact that they had successfully bombed Hambrucken, receded into his subconscious. There was still the eternity of the long journey back to Archbury, but thankfully the engine fire had finally gone out.

Occasionally the sky would, again, become mottled with enemy fighters. But their attacks were sporadic, because the Germans, too, had fought themselves out.

Suddenly, Savage glanced down at his map, then called the navigator.

"Pass Control Point eight, at twelve miles north of course", he said. "Got it?" "Twelve miles north of course at Control Point eight. Roger."

There was a pause, then the navigator called back. "That'll take us right over Luftstalag Nine, sir", he said. "That's a Roger", answered Savage.

Half an hour later, Jesse Bishop, sitting on the steps of a barracks at Luftstalag Nine, heard a deep, low rumbling in the sky. Slanting his eyes upward, he made out a long column of black specks - fifteen miles long.

His eyes opened wide and his lips parted.

"Hundreds of 'em! There must be hundreds of 'em!"

He turned to a pilot standing next to him, who was also staring skyward. "It's Savage", Bishop cried out! "I know it's Savage, and the 918th."

Twenty thousand feet above Luftstalag Nine, Savage, having delivered on his promise, hoped that Bishop, and the others, had seen the B-17s.

One hour later, and feeling like a man recovering from an anesthetic, Savage heard the navigator call out, happily.

"I can see the coast. sir."

It was true. Savage caught a glimpse of sunlight flashing off the expanse of water in the distance.

The gunners, surrendering to the reaction from the long hours under the tense strain, began to chatter excitedly. Savage calmed them down, cautioning them to stay on their toes, because the friendly fighters, fogged bound at their bases in England, had not been able to keep their rendezvous.

At last, the English Channel appeared, and they were leaving the enemy coast. Savage nosed the Piccadilly Lily down, into a gradual decent, toward England.

And then, McIllhenny shot a final squirt of adrenaline into everybody's weary bloodstream, with the warning . . .

"Four fighters at five o'clock low!"

Savage immediately called the other Group Commanders and alerted them. This was just the kind of situation that could be fatal, as more than once, enemy fighters had shot down B-17s, whose gunners had already removed the barrels from their mach- ine guns, when they were almost home.

Twelve O'clock High

The unidentified fighters finally came into Savage's field of vision - three FW-190s and the same red Me-110. They were climbing fast, above the horizon, and far ahead.

Suddenly they turned, and dived directly for the 918th. With her nose guns shot out, the Lily had only its two top turret guns to defend itself with, as the fighters swelled into close range and were apparently aiming right at Savage's cockpit.

In another second, with the leading edges of their wings blinking tiny flashes of light, they shot, head-on, through the 918th's formation. The number 1 and number 4 engines were hit and quit, almost immediately, leaving the Lily with only one oper- ating engine.

Savage shoved the control column forward and dove straight for the water. There was no longer any doubt in his mind that somebody, probably Adolph Galland, was out to get him, person- ally.

The tail gunner called.

"Keep agoin', General. Them bastards are tailing us!"

Savage gradually pulled out of the dive, as close as he dared get to the water, hoping that the B-17, relieved of the weight of nearly all of its fuel and ammunition, might reach the English coast on one engine. It had been done before.

He order the ball turret to be dropped and all equipment on board jettisoned, except guns, ammunition and ditching gear. The aircraft began slowing down, from 250 K.I.A. (Knots Indi- cated Airspeed) to 150 knots, then to 100 knots, and finally to 90 knots.

Pulling maximum manifold pressure, the number 2 engine rapidly overheated, and began losing power. Savage looked out and saw that the fighters were circling, unable to attack from be- low, and apparently reluctant to take a chance of diving and pull- ing up too late, to avoid hitting the water.

"Stand by for ditching", ordered Savage! "Acknowledge."

The men called back from their stations, one by one. Just above wave-crest level, Savage cut off the last engine.

"Here we go", he called. "Get set!"

The B-17 settled into the water with a huge cloud of spray and decelerated violently to a standstill, its tail high and the cockpit partly submerged. The eight survivors, acting automatically from the habits instilled in them from their ditching practice drills, scrambled through the escape hatches, then released the two dinghies from on top of the fuselage, clambered aboard and shoved off from the slowly sinking Flying Fortress.

"Look out", screamed a voice!

A second later, a stream of bullets stitched a series of foaming puddles across the water, a few feet from Savage's dinghy. And they were followed by the roar of the red Me-110, as it pulled out of a shallow dive. The three 190s had disappeared and only the 110 had lingered around for the kill.

Without hesitation, Sergeant McIllhenny dove from Savage's dinghy and swam, with powerful strokes, back to the B-17. He climbed up on the wing, before Savage, who was watching the German fighter, knew what was happening.

"Hey! McIllhenny", yelled Savage! "Come back! Do you hear me? Get the hell back in this dinghy . . . quick. That's an order!"

But McIllhenny paid no heed. And he began lowering himself through a cockpit window, pausing only to glance up at the German fighter, which was maneuvering into position for yet another pass at the stranded men.

McIllhenny disappeared for a moment, then Savage saw his head emerge in the blister of the top turret, which, except for the aircraft's tail, was the only part of the Lily above water. Over his shoulder, Savage saw the fighter begin its approach, but his attention was still focused on McIllhenny, at whom he and the other crew members were frantically calling.

McIllhenny held his fire until the German was within range. Then he let loose his twin fifty calibers, spouting streams of lead.

As the Piccadilly Lily began settling towards her final plunge, the water rose over the top of the turret, until only the muzzles of the guns, still smoking, showed above the surface. But, they too soon disappeared beneath the waves.

The Me-110 roared past and this time it was trailing smoke, because, before he died, McIllhenny had gotten a piece of it. And, apparently, Galland had had enough, as he turned and soon faded south toward the French coast.

Twenty minutes later, an Air Sea Rescue launch of the R.A.F. arrived, along side of the two dinghies. In them, they found six men, who greeted them with cheers, and a weary general who looked up at them with eyes like those of a dead man.

CHAPTER TWELVE

THRESHOLD

No mission had been scheduled, but Savage and the combat crews were wearing their flying clothes, when the general walk- ed into the Briefing room, two mornings later, at 10 A.M.. Even to the men in the front row, the general did not appear to be suff- ering any ill effects from the mission to Hambrucken.

He was freshly shaved, his eyes were clear, and his whole manner exuded drive and energy, somewhat of a contrast with most of the crews, many of whom were suffering from a reaction that left them hollowed-eyed.

"Well, men", began Savage. "We've got a job in front of us. I want you to start looking ahead . . . not back, at what happened the day before yesterday. We lost a few. Other Groups lost more. And for a day on which the Eighth Air Force, as a whole, lost sixty-six bombers, we got off fairly light.

The bombing should have been better, and that's what I want to talk to you about."

He glanced down, organizing his thoughts. And when he looked up, the men experienced that familiar illusion that he was talking to each of them individually.

"We have a good Group, in the 918th", he continued. "But I'm not satisfied. We have got to make it better, and we will.

Half of our low squadron was taken right out of the play on the first pass, and I feel that better gunnery might have prevented it. So, -" he was speaking sharply now - "we are going to have better gunnery.

To start, no one present will be permitted to leave the station until further notice. After this Briefing, when you gunners check your bulletin boards, you'll find that, when you're not eating, sleeping, using the latrine, or flying, you'll be sweating out your time on the gunnery trainers and at the target range.

Pilots. We're going back to school. Practice missions and fundamentals. Our formation flying isn't perfect, . . . yet!

Navigators. Frankly, I am fairly well satisfied with your navigation. But some of you weren't so hot with your nose guns, and that's got to change. What I said about the gunners goes for all of you, too. You're going to fire a lot of practice rounds.

Bombardiers. All lead bombardiers will drop at least one stick of practice bombs a day, up at the Wash, until further notice. That means you will stand by in cockpit-readiness, when the weather is doubtful, in order to take advantage of even an hour- and-a- half's break in the weather. Understood?"

He paused, briefly. "Gately", he said! "Yes, sir."

"I'll hold you responsible for the lead crews." "Yes, sir."

Savage looked at the floor again, unhurried, thinking.

"One more thing", he said. "I don't want any of you getting the idea that the Old Man is bearing down on training all of a sudden, just because he's got some kind of wild hair up his butt! And, I don't want anyone merely going through the motions!

It's no secret that you'll walk in here some morning, before long, and see a string stretching to Berlin."

He paused.

"So, now's the time to start getting ready. Dismissed!"

During the next few days, Colonel Stovall marveled at the way the general, always tireless, drove himself and all of the men at Archbury Field. Savage, he reflected, had the resilience of a rubber ball. The harder you slammed him against the wall, the harder he bounced back.

Twelve O'clock High

No combat missions were scheduled. But the station was seething with such a constant uproar of training activity, that only a hardy few showed up at the Officers' C lub any more, before hitting the sack early.

Pamela had called twice. On one occasion, the general had been in the air. On the other, after a messenger had interrupted him lecturing a group of new replacement crews, he had sent word that he could not come to the phone.

Even General Henderson, who called to notify Savage, personally, that higher headquarters had just approved a Distinguished Service Cross, for his leadership of the Hambrucken mission, had to wait for more than an hour, before the general could be located.

Savage was at the wheel of a jeep, with Gately sitting beside him, as they drove toward Savage's hard-stand. Stovall shared the rear seat with the flight gear of the two fliers.

Shedding red light across the airfield, the rising sun filtered through the remains of a thin mist. Pamela had wired him that she would coming home for a week's leave, but Savage had thrust the thought from his mind, as it had the sting of pouring salt on an open wound.

With an equal effort of will, he had previously dismissed McIllhenny from his thoughts, except for a brief moment in his office, when he had signed two papers. Sergeant McIllhenny had missed his Air Medal by only one mission, of the five usually considered a minimum. But Savage had signed a recommend- ation for the Air Medal, anyway - in addition to his recommend- ation for a posthumous Congressional Medal of Honor.

For now, Savage was concentrating on the larger thought. BERLIN This was the day he had lived for. This was the culmination of seventeen years of training as a military pilot and commander.

Furthermore, he believed that this day would mark the beginning of the end for Adolf Hitler, and his blood-smeared henchmen.

Harvey Stovell sneaked a look at the general's face. His eyes looked calm, but dangerous, and his features had the solidity of granite.

Stovall knew that he was looking at a man living the supreme hour of his life. He felt profoundly confident that all the minions of hell could not stop Frank Savage from leading the Eighth Air Force to Berlin, and getting home safely, on this day.

"Six minutes before start-engine time", said Gately, after they had unloaded the general's gear at the hard-stand. "Time for a smoke, sir."

Gately lit a cigarette with a steady hand, as Savage drew a few last puffs on his cigar, before throwing it down and stepping on it. And then, for a moment, he stood there and stared, at his brand new B-17, sinister looking and complacent, squatting on its fat tires.

"Might as well get started", he said, smiling at Gately. "Good luck, Ben." Then, he winked at Stovall.

"I'll try to get home this time, Harvey", he said, "without getting my feet wet."

He picked up his parachute bag and walked purposefully toward the Flying Fortress, until he was standing beneath the nose hatch. He tossed his chute bag inside the nose, then reached up and gripped the edge of the hatch to hoist himself up, his biceps standing out, below his rolled up sleeves.

And then, Gately and Stovall, watching him, saw a strange thing happen. Savage didn't pull himself up, he just continued to stand there with his hands gripping the hatch edge, his arms straining.

The two men hurried over and saw that the general's face was an ashen gray. Sweat was pouring down Savage's face and, invisible to the two men, sweat was also streaming down his shoulder blades and the back of his legs.

His body shivered and his teeth chattered. His eyes, still fixed upward toward the nose hatch, were stricken, despairing, struggling, like those of a drowning man. He made another attempt to pull himself up, against the unseen weight of some crushing load.

As Stovall and Gately hurried to his side, scarcely believing their eyes, both men understood, in a flash, what was wrong. The incredible had happened. Brigadier General Frank Savage, the man everyone looked up to for support, had mentally broken down.

Too many missions. Too many near misses from flak and cannon shells, buried in the subconscious. Too many drains on the adrenaline discharged into the bloodstream, to enable a man to cope with dire emergencies. Too many hours spent sitting helplessly, unable to retaliate, against the airborne firing squads of the Luftwaffe. Too many sleepless hours spent staring at the ceiling of the bedroom, under the pressure of his responsibilities. Too incessant and excessive a demand on the physical resources of even the strongest human body, when deprived of the opportunity for recuperation. Too much emotional stress, from the perpetual denial to himself, that he and his men were only flesh and blood, with a right to live. And too long a residence in the halls of the living dead.

But even in this final crisis, Savage's heart and mind had not failed him. All of the old determination was still there, and all to no avail, against the paralysis of nerves and muscles.

Glowing with false brilliance in the days since the Hambrucken mission, like a light bulb just prior to its burning out, his faculties had failed him, simultaneously, under the nose hatch. His body ignored the commands from his brain, and he was literally incapable of climbing into that aircraft again.

Fighting to compose his features, as he labored to walk away from the aircraft's nose, with Gately's assistance, the general turned to him, with tortured eyes, leaned on his shoulder, and said, barely audibly.

"You take it, Ben."

Without a word, Gately reached out and put Savage's quivering arm over Stovall's shoulder, then went back and quickly hoisted himself up through the nose hatch.

With his friend, who was too stunned to utter a syllable, help- ing him, the general staggered back to the jeep. Then, after climbing onto a seat he simply collapsed and slumped back.

Leaving Savage in the jeep, but feeling instinctively that the best thing was to leave him alone, Stovall hurried over to the operations jeep, parked nearby, which always stayed around until the general had taken off.

"Get a pilot from a spare crew over to Colonel Gately's plane, now", said Stovall, to a somewhat startled lieutenant!

"YES, SIR", said the lieutenant, as he sped away, down the perimeter track.

Stovall walked slowly, back to Savage's jeep, and climbed in beside him, just as Gately's engines began exploding into life. Savage was staring straight ahead, unseeing, until Gately taxied out.

Then he turned his head, wearily, and watched the long procession of bombers, jockeying along the perimeter track, toward the head of the runway, behind Gately, like a clumsy herd of elephants, their heads to their tails. Soon, a red flare streaked out over the grass from the Control Tower.

Gately's B-17 began to roll forward, accelerating slowly with its overload of fuel and bombs, and finally, after covering almost the entire length of the runway, it lifted itself from the ground and roared straight ahead in a flat climb, with its wheels curling up into the inboard engine nacelles. At thirty second intervals, another B-17 was airborne, until all of the bombers had cleared the airfield.

They circled at one thousand feet, asembling with the precision of veterans, into their squadrons, and then into a single group. Returning directly across the field, with the Group closed up in solid battle order, Gately rocked his wings three times.

Then the 918th Bombardment Group set course for the Wing assembly point, to assume the lead, once more, of the Eighth Air Force, and rapidly faded from sight. Savage watched until the last speck was no longer visible Arriving at Savage's living quarters, Stovall helped the gen- eral to his room and then called for Doc Kaiser. When the Flight Surgeon entered the room, Savage was sitting in a chair, quiet, and not moving. He was sitting as if he were in the cock- pit of his aircraft, and just staring at a wall.

"What happened to him?"

You know what happened, Don, . . . he broke down", said Stovall.

"Yeah, I've been expecting it for some time now. The way he's been pushing the Group, and himself, it was inevitable."

"Well, what can we do?"

"Nothing, . . yet. We'll just have to see what happens in the next few hours."

Waiting, . . that's the hard part, but that's what they did. They stayed there and waited. They waited for the Group to come back from the mission, and they waited to see if Savage would come back too. However, waiting wasn't always good enough for Harvey Stovall and he'd decided that he wasn't going to just sit there and watch his friend fold up.

"Frank", said the colonel. "Frank, I know what you're going through. You think you've failed. You think you've failed your men, and you feel that you've failed yourself. Well, you're wrong, Frank. I'll tell you what a failure you turned out to be!"

His voice became impassioned.

The only thing you've done is that you failed to realize that your boys have grown up. They're good at their jobs, Frank, and that's because of you. You think that because you're not leading the Group to Berlin today, you've failed. Well, hell, Frank, who do you think is leading it? A no good loafer you pulled out of the wastebasket, and turned into a man! A combat leader. And that's because of you. You, Frank."

He stopped to take a breath.

And he's not the only one. Frank, . . . you're in every aircraft up there. You're riding up there right now, in every cockpit and every crew position. Those men up there are young and tough, and they're the ones who're going to win this war.

And, that's because of you."

Savage didn't move a muscle. It was as if he hadn't hear a thing. Then, Harvey Stovall's voice hardened.

"Frank, . . don't you see, it's over? You've done your job, and you've done it well. But, Frank, . . you're fighting after the bell."

Stovall was surprised at what he had just said, but he knew he had had to say it. Savage still didn't move. But, he did seem to relax just a bit, and some color seemed to come back into his face.

Now that he had discharged his outburst from his system, Stovall was beginning to feel awed. He felt humbled in the presence of greatness.

For all these many months, he had thought of Brigadier General Frank Savage as a superman, Now, he knew that Savage wasn't a superman . . . that he never had been.

Rather, he saw Savage as a man who had made a superhuman effort. A man capable of giving everything that was him . . . and then giving some more.

Furthermore, he knew that it would be useless to try to tell Savage that he wasn't a failure. Men like Savage would always be failures . . . in their own eyes, always short of the level of attainment toward which they strove.

After about an hour, or so, Keith Davenport came into the room. "How is he, Harvey?"

"No change since I called you", said Stovall. Davenport turned to Doc Kaiser, and asked. "Well, Doc, what's your prognosis?"

"It's unknown. Some people call it combat fatigue, but I call it 'maximum effort'. It could last a few hours, a few days, or . . . . . who knows? Who will ever know?"

The three men stood around their friend and hoped for the best.

A short time later the phone rang. Harvey Stovall picked up the receiver and after a few minutes he put it back down. Turning to Davenport and Kaiser, he said.

"The results from the mission are starting to come in, and so far it's looking really good. Fighters and flak were both as heavy as expected going in, but the 918th is keeping its forma- tions tight and no losses have been reported. Ben reported that they plastered the target area and that they're on their way home."

Davenport turned to Savage and put his hand on the general's shoulder. Leaning over, he half whispered to his friend.

"Did you hear that, Frank? Ben said the 918th is doing great." Savage didn't move.

After a few hours, for what seemed like an eternity, a distant droning could be heard. Slowly it grew in intensity until it felt like the whole room was vibrating. Stovall was standing by an open window, looking out, as Keith Davenport and Doc Kaiser went outside to watch. Standing outside and near the same win- dow as Stovall, they looked up and began counting the aircraft.

Flying low, but not quite in the tight formation that it had left in, the 918th Bomb Group was returning. And, as they flew over the base, Davenport started counting, aloud, "Three, . . . seven, . . . ten, . . . twelve, ... fourteen", muttering more to himself than to the others.

"Sixteen, . . . eighteen, nineteen, ... twenty, twenty-one", continued Kaiser. "They're all back, Harvey", said Davenport.

"Good", said Stovall.

Turning to tell the general that all his men had come home, Stovall was surprised to see Savage standing at the telephone, the receiver in his hand.

"Operations", he said, and then pausing for someone on the other end to answer. "Operations, . . this is Savage, what's the count?"

After a long pause, Savage said thanks and then hung up the phone. By this time Davenport and Kaiser had re-entered the room and, standing with Stovall, they watched as the general turned and sat on his bed. Then, Davenport asked.

"Frank, . . are you okay?"

Doc Kaiser moved over next to him and asked. "General Savage, how do you feel?"

Almost as if he didn't notice the doctor, Savage looked at his Ground Exec., and said. "The boys did good, Harvey. A few wounded, but that's all."

"How do you feel, General", asked the doctor, once more?
"I'm fine, Doc, it's just that, ... I'm awfully tired."

And with that, Savage laid down.

"Okay then", said Kaiser, "I'd better get over to the hospital and check on the wounded."

Turning to leave, the "Doc" told Davenport and Stovall that, for now, the best thing to do was just to let the general sleep, and that he would check on him later. With that, Kaiser left to tend to his duties at the hospital.

Then, both Harvey Stovall and Keith Davenport walked over to where Savage lay. Stovall went to the end of the bed and proceeded to remove the general's flight boots, while Davenport took a blanket and covered his friend.

The general awoke to a room darkened by the black-out curtains covering the windows. He turned on the light that sat on the small table next to his bed, and looked at the clock that sat under the lamp.

It read two o'clock. He didn't know if it was morning or afternoon, but he did know that he felt better than he had for some time. He also felt hungry. So he got up, then noticed that he still had on his flight suit and jacket.

Taking off his jacket, he went over to the windows to look outside. When he parted the curtains a bit, the light from outside just about blinded him. Closing his eyes because of the bright-ness, he opened the curtains all the way and then turn around. With his eyes quickly adjusting to the light, he walked over to the table and turned off the lamp. Wiping his hands across his face, Savage felt the stubble of a beard and decided it was time for a shave and a shower.

After stopping by the Officer's Mess for a bite to eat, the general headed for his office. And when he entered the outer office he noticed Colonel Stovall sitting behind his desk, engrossed in something that he was reading.

"Afternoon, Harvey", said Savage.

Startled, Stovall stood up and looked at Savage in wonder. "Good afternoon, General, how are you feeling?"

"Just fine, ... thanks."

Turning to go into his own office, Savage stopped and asked. "How's the Group doing?"

"Everything's going just fine, sir. We're on a stand-down for the next few days, and getting some replacements for the ships that were too badly shot up on the Berlin mission. The wounded have been cared for, of course, and I took it upon myself to issue some forty-eight hour passes."

"That's good, Harvey", said Savage, where upon he went inside his office.

Closing the door behind him, the general walked over to his desk. On the desk was a mission report, but Savage ignored it, for the time being, and opened a side drawer in the desk. He pulled out a letter that he had received a while back, and read it again.

SUBJECT: O.T.U. training in the Continental United States, Zone of the Interior.

TO: Commanding Officer, 918th Bombardment Group (H)

1. Effective immediately, you will refrain from further partici- pation in any combat action (missions) without specific prior authorization from this Headquarters.
2. The Commanding General, United States Army Air Forces, Eighth U.S. Army Air Force, has been requested to return a suitable General Officer, qualified by outstanding experience in combat, to the United States, Zone of the Interior, for urgently important duties in connection with the training of heavy bombardment groups for combat. You are here- by advised that in the opinion of this Headquarters, no officer, other than yourself, can meet these subject require- ments.
3. Pursuant to para. 2, above, you will consider yourself in readiness for re-assignment to this important duty, to which you will be ordered as soon as practicable. Mean- while, you will take appropriate action relative to term- ination of your present duties at a reasonably early date, of which you will be advised in due course.

SIGNED: Henderson, Brigadier General, U.S.A.A.F.

Headquarters, Eighth U.S. Army Air Force Although he had fought the order before, he now felt that it was time to move on. He picked up the phone and told the oper- ator to get General Henderson on the line. When Ed Henderson came on the phone Savage said, calmly.

"Ed, Frank Savage, here. you can go ahead and cut that order on me. Yes . . . that's what I said." Before Henderson could really say anything, Savage hung up, while Henderson was still talking.

He then pulled out a bottle of whiskey and a glass from a bottom drawer of the desk, poured himself a shot, and swallowed it all in one gulp. After placing the bottle back in the drawer he stood up, then headed out the door.

"Harvey", he said, "I'm going to take one of those forty-eight hour passes you've been handing out and go over to visit Desborough Hall. If anything comes up, you take care of it."

"Yes, sir", replied the colonel. "And, sir, ... good luck." "Thank you, Harvey, thanks very much."

Both men smiled as Savage left the room. And, a short time after leaving the base in his jeep, the general turned off the highway and onto the old road leading to Desborough Hall.

Savage started up the road to Desborough Hall, riding with the windshield down, beneath the arching elm trees. He still saw the trees and fields around him in the dead, gray hues, in which they had registered in his brain for months.

And then, gradually, subtly, he began to see color. In the fading sunlight, he saw the greens of early spring on the hedges, and on the tips of tree branches. He heard the tinkle of a cow-bell and smelled the fresh pungency of the earth, and he detected the scent of wood smoke.

He had never noticed, before, how beautiful the moss was, growing from the cracks, of that tiny stone bridge, across the creek. Or that doe, with the two fawns following her. Or that flock of pheasant, with their brilliant, shiny plumage, ignoring the jeep's approach, as they leisurely cross the road. Why hadn't he seen any of them before?

Dimly, Savage commenced to realize that the world of living things about him was transforming from black and white, into Technicolor. His senses of sight, hearing, and smell, were awakening from their long hibernation, into acute awareness.

Almost physically, Savage's burden began to grow lighter by the second. His face broke out into a smile, that mirrored the sense of almost intolerable relief that suddenly buoyed him.

Three lines, from an old Northhumberland fighting song, which he had memorized during a convivial evening at a British bomber station, crossed his mind once more.

I am hurt, but I am not slain.

I'll lay me down and bleed awhile And then I'll rise and fight again.

Savage gripped the wheel tighter, pressed down harder on the accelerator, and opened his mouth wide to gulp the rushing wind In a cloud of rising dust, the jeep vanished around the next bend in the road.

Made in the USA
Columbia, SC
28 February 2024

11b94195-f23d-4b1c-8caf-824153e8391bR01